CW00349601

BOLTED

By

BRIDGET BERESFORD

BOLTED copyright © 2012 by Bridget Beresford.

All rights reserved. No part of this book may be reproduced or transmitted in any form or by any means, electronic or mechanical, including photocopying or recording without the permission of the author.

Cover by www.spiffingcovers.com

1st edition.

This book is a work of fiction. Names, places, characters and incidents are the product of the author's imagination or are used fictitiously. Any resemblance to events, locales or persons living, or dead, is coincidental.

Acknowledgements: Many thanks to Sally Rees M.R.C.V.S. for her veterinary advice, also to Paul H and Sue Cameron.

Dedication: This book is dedicated to all those competitors, owners, organisers, and volunteers who make our British equestrian sports so Great.

CONTENTS

CHAPTER ONE

The driver of the lorry was way off course. His GPS had taken him on a route that was far too narrow for his articulated monster. He jammed on his brakes as he turned a corner. The weight of his load carried him helplessly forwards and he could only watch as a horse and rider galloped towards him. The horse's mouth was wide open, its lips drawn back. The rider sat rigid with fear in the saddle, a look of horror on her face.

The vehicle took up all the space in the lane between the high banks.

***

Maddy Richards was having breakfast in her farmhouse kitchen. The smell of horses filled the room and bandages belonging to various equines dried on a rail in front of the Aga.

Her property, October Farm in Sussex, was a thriving equestrian business. As Maddy was finishing her coffee she looked up at the photo of her husband, Captain Jonathan Richards. He had never returned from a war in the Middle East. His good-looking tanned face grinned down at her from the mantel above the Aga. She smiled back, twirling her long dark hair around a finger. 'It's such a lovely day, perfect for riding. I think I'll start with Hyperion.' Hyperion was a black Hanoverian stallion. He was named after the Greek Titan god, the mythical father of the Sun, the Moon and the Dawn. He meant all of those things to her.

The phone rang. She looked at the display, delighted to see the name Tamsin Coulson, her long-time friend and fellow rider. She picked up the receiver. It was Emma, Tamsin's daughter.

'It's lovely to hear from you,' replied Maddy. 'How are you?' She adored Emma; their family lived in Devon so she didn't get to see them as much as she would have liked.

'It's Mummy…' The hollow tone made Maddy grow cold and the smile left her face.

'Whatever's the matter?'

Emma burst into tears.

'What's happened,' asked Maddy.

Emma sobbed. 'I can't…'

The line remained open and Maddy heard someone pick up the

phone.

'Hello,' said Tamsin's housekeeper.

'Anna,' gasped Maddy. 'What's happened?'

'It's Tamsin. She's... had an accident.'

'What sort of accident? Is she all right?'

'No, I'm afraid not. Her horse was hit by a lorry... She... She was killed.'

'My God! Where's Simon?'

'The Colonel has gone to Sandhurst... to break the news to his son.' Simon Coulson had left the army but Anna always called him by his rank.

'My God!' repeated Maddy. 'How did it happen?'

'She was riding along the lane over to Southways Cross yesterday afternoon and a lorry ran right into her horse. They were both killed. Nobody really knows how it happened.'

'I...' Maddy felt numb. 'How's Emma?'

'Poor little maid, she's devastated. She didn't sleep a wink last night. She looks like a ghost, she's not eating, and I'm that worried about her. Please would you come down?'

'Of course. I'll leave now.'

'Thank you Maddy, that would be a great help.'

'I'll see you later.' Maddy put the phone down and stared out of the kitchen window. She had to go to Devon and she had to break the news to Ruth, her head girl. She couldn't move and she couldn't cry.

Ruth came cheerily into the kitchen. 'It's a beautiful day. Are you coming to do any work this morning? You've been in here for ages.' She saw the look on Maddy's face and stopped. 'What's happened?'

'Tamsin's been killed.'

'What? How?' Ruth sat down heavily at the table and listened aghast as Maddy told her what she knew of the accident. 'I can't believe it,' she murmured.

'Neither can I.'

'Tamsin, of all people... one of the best riders in the country. Maddy I'm so sorry.'

'I'm going down there today. Will you be all right?'

'Of course I'll be all right. Does Simon know you're going?'

'I don't think so. I know he's not going to like it, but if Emma wants me there, then that's more important.'

'Yes, I agree. You'd better go and get ready. How long are you going for?'

'I don't know. You're going to need some help with the horses.'

'I can find help, don't you worry.'

'I'll ring Sally,' Maddy suggested.

'She's coming to ride later. I'll tell her.' Ruth stretched across the big pine table and picked up the desk diary. She flicked through it. 'I'll sort things out. Will you please get going?'

'Thank you Ruth,' Maddy smiled weakly. 'You're a star. What would I do without you?' She went upstairs, followed by her two dogs, Zippy, a whippet and Jock the Border Terrier. They hardly ever left her side and anxiously watched her as she threw some things into a suit case.

When Maddy went outside, she found Ruth in Hyperion's stable. 'Well, I'm off.' She patted the big horse. 'I hope you'll all be okay.'

'Yes, we'll all be fine.' Ruth gave her a hug. 'Drive carefully, send my love to Emma and let me know when you arrive.'

***

As Maddy drove down to Devon she had plenty of time to think and to worry. She was sure that Simon Coulson didn't know she was coming, and she knew he wouldn't like it. She recalled how dogmatic and arrogant he could be and how he was always able to annoy her with his high-handed remarks.

She and Tamsin had been friends for years, but when Jonathan had been killed things changed. Maddy grew angry as she remembered staying with Tamsin soon after Jonathan's death. Simon was away, having been posted to Northern Ireland. There were several bogus telephone calls; the caller would hang up as soon as they heard Tamsin's voice.

Tamsin didn't seem to worry, but Maddy became suspicious. A few days later when Tamsin was taking one of Simon's suits to the cleaners she found a bill for a dinner for two in London. It was dated on a day when Simon was supposed to be on an army exercise. Maddy was furious.

When she got home she rang around her old army friends and found out that Simon was seeing a pretty voluptuous girl in her twenties. She told Tamsin, instantly regretting her rash action. She went cold as she remembered how furious Simon had been when he had had to come back from Northern Ireland to sort out his marriage.

But he still persisted in flirting with other women and Maddy couldn't understand why his wife couldn't or wouldn't see what he was up to. She stopped discussing him with Tamsin, and managed to avoid seeing him. This was going to be their first meeting for a long time.

Maddy was tired and miserable when she eventually turned into Simon's drive. The large granite-built Victorian manor house faced north and Maddy always thought it looked rather austere but today, as she caught sight of it, it looked bleak. She passed a large sign which read: *MOORSEND MANOR straight on. All traffic for MOORSEND EQUESTRIAN CENTRE fork right.* She faltered and then took the right fork.

A modern complex of stables with an indoor school and a very large outside jumping arena replaced the old farmyard. Maddy pulled up and parked her 4 x 4 as close to the house as she could.

It wasn't until she got out of the car that she felt the atmosphere. The place was usually buzzing with activity, a radio playing or someone whistling, but today there was an unnatural hush. There seemed to be a black cloud hanging over the yard; even the horses seemed to be strangely quiet.

Maddy walked under a stone archway into the old stable yard and shivered. She passed quickly through a small, thick oak door in the corner of the yard and past the outbuildings at the back of the house. She opened the scullery door and walked on into the large kitchen. Herbs dried on an elevated rail and there was the smell of a freshly baked cake.

Anna, a large woman with big hands and heavy features, was putting the kettle on as Maddy walked in. She turned and smiled. She looked haggard and her eyes were red from crying. 'Hello. I saw you coming through the back. What a terrible time. I don't know what to think. I can't take it in. I can't get used to it.'

'I know, even the horses seem to sense something awful has happened. You look really tired. Where's Emma?' Maddy gave the comfortable woman a hug.

'She's upstairs, poor little maid. I haven't had much sleep, none of us have. I'm glad you could come. Emma always thought the world of you. Poor little maid,' she repeated as the tears spilled over. 'We'll have a nice cup of tea, shall we? I'll give Emma a call.'

Maddy suddenly felt very hungry. She looked at the cherry cake that stood on the table. 'Yes, that would be lovely. I can hear Emma coming now.'

A slim blonde girl came into the kitchen, closely followed by a black Labrador. She looked a ghost of her normal bouncy self, her eyes were red and she sagged like a rag doll. Maddy's heart went out to her. She stood up and they put their arms around one another. Maddy felt inadequate; she wished she could take away the girl's grief.

At last Emma broke free, saying, 'Thank you for coming.' Maddy made a gesture and Emma continued: 'I feel wretched. I don't want to do anything. I haven't been out to the stables. I just can't. Not even to see Tempie.' The Temptress was her chestnut mare who she adored. 'I keep thinking Mummy's out there, and I can't bear to look at Troubadour's empty stable.'

Maddy hadn't asked which horse Tamsin had been riding; she was shocked to hear it was one of her best horses. It made the whole thing even more appalling. 'You don't have to go out there today,' she said. Nobody would expect you to. Monica will have everything under control.'

This won a smile from Emma who said, 'No, you're right. Even Daddy told me to stay indoors'.

'There you are then, the master has spoken.' Maddy smiled.

'I knew you would make me feel better. I just don't want to let people down.'

'You're not letting anyone down. Don't be daft. Now come and have some tea. I can't look at that cake for much longer without eating a piece.'

'You know,' Emma stared out of one of the high windows. 'I don't understand why mummy was galloping down the road. She would never gallop on the road.'

Maddy looked up. 'What do you mean?'

'Well, the lorry driver said that mummy was galloping towards him up the road. I don't believe him.'

'No,' Maddy agreed.

'I think it's his fault. The police should arrest him.' She turned to Anna. 'Why haven't they?'

'I don't know,' Anna replied, looking at Maddy for help. 'Your father is dealing with it all. You must ask him when he comes in.'

Maddy responded to Anna's quick glance by saying, 'If it was the lorry driver's fault, then your father will have him crucified. You can be sure of that.'

'Yes he will, and the sooner the better.' Emma shook her head and added, 'I don't want to talk about it anymore.'

Silence fell until Maddy asked, 'When's your father coming

home?'

'I don't know, he said he would ring when he was on his way.'

Maddy was becoming increasingly anxious about meeting him and was desperately trying to think of a way of warning him that she was there. She didn't want to see the look of fury on his face when he first laid eyes on her.

'I've forgotten to tell Monica something. It's about Tempie's feed.' Emma looked imploringly at Maddy.

'Don't worry, I'll go and tell her. What is it?'

Emma gave her the message and Maddy made her way down into the stable yard to the head girl's cottage.

Monica caught sight of her and threw open the door. 'Maddy,' she cried, smiling. 'Someone told me you were here. I'm so pleased to see you. Come in, have a cup of coffee, excuse the mess.'

Maddy followed her into the small kitchen saying, 'Never mind the mess, you should see my house. How are you? You look shattered. I felt the atmosphere in the yard, it was horrible.'

'Yes, it's awful.' Monica had tears in her eyes. 'I don't know how I got through the day. I don't know how I'm going to get through tomorrow for that matter.'

'Take each day at a time. Just keep working. It gets easier... eventually.'

'Oh Maddy!' Monica stopped making coffee, turned round and put her hand on Maddy's shoulder. The tears were now running down her drawn, tired face. 'I'm so sorry. I forgot. It was round about this time of year...'

Maddy nodded, her own eyes were filling up. 'Yes,' she replied. She couldn't bring herself to say that the anniversary of Jonathan's death was, in fact, the next day. 'Don't worry about me,' she continued, 'I'm a seasoned campaigner. I'm far more worried about Emma.'

'Yes, poor kid. Come into the front room.' Maddy took her mug of coffee and followed the stocky girl into the tiny untidy room.

'Some people want to leave now,' said Monica. 'Honestly, like rats leaving a sinking ship. Can you believe it?' She was in her late thirties and had been with Tamsin ever since she was twenty. She had qualified to become a riding instructor but decided to gain some experience working with event horses for a short while. She went to work for Tamsin and had never left. 'I don't want to stay here in the long run. Of course I'll wait until things are sorted out. I don't really want to work for Simon. God! I wonder what he'll do with it all. I know its early days yet but I've been thinking about it all day. Sam Hamilton, the New Zealand rider, is always asking me to go and work for him.'

'He's gorgeous, and a good rider,' remarked Maddy.

'Yes, he spends the horse trials season in this country and then he goes back to New Zealand. He'll probably be in their Olympic team. He would want me to go back with him to New Zealand too.'

'That would be fabulous.'

'I know. But I feel a bit disloyal even thinking about it at the moment.'

'You mustn't. You have to move on and you have to think of yourself, however hard that sounds.'

'Yes.' Monica gave a sigh. 'But as I said, it's early days yet.'

Maddy took a deep breath and, feeling awkward, asked, 'Emma said Tamsin was galloping down the lane, is that right?'

'That's what the lorry driver said. The police have been examining the place where it happened. The road has been closed all day, it might still be closed. I expect we'll find out more tomorrow. She was riding Troubadour which makes it even worse in a way. Not that it could be much worse. He was so well behaved, and he was good in traffic. Tamsin thought the world of him; he was a fabulous jumper and he could do a good dressage. Everything you need for a top class horse; she always said he was too good to be true and something would happen to him...' Monica paused and took a swig of coffee. 'God! I need something stronger than this.' She got up and fought her way through the clutter to a cupboard. She had to move a marmalade cat who was sitting on a pile of ironing before she could open the door. She produced a bottle of sherry and two glasses.

'This'll have to do.' She poured out two large measures and gave a glass to Maddy. 'I don't really drink sherry but it's all I've got at the moment. It was a Christmas present.'

'Thank you.' Maddy took the glass and swallowed a large mouthful, nearly choking. 'Nor do I, but it should do the trick. What have they done with Troubadour?'

'They've taken his body to the hunt kennels.'

Maddy looked horrified. 'You don't mean they're going to...'

'No, no the hounds aren't going to eat him. It's just because they have a cold room there: they're going to keep him until Simon and the children decide what to do with him. Simon didn't want him back here.' Monica shuddered. 'He's not a pretty sight, I understand.'

'No.' Maddy put her hand to her mouth and paused. 'Wa... was he all right in the morning, I mean before he went out?'

'Yes, he was absolutely fine. Simon asked me that.'

'Talking of Simon, could you do me a favour? I don't think he knows I'm here. Please could you ring him and tell him.'

Monica stared at her. 'Why?'

'He doesn't like me and I want to warn him.'

Monica smiled. 'I know he doesn't like you.'

'Is it that obvious?' Maddy was a little affronted.

'No, but you're always telling me. Anyway, why doesn't he like you?'

'I'll tell you one day. Please, please ring him. It could be so embarrassing if he arrives and finds me here. Anna and Emma don't really know the whole story.'

'Well, neither do I.'

'I'll tell you one day,' repeated Maddy.

'Okay, okay,' Monica laughed. 'I've got to ring him about something actually. Honestly, you're behaving like a teenager. It all sounds very peculiar.'

'It's quite simple. I'll feel very uncomfortable if he suddenly finds me in his house unannounced.'

'All right, as long as you tell me the big secret.' Monica smiled as she picked up her phone and dialled Simon's mobile.

***

Simon Coulson was driving home feeling emotionally drained. The meeting with his son at the Royal Military Academy Sandhurst had been far worse than he had anticipated. Richard's look of anguish had been tragic. Simon did his best to comfort the lad but felt that he had failed miserably.

When his mobile rang he answered it with a sharp, 'Yes... Oh it's you Monica.' His tone softened as he talked, then his face hardened again. 'What did you say?'

'Maddy's here, Emma asked her to come down,' repeated Monica.

Simon was far from pleased, but he replied calmly, 'Good, I'll look forward to seeing her. Tell them I'll be back in an hour.'

He had never forgiven Maddy for prying into his private life. 'She'd better keep her nose out of this business,' he muttered to himself. Tamsin had been very young when they married, Richard was born when she was only twenty and Emma followed eighteen months later. He felt wretched as he recalled what had gone wrong in his marriage and why he had started having affairs with other women. He only chose married women, never friends or girl grooms. He always told them right from the start that there would be no involvement, only sex and fun. 'How come I managed to break my own rules?' he asked himself as he gripped the steering wheel. He brought to mind the sexy girl in her twenties who, he considered, had acted like a Siren and led him astray. She wasn't particularly good looking but she had a fabulous body and was good in bed. Everything was going swimmingly until she became clingy and wanted him to leave Tamsin. He was in line for promotion at the time.

'I certainly wasn't going to jeopardize that or my marriage,' he said aloud to himself. 'I had to get rid of her. She knew the score.' Just as things were becoming very awkward he had been posted to Northern Ireland. Simon was convinced that if Maddy hadn't interfered the whole thing would have blown over.

He seethed as he remembered having to come home to sort things out with his wife. When he left Ireland he considered that he was shirking his duty. He set himself a high standard of conduct as an officer and he considered that being called away on a domestic matter had made him look incompetent. To make matters worse, while he was in England there was an IRA incident and two members of his unit were killed.

***

Maddy sat having a drink with Emma in the cosy room that used to be the children's playroom and was now the snug. She stared bleakly at a large photo of Tamsin jumping a huge cross-country fence in Lexington, U.S.A., which hung over the mantelpiece. Maddy felt cold and turned to watch the flames dancing and crackling in the grate. She was so absorbed in her own thoughts that she didn't hear Simon come into the room.

'Daddy,' cried Emma. She jumped up and threw her arms around her father. Maddy stood up and spun round but Simon appeared not to notice her as he hugged his daughter.

Maddy thought how immaculate he looked in spite of the long day. He wore a well-cut dark, three piece suit with a black silk tie. She noticed that his neatly-cut dark hair now showed a hint of grey. He broke away from Emma and turned towards Maddy. His steel grey eyes bored into hers, making her feel very uncomfortable. His face remained inscrutable as he walked over and gave her a polite peck on the cheek.

'So kind of you to come,' he said in his deep cultured voice.

'It's the least I could do. I'm so sorry…'

'Yes.' Simon cut her short and turned back to Emma. 'Richard's coming home tomorrow so he'll be here to look after you.'

'Oh, good. How come he can get away?'

'I spoke to the Camp Commandant today and he's letting him have some time out.'

'You know you can call me at any time, don't you?' said Maddy. She glanced at Simon and suddenly felt frightened by the look of anger on his face.

His eyes glinted as he replied urbanely, 'Yes, of course.' He glanced at the fire and abruptly changed the subject. 'It's very cosy in here. It's becoming quite chilly outside.'

'Yes, that's why we decided to light the fire.' Maddy tried to smile.

Simon spoke to Emma. 'That was a good idea.' He walked over to a glass-fronted drinks cabinet. 'What are you drinking?' he asked Maddy.

'A whisky, please.'

'Do you still take coke with it?'

'You've got a good memory,' she replied, feeling more cheerful.

'Yes, I have.' His face hardened as he handed her the drink. He left her in no doubt as to what he meant. He poured a drink for Emma and himself, and then sat down and chatted to his daughter with his back turned towards Maddy.

She felt humiliated and close to tears; she twirled her glass round in her hands and stared at the fire. She thought of Jonathan and desperately wished that he was there.

'Maddy.' Simon spoke to her, but she didn't seem to hear. 'Maddy,' he repeated louder. She jumped and the glass flew out of her hand and shattered on the stone hearth.

'I'm so sorry.' She stared at the broken fragments, feeling mortified.

'Not to worry,' Simon was almost kind. 'Would you like another drink?'

'No… no thank you, excuse me, I need to go…' She grabbed her handbag and fled from the room. Once in the downstairs cloakroom she burst into tears of anger and embarrassment for herself, mixed with grief for Tamsin and Jonathan.

When she recovered she took out her mobile and rang Ruth; she told her how wretched she felt. 'I bet he got Richard out of Sandhurst just to get rid of me.'

'I'm sure he didn't. It would be the obvious thing to do.'

'I'm coming home tomorrow, but not before I look at the accident scene because there's something very fishy about all this.'

'What on earth do you mean?' Ruth sounded startled.

'It doesn't add up. I don't like it. I'll tell you when I see you,' Maddy whispered.

'You be careful and don't go treading on Simon's toes, you know how nasty he can get.'

'I'm not bothered about him,' said Maddy airily. 'I'd better go. Dinner will be ready in a minute.'

'Please take care,' said Ruth.

Maddy rang off. She repaired her makeup and tidied her hair. She took a deep breath, drew herself up to her full height and walked back towards the snug just as Anna arrived to say that dinner was ready.

Simon politely stood aside as he and Emma joined Maddy in the hall and allowed her to enter the dining room first. She looked up at an oil painting of Tamsin on a horse and her spirits plummeted again. She glanced dismally round the large room at the military photos of Simon, and then at the plaques bearing the regimental insignia.

Simon sat at the head of the table with his daughter on one side and Maddy on the other. She stared at an intricate silver statue of a huntsman on a horse surrounded by hounds that stood in the centre of the large oval mahogany table. It seemed to be the only thing in the room that was safe to look at: everything else brought back painful memories. She had packed all Jonathan's plaques and army photos away in a cardboard box and put them in the attic. She suddenly felt guilty about that.

Anna brought in a trolley laden with food and, as Simon lifted the lid of the silver entrée dish, Maddy, who had only eaten a piece of cherry cake since breakfast, smelt the mouth-watering aroma of a home-made beef bourguignon and realised how hungry she was.

'That smells fabulous,' she said as Simon served her a large portion.

It was heaven, the meat melted in her mouth. Simon filled her glass from a bottle of Premier Cru Château Margaux. Maddy took a large sip of the wine which went down like liquid velvet. She began to feel better.

'What time is Richard coming tomorrow?' asked Emma.

'Probably lunchtime.'

'Will you be here, Daddy?'

'Yes, I'll be here until Richard comes, then I've got one or two things to do in the afternoon.'

'I wondered...' Emma stopped in mid-sentence.

'Yes?' said Simon.

Well... I don't know...'

'What is it darling?' he asked gently.

'Could I see mummy?' Maddy started and reached for her glass of wine.

'Of course, if that's what you want,' Simon replied with barely a pause.

'Yes, I do, I need to say goodbye. Where is she?'

Simon answered softly, 'She's in the Chapel of Rest. I'll take you there tomorrow morning'.

'Thank you.' Emma looked down at her plate. Maddy smiled warmly at her and Simon looked inscrutable.

Emma broke the silence. 'Maddy do you want to come too?'

'I... I can't. I have to get back. I must leave tomorrow morning. Ruth rang while I was in the loo. Thank you for asking me though.' She glanced at Simon, who picked up the wine bottle and refilled her glass.

'There's no need for you to rush off,' he said courteously.

Maddy turned, looked him straight in the eye and said, 'Yes, I'm afraid there is.'

'Maddy was telling me about Hyperion,' said Emma. 'She's doing high level dressage now.'

'That's good.' Simon sounded bored.

'You'll be in the British Dressage team soon,' said Emma.

'No I won't. I have to do Grand Prix to get into the proper team.'

'You're nearly there.'

'Not really. Anyway I'm not good enough.'

'Yes you are; she is, isn't she Daddy?'

Simon was spared from answering as his mobile rang; he looked at the display, stood up and said, 'Excuse me.' He walked into the hall with a strange look on his face. Maddy strained her ears as she tried to hear what he was saying.

'I'm sorry I dragged you all the way down here,' said Emma.

'Don't worry about that.'

Just as Emma said something else, Maddy leant down and looked at the floor, as if she had dropped her napkin, so that she could listen to what Simon was saying. She managed to hear him say: 'Okay, thanks for letting me know, Bob. I'll ring Andy now and get the details, just keep this under your hat. See you tomorrow afternoon.'

Maddy knew that Bob was the huntsman, Andy was Simon's vet and that Troubadour was at the hunt kennels.

'I was talking to about Rhona Whitehaven, I know you don't like her, but there was no need for you to disappear under the table like that as soon as I mentioned her name,' said Emma as Maddy's head bobbed up again.

Maddy laughed. 'Sorry, I dropped something. No, I can't stand her, what's she done?' Rhona Whitehaven, like Maddy, was a dressage judge.

'I was just saying that she was eventing at Taunton the other day.'

'Not judging? That's a hell of a long way for her to come and judge, she lives near me.'

'No, she was riding.'

'You're joking, she can't ride. I bet she didn't get round the cross country.'

'She did. She finished fourth in her section.'

'Good God! The course must have been easy.'

'Not that straightforward; the fences were up to the full height. Mum rode two horses in the same novice section and said that they were plenty big enough. She won with one horse, but the other, who's a brilliant jumper, didn't come anywhere because he was naughty in the dressage.'

'How on earth did Rhona manage to come fourth?'

'I don't know. She was with that Jilly Rich. They both upset mum.'

'Silly Jilly.' Maddy laughed. 'So she was there too. Well she would be. They go everywhere together. What did they do to upset your mother?'

'I don't know exactly, it was something to do with Rhona's horse, I think.'

Just then Simon came back into the room without offering any explanation as to whom he had been talking. Maddy thought that maybe he often made a habit of going out of the room in the middle of a meal to talk on his mobile, but, given his amorous habits, she wasn't surprised.

'Who are you two talking about?' he asked as he sat down to finish his meal.

'Rhona and Jilly Rich, they were at the Taunton horse trials. Rhona was riding and came fourth,' replied Emma.

'Good God! That old harridan; was she riding a broomstick?'

'No.' Emma laughed. 'She was on a very nice horse that she has only just bought. It's an eight-year-old but hasn't done very much yet.'

'She hasn't had time to ruin it, then,' remarked Simon.

'I didn't know you knew her,' said Maddy.

'I don't know her that well, only her reputation as a bad judge. I didn't know she could ride.'

'She can't, and however good her new horse is now, you're right, she'll end up ruining it.'

'Jilly Rich was telling mum, quite nastily actually, what a good rider Rhona is,' said Emma.

'She would say that. Jilly creeps around Rhona because she has money and lives in a big house with her own yard. The silly woman tries to get in with everyone whom she thinks is important.'

'But Rhona isn't important,' said Emma.

'No, not now, but she used to be an "in" person in the dressage world; she had a very good horse that some bloke used to ride. It won everything. There was talk of it being in the British team, but in the end it went lame and disappeared off the scene. She won't talk about it, so no one really knows what happened to it. I can't think of its name, it was the same as a racehorse, like Hyperion.'

'Singspiel,' said Simon.

'Good Lord, how did you know that?' Simon looked uncomfortable and for a second Maddy supposed that he might have had an affair with Rhona. However, she instantly dismissed the idea because she thought that even Simon wouldn't stoop that low.

Simon evaded her question by replying, 'Yes, they were both good racehorses and good sires.'

'Good racehorses! That's an understatement. Hyperion won the Derby in 1933 and sired a dynasty of great horses.' Maddy unwittingly allowed Simon to swing the conversation around to the safer subject of racing and thoroughbred breeding.

***

After the meal Maddy thought that Simon had mellowed, but when they returned to the snug he continued to talk to Emma with his back towards her, excluding her from the conversation.

She stood up. 'I really must go to bed.' She gave Emma a hug. 'Good night, see you in the morning.' Then she turned to Simon and said, 'May I have a word?'

She could see that he was irritated. He followed her out of the room into the hall. 'Yes?' he asked impatiently.

Maddy took a deep breath and turning to face him looked him straight in the eye. 'I just want to say that I think your behaviour towards me has been rude, uncalled-for and hurtful.'

Simon looked furious. He opened his mouth to say something, so she continued quickly: 'I didn't come here to annoy you. I came down because your daughter asked me to. I'm disgusted at your attitude, and if either Jonathan or Tamsin were here you wouldn't be behaving like this. I wanted to tell you how devastated I am by Tamsin's death and perhaps we could bury the hatchet. I can now see how wrong I am. You clearly have no intention of doing that. Nevertheless, I offer you my deepest sympathies. I hope I don't have to see you again tomorrow morning, so thank you for your hospitality.' She swung round to go, then quickly turned back. 'By the way, we'll always share the same anniversary because Jonathan was killed five years ago tomorrow. Good night.' She turned on her heel and walked up the stairs.

Simon stood and stared after her; he had forgotten that Jonathan's death had been at this time and he suddenly realised how Maddy was feeling. Also he thought how pretty she looked. Her turquoise figure-hugging sweater enhanced her skin tone and brought out the colour of her deep blue eyes. He wanted to call her back and apologise. Instead he turned and walked slowly back to the snug and his daughter.

CHAPTER TWO

Maddy woke early the next morning after a fitful night's sleep. As soon as she heard Simon drive away she felt it was safe to go downstairs to the kitchen. She found Anna and Emma finishing their breakfast.

'What would you like to eat, m'dear?' asked Anna.

'Only toast and coffee, thank you, I have to hurry back home.'

'Stay for lunch and see Richard,' Emma suggested.

'No, I'm sorry, sweetheart, I would love to but I can't.'

As soon as she finished her breakfast she hugged Emma tearfully, said her goodbyes and left the house as quickly as she could. She felt like a coward running away in the face of enemy fire as she walked through the old stable yard on the way to her car. Some of the loose boxes were vacant as their occupants were out on exercise which made Troubadour's empty stable look less obvious.

She threw her case into the back of the 4 x 4 and sat down gratefully behind the wheel, feeling safe at last. She quickly reversed and as she turned the vehicle around she caught sight of Simon coming down the drive in his silver Mercedes. Luckily he turned left and parked in front of the house. She heaved a sigh of relief and drove away, thankful to be able to leave the beleaguered house behind.

Instead of turning right for the main road and the way home, Maddy turned left towards the moor and drove to the scene of the accident. When she arrived at Southways Cross, she stopped the 4 x 4 and got out. She saw no sign of a collision. The road which had brought her to the junction carried on straight ahead and another lane joined it from the right. The fourth side of the "cross" was an old track which led up to the moor through a field to the left.

Maddy walked into the field and immediately saw long deep skid marks left by a horse galloping headlong down the hill. She was surprised as she noticed that the tracks continued on to the road and straight down the lane opposite to the gateway. It appeared as if the horse had been out of control and going too fast to make the right-hand turn towards home.

She followed the grey scuff marks of metal horseshoes on the road. The horse's hooves had hit the tarmac with such a violent impact that in places whole impressions of a horseshoe, including the nail marks, were imprinted in the tar.

Going back to her car, Maddy drove slowly down the lane, leaning out of the window whilst following the intermittent hoofmarks. She was so absorbed in looking for the tracks that she didn't notice the accident spot until she came across a thick covering of sand. She felt sick and stopped the car, her hand shaking as she switched off the engine. Although she wasn't particularly religious, she crossed herself and offered up a little muddled prayer for Tamsin.

She forced herself to get out of the car and walked unsteadily to the accident scene. Although every piece of debris had been cleared away she could still make out the point of impact. She could see how narrow the lane was, and that one side of the lorry had carved out a piece of the high bank as if trying to avoid the horse.

Maddy felt cold and dizzy. She ran to her car and rapidly reversed back to Southways Cross. She swung into the field and put her 4 x 4 into four-wheel drive. She said 'Come on,' as if it were a horse and drove up the steep, partly stony and gassy track to the moor.

The gate at the top was shut, so Maddy parked beside it. She put on a pair of stout walking boots, took her mobile phone with her and locked her handbag in the car.

As she opened the gate on to the moor she noticed the hoof prints of the horse as it had slipped and slithered hurriedly through the gateway. The ground had been damp on the day of the accident but the weather had been dry and sunny since then, so the footprints were well preserved.

Maddy followed the hoofmarks which came down a cart track. It appeared as if the horse had gathered speed as he approached the gateway.

She walked to the top of the hill and the view which met her took her breath away. Exmoor stretched away down in front of her, gorse and heather painted the rolling hills purple and yellow. Bare trees stood in small clumps of woodland, their branches laden with budding leaves not yet open. Maddy could just see a glint of the sea on the horizon.

As she stared at the view she began to relax. She sighed and walked on, but her anxiety came back once she realised that someone else had been doing the same as herself. She could see large footprints, probably belonging to a man wearing Wellington boots, walking along the path. Whoever it was had been careful not to step on the horse's hoofmarks.

The hoofprints came to a standstill beside a thick cluster of gorse bushes. It was obvious that the horse had stood still and then fidgeted as if eager to get on with his work whilst the rider spoke to someone. A weather-beaten hawthorn tree bent like a petrified, tattered wind-sock grew out of the thicket. Maddy shivered as she noticed a second pair of human footprints coming out from under the grotesque distorted tree. She walked up the narrow path into the thicket. *A secret place*, thought Maddy when she looked around at the thick walls of gorse which concealed a little clearing in the middle of the undergrowth. She thought it might be used by lovers in the summertime or that it could be a hide for birdwatchers. She glanced at the ground and noticed a number of small holes, about the size of a finger, in the earth floor, also several clear footprints. Someone had recently been sitting in the tiny copse on a shooting stick.

Maddy came out of the bushes feeling frightened: something had happened to make Troubadour bolt. Tamsin must have seen someone standing by the tree and stopped to talk to them. She trembled, as for a moment she felt that she was being watched.

She put her hand in her pocket and touched her mobile phone for reassurance. Then she suddenly thought of Jonathan and wished that he was standing behind her with his machine gun. She heard a rustle and spun round. There on the track in single file stood a small family of red deer with a splendid stag at the rear, his proud head of antlers held high. Maddy stared at him while he gazed back at her, and then, as if in response to some hidden signal, all the animals moved off as one and disappeared. Maddy stood looking at the empty space on the track. The deer had broken the tension and she felt calmer.

She decided to take another look inside the thicket. She crouched over the little holes in the ground as if she were sitting on a shooting stick and noticed a gap in the gorse which allowed her to see clearly up the track in the direction from which Tamsin must have arrived earlier that day.

Maddy looked at the footprints and wondered how she could memorise the pattern of the print on the sole. She fished around in her pocket for a pen and a scrap of paper, but found nothing. She was thinking of going back to the car to find something when she felt her mobile again. She used it to take a couple of photos, and then she took some more looking out of the hide and up the track.

The sun went in behind a cloud. She felt cold and wanted to get back to the safety of her car. Her mobile rang. It was so unexpected that she jumped, fell forwards into the gorse and dropped her phone. It lay in the middle of the gorse bush playing the Post Horn Gallop, loudly advertising her presence in the thicket. Maddy wrapped her coat around her hand and shook the gorse bush as hard as she could. The phone eventually fell to the ground just out of reach but it stopped ringing.

She searched around the little den and found a dead branch. She got down on her hands and knees, crawled as far under the bush as far as possible and managed to drag the phone towards her. The dragging process was impeded by pieces of newly cut gorse that lay on the ground and got caught up on the phone.

The call had been from her friend Sally who left a message, wanting to know where she was and when she would be home. Maddy rang her straight back, whispering, 'What do you want? You frightened me to death and now I'm all scratched and bleeding. I'll probably get gorse poisoning. Oh my God,' she exclaimed, horrified at what she had just seen stuck to her knee.

'What are you doing and why are you whispering?' asked Sally.

'I'm on Exmoor and there's a used condom stuck to my knee. Ugh, ugh!' Maddy flapped at her jeans with her free hand.

'For goodness sake talk sense. Are you drunk?'

'No, I'm not drunk. I'm in a hide and there's a condom stuck to my knee.' She managed to dislodge it and it fell to the ground, revealing four fingers and a thumb. Maddy gave a gasp of relief and continued: 'Thank goodness, it's a latex glove. What on earth is that doing here?'

'For the hundredth time, where are you?' Sally sounded exasperated.

'I told you I'm on Exmoor and I'm coming home now. I've had enough for one day.'

'What are you doing?' repeated Sally.

'I'm collecting evidence,' whispered Maddy.

'What are you talking about?'

'I expect Tamsin's accident has been on the news and in the papers. She was virtually a household name.' Maddy ignored Sally's frantic questions.

'No, nothing has been mentioned anywhere, not on the radio nor the TV, nor in the newspapers for that matter.'

'I think that's very odd, don't you?'

'I don't know, I suppose so.'

'Well I do, and it wasn't an accident, it was contrived. I know it was.'

'You're doing something silly, aren't you? Where exactly are you, if I have to tell the police when you disappear?'

'Don't be stupid.' Maddy hoped that she sounded more confident that she felt, although she thought it might be a good idea if someone did know where she was, so she said, 'I'm just above Southways Cross, in a sort of hide on the ridge. My car's in the field and I'm now going to make my way home.'

'Okay,' replied Sally. 'I'll come round this evening with a take-away and a bottle of wine. You can tell me all about it then.'

The thought of normality after the last twenty four hours sounded wonderful to Maddy and, suddenly feeling close to tears, she said, 'I'd better hurry, I probably won't be home until about five. Can you tell Ruth, please?'

'See you later.' Sally rang off.

Maddy felt very alone and anxious to get away from the thicket; on the spur of the moment she decided to take the glove. She picked it up by sticking a twig into one of the fingers, and carried it upright in front of her like a trophy. As she left the thicket her instinct told her to hide it; so she moved it close to her body under her coat.

She felt a rush of relief as she unlocked her car. After she had put the glove in an old plastic bag that she found lying in the boot she changed back into more comfortable shoes and cleaned her sore gorse-scratched hands with an antiseptic wipe. She drank some water and felt a little more human, congratulating herself that no one had seen her.

***

'It's so nice to be home,' said Maddy with feeling, as she and Ruth walked into her kitchen. Her dogs were prancing at her heels, ecstatic to see her and eager for attention.

'How did it go?' asked Ruth.

'It was dreadful, worse than I thought. Simon was horrible. Do you know he never mentioned Tamsin's accident? Don't you think that's odd?'

'N.. no…' said Ruth tentatively, 'perhaps he was too upset.'

'Maybe.'

'How was Emma?'

'Not good, poor kid; it was awful.'

'I didn't think it would be a picnic.'

'No, it certainly wasn't that. Sally rang and said she would bring a take-away.'

'Here she comes right on cue.' Ruth smiled, looking out of the window. 'She's been working here for most of the day. A horse bit her.'

'Which one?' Maddy laughed.

'Jupiter. She was changing his rugs and you know how crabby he gets sometimes? Well, Sally said she would risk it without tying him up and he got her on her arm just as she looked away.'

'Oh dear. I think he's bitten all of us at one time or another, just like his owner.'

They both laughed, Jupiter was a horse belonging to a woman called Angela Tidebrook, the only owner in the yard who was difficult.

'What are you laughing at?' asked Sally as she walked into the kitchen laden with foil boxes in plastic bags. She was tall and slim with brown eyes and straight dark hair cut shorter at the back, the sides swept forwards framing her face. 'Thank goodness you're back in one piece.' She unpacked the food.

'We were laughing at your exploits with Jupiter,' Maddy answered her question.

Sally showed them the blue, purple and yellow bruise which adorned her upper arm. The horse's teeth marks stood out in two semi-circles clearly showing his upper and lower jaw. Maddy winced. 'That looks sore.'

'Tell us what happened at Moorsend,' Sally asked as they started to eat.

'The accident only happened on Monday and it's now Wednesday. It seems as if I've been away for a week. Has it been on the news yet?'

'Yes,' Sally answered. 'It was on the lunchtime news today. They mentioned the road accident and Tamsin's death, no details.'

'I thought it was strange that it wasn't mentioned on Monday,' said Maddy.

'Yes, I agree,' said Sally.

'It's all very odd.' Maddy continued. 'Tamsin was riding Troubadour who was the ultimate gentleman amongst horses. He never put a foot wrong yet he gallops uncontrollably down a hill, along a road and straight into a lorry. Why?'

'The horse probably bolted. You know even the quietest of horses can take fright and bolt,' said Ruth.

Maddy nodded. 'I know, but there's more to it than that.' The others stared at her. 'What do you mean?' asked Ruth.

'What did you find on the moor?' asked Sally.

'Tamsin had been riding along the ridge, above Southways Cross. You know where that is?' They both nodded. 'She often used it as a good place to get the horses fit: a steady hill leads up to the ridge and then the path is straight and flat for nearly a mile. She had been cantering steadily along the track.'

'How do you know?' asked Ruth.

'Because I studied the footfalls of the horse.' Maddy went on to tell them about the hide and the tree, and then described the human footprints that she had seen. 'It looked to me as if Tamsin had slowed down quite steadily and pulled up by the tree. I think she stopped to talk to someone and I believe that they had been waiting for her in the hide. I could see where Troubadour had fidgeted by the thicket. As Tamsin rode on, the horse's footfalls became deeper as if he was going faster. By the time he reached the gateway out into the field it looked as if he was galloping, because there were some very long skid marks when he turned to go through the open gate.'

'You think someone did something to him?' exclaimed Ruth.

'Yes, I do. Then he galloped down the hill across the field towards the road. Tamsin was an event rider for goodness sake, how many hills has she galloped down with huge fences to jump at the bottom? It was part of her everyday life, galloping down hills. When the field flattens out there is enough room to turn the horse in a circle before the road. We've all three been bolted with and we know that if you can keep turning in a circle, the horse will eventually stop. But Troubadour galloped towards the road without the hint of a circle, and then straight down the lane away from Moorsend. The turn towards home wasn't all that sharp, he could have made it.'

'Most horses will always head for their stable,' Sally nodded.

'Troubadour often went that way,' added Ruth. 'He would have known exactly where he was and which way was home.'

'Yes,' Maddy continued: 'But he galloped on down the lane away from Moorsend. He carried on for about half a mile and straight into a lorry. The lorry tried to stop. I saw the skid marks. The road was too narrow for a horse to get past, they had no chance. It was horrible.' Maddy shivered.

'What did Simon say about it?' asked Sally.

'Nothing, we didn't discuss it. Emma thinks the driver was drunk, but I doubt it. Well, actually I don't know if he was or if he wasn't, but that didn't seem to be the cause of the accident. The cause was a runaway horse ridden by a medal winning event rider.' Maddy was becoming emotional and her tears were very close to the surface as she added, 'Horse trials riders are the best all-round riders in the world and Tamsin was one of the best'.

They all fell silent for a while. Sally topped up Maddy's glass and broke the silence. 'You mentioned a rubber glove on the phone. What significance does that have?'

'Yes, I found a rubber glove in the little hide. I thought it was…'

'I know. You made enough fuss about it.'

'So would you if you thought you had knelt in someone else's…'

'Someone else's what?' asked Ruth.

'Never mind, I'll tell you when we've finished eating. I'll bring it in later.'

'Bring it in! You haven't got it with you?' Sally was horrified.

'Yes, I brought it home. It's in the back of my car.'

'I can't believe you did that,' said Sally. 'What on earth are you going to do with it?'

'I don't know. I've also got some photos of the footprints in the hide on my phone. I'll print them out tomorrow on my computer… Actually, I can show them to you now. Where's my phone?' Maddy found her mobile, brought up the first photo on the display and passed it to Sally.

'It's not very clear.' Sally passed it on to Ruth.

'Oh, I don't know.' Ruth scrolled down. 'This one's better. The footprints look as if they belong to a walking boot.'

'That's what I thought,' remarked Maddy.

'Yes, but what size?' asked Sally.

'Well I take size seven, and these were just a bit bigger. They're probably an eight.'

'Could be a man or a woman,' remarked Sally.

'Yes, but a woman with big feet!' replied Maddy.

'What's this?' Ruth scrolled down to the next photo.

'That's the view from the gap in the hide.'

'Let's have a look.' Sally took the mobile. 'Yes, you can see right along the top of the ridge. It's blurred in the distance but you can get the idea of the layout. It's a bit odd isn't it?'

'What is?' asked Maddy.

'Well, this hole in the gorse. It seems to have been very conveniently placed for watching the track. If you were bird watching, wouldn't you look on to the moor, straight in front?'

'Yes, you're right, I hadn't thought of that.' Maddy pondered. 'Now you mention it, when I was rescuing my phone from the ground underneath the gap, it got caught up in some freshly cut pieces of gorse… Someone had cut that hole very recently.'

'I think you're right, someone was waiting there. How horrible.'

Sally blanched.

'Would they have been able to see the horse as it careered down the field while they were standing on the track outside the hide?' Ruth asked.

'Oh yes, easily. And someone must have previously opened the gate for Tamsin because the horse galloped straight through the gateway.' Sally and Ruth stopped eating and stared at Maddy.

'Suppose we're right, who would want to kill Tamsin?' asked Sally. 'Everybody liked her. She was one of the most popular riders on the circuit.'

'I know, I thought of that as I was driving home.'

'It's a bit of an unreliable way to try and kill someone. I mean Tamsin might have bailed out, or she might have stopped Troubadour, then she would have known exactly who had tried to harm her horse, and then what would have happened?' said Ruth.

Sally trembled. 'That's horrible. But who would want to do such a thing?'

'Simon has lots of enemies,' replied Maddy.

'Only you, everyone else likes him. I do,' remarked Sally.

'You fancy him, that's different.'

'You fancied him once,' retorted Sally. 'Anyway I like him, so does Ruth, don't you?'

'Yes I suppose so, although he is a bit up himself,' answered Ruth.

'A bit,' exclaimed Maddy. 'That's the understatement of the year. Anyway, I'm not talking about his social life. I'm talking about his army career. He was in Northern Ireland and in dangerous places in the Middle East. It could be a terrorist revenge attack.'

'Oh my God! You've got someone's rubber glove in your car and photos of their boot prints on your phone,' cried Sally.

'Yes, but they don't know that, do they?'

'I hope not. If this person is a terrorist, then for God's sake don't do anything, let Simon deal with them.'

'But we don't know who they are,' replied Maddy. 'Anyway, I think he is dealing with it.'

'You just said he didn't talk about it.' Sally helped herself to more wine. 'So how do you know?'

'I think he was up on the ridge doing what I was doing.'

'What do you mean?' exclaimed Sally.

'There was another set of footprints up on the moor. They looked like Hunter wellies because I've got a pair and the soles are distinctive. I saw Simon's Hunters in the boot room at Moorsend. They were muddy, and before you say anything I noticed them because I nearly fell over them when I was leaving this morning. I thought at the time it was a bit unusual because you know what a tidy freak he is.' She added, imitating Simon's cultured voice, 'One can't leave one's muddy boots lying around, don't you know'.

The others laughed and Sally got up to make some coffee. 'Well, I must say that's a relief if Simon's on the case.'

'Is it?' asked Maddy, 'I'm not so sure.' Both women stared at her.

'I suppose there'll be an Inquest,' said Ruth.

'I expect so,' replied Maddy.

'Will you go?' asked Sally.

'No, but I'll get the Notes of Evidence from the Coroner's Office after the Inquest. They'll tell us what the witnesses say, etc.'

'If there are any witnesses,' said Sally. 'Are you sure you weren't seen up on the ridge?'

'Yes. No one saw me. Why?' Maddy suddenly took a sharp intake of breath. 'Only...'

'What?' Sally asked.

'Well... there might have been a car. I think I saw one driving away to my right as I joined the road at the bottom of the hill.'

'Oh my God, suppose they followed you back here,' said Sally.

'Don't be silly, I would have noticed.' Silence fell.

'We have to do the late night feeds.' Ruth broke the silence.

'We'll all go out together,' said Maddy.

They trooped out into the yard, taking the dogs with them. Sally went to see Poppy, her pretty dark bay Trakehner mare, and Maddy topped up Hyperion's water bucket and gave him some hay. She loved being out in the stables at this time of night looking over the warm, contented horses as they munched their hay. She stood for a moment in the barn thinking how lucky she was to have them, and then she thought of Jonathan. In the peace and quiet of the stables she could almost feel his presence. 'Thank you for giving me this place and please look after Tamsin, wherever she is,' she whispered.

'Who are you talking to?' asked Sally.

Maddy jumped. 'I didn't hear you come in.'

'Didn't you hear me calling?'

'No.'

'We've finished,' said Ruth as she joined them.

'Where are the dogs?' asked Maddy.

'They're in the feed shed, hunting,' replied Ruth.

Maddy called the dogs and they came out of the shed reluctantly leaving a very promising rat hunt. She locked the door. 'You know, I'm thinking of getting CCTV cameras set up in the yard. You never know who might be prowling around.'

CHAPTER THREE

The telephone rang. Maddy looked at the number on the display and realised that it was unpleasantly familiar. 'Hello,' she said reluctantly.

'Hello, Maddy. Rhona Whitehaven here.' Rhona spoke very quickly. 'I'm sure you've heard the awful news. I saw it on the television last night, dreadful isn't it? Are you going to the funeral? Well, you must be. I think we should all go together, with Jilly too. We local judges must all stick together. What happened? You're a friend of the family. When's the funeral?' Rhona stopped talking as abruptly as she had started.

'I…I don't know yet.' Maddy felt uncomfortable.

'What happened?' Rhone repeated.

'It was a road traffic accident.'

'Is that all you know? As you were so friendly with the family I would expect you to know more.'

'I don't.' Maddy was becoming annoyed.

'Haven't you spoken to them yet?'

'Yes, but…'

'I saw Tamsin the other day at the Taunton Horse Trials. She was in the same section as me, I came fourth. I beat her. Well she did such a bad dressage test, I mean really, for an Olympic rider. She liked my horse; he's an Irish Sports Horse by a good eventing stallion. He's only six and his first time out with me.' Rhona went on to describe in detail how the horse went in each stage of the event. 'So,' barked Rhona, making Maddy jump, 'you will let me know about the funeral.' Before Maddy had a chance to say anything, Rhona hung up.

'Bloody woman!' said Maddy.

'What on earth's the matter?' asked Ruth as she came through the back door.

'Rhona… on the phone. She wants to go to the funeral with me.'

'Why? You're hardly friendly with her.'

'I know and I'm not going anywhere with her or her silly friend,' replied Maddy. 'She was fishing for gossip and going on about her new horse. She said she beat Tamsin, which she didn't. Tamsin won her section on one horse. Then she said that Tamsin liked her horse. But Emma said that Tamsin was really annoyed about her horse.'

***

Later that day Ruth and Maddy were talking in the tack room, sorting out saddles and bridles for a dressage show that they were all going to the next day.

'I'll take this one for Hyps,' said Maddy, picking up a black double bridle with a glittery brow band.

'What about Jupiter?' asked Ruth. 'Is Angela going?'

'No, of course not,' replied Maddy, not noticing that Angela had come in and was standing in the doorway. 'She never wants to do anything.'

'You never asked me if I wanted to go.'

Maddy spun round. 'I'm sorry, I didn't see you there.'

'Obviously not.' Angela grabbed her saddle and bridle and stalked out.

Maddy followed her and, trying to make amends, said, 'Do come with us.'

Angela stopped and looked angrily at Maddy. 'You know it's too late and I haven't entered.' She turned and walked away.

Maddy went back to the tack room. 'Oh dear,' she said to Ruth, 'I didn't mean to upset her.'

'She's feeling left out,' replied Ruth. 'She said as much to me the other day.'

'When?' Maddy broke off as a police car drove up the drive. 'What's this?' She and Ruth stopped what they were doing and looked at each other in dismay.

'Oh my God!' said Maddy. 'Do you think they're after the glove?'

'Don't be stupid.' Ruth sounded unsure.

'Come on. We'd better go and find out.'

'Good morning, madam.' A tall policeman got out of his car. 'Are you Mrs. Richards?'

'Yes.'

'I believe you're a member of the Horse Watch Committee for this area?'

'Yes, I am.'

'We've been informed by our colleagues in Hampshire and West Sussex that horses have been found slashed with knives.'

'What do you mean?'

'Horses have been found mutilated. One had its ear cut off,' replied the policeman looking down at Maddy and Ruth. 'I would like you to warn the horsey people in this area, if you would, please.'

'Yes... Yes, of course.'

'We're asking everyone to be especially vigilant. Do you have CCTV?'

'No, but funnily enough the other night I was talking about getting a camera.'

'Good. Although the attacks seem to be on horses out at grass, and of course you can't always watch a field. There haven't been any incidents in this area yet, but they do seem to be getting nearer.'

'How awful. Who could do such a thing?' Ruth was appalled.

'There are some very nasty people in this world, Miss,' replied the policeman. 'So if you would pass the word on, please?'

'Yes certainly,' replied Maddy. 'I'll do it now shall I?'

'If you wouldn't mind.' The officer got back into his car. 'The sooner the better.'

Maddy sat at the kitchen table ringing all the people on her Horse Watch list. She found it very tedious, repeating the same thing over and over again. Everybody was frightened and angry. At last she came to the end of the list and she put the phone down feeling tired and troubled. It rang again. Her heart skipped a beat as she saw *Tamsin* on the display.

'Hello,' said Emma and without any preamble continued in short staccato sentences. 'Mummy's funeral is on Monday. At 2 o'clock. In the village. At the church. She's being buried. Can you come?'

'Of course I'll be there.'

'Come to the house at 1.30. It's going to be awful. Uncle Nicholas and Aunt Amelia are coming, and Granny Monk, and a load of other relations who I hardly know. The house is going to be full of them. I don't think there'll be enough room for you to stay. I feel dreadful about that.'

Maddy felt quite relieved; she didn't relish the idea of staying at Moorsend with all Simon's relatives. 'Don't worry. How are you? Is Richard with you?'

'Yes, he's staying for a couple of months. He's being great...' she paused. 'There was an Inquest. They said it was an accident.' Emma's voice suddenly sounded very tired. 'I don't believe it. Mummy wouldn't gallop on the road.'

'I know,' said Maddy. 'Perhaps something frightened Troubadour.'

'Maybe.'

'How's Tempie?' asked Maddy.

'She's fine. I'm riding her every day. She makes me feel close to mum. I can hear her voice telling me off when I do something wrong and she's really pleased when Tempie goes well. Do you think I'm mad?'

'No. I know exactly what you mean,' Maddy smiled.

'I knew you would understand. Monica is being brilliant too.' Then she said in a small voice, rather hesitantly, 'I wonder if Tempie and I could come and stay with you after the funeral… When the relations have gone, and Richard goes back to Sandhurst.'

'That's a marvellous idea,' said Maddy. 'We would love to have you. Ruth will enjoy having you here too, and Hyperion. You know he fancies Tempie.'

'Thank you, I'd better go now,' said Emma. 'It's been lovely talking to you. You're so normal. Bye.'

Maddy felt tearful when she came off the phone and Ruth found her rubbing her eyes as she came into the kitchen.

'Oh dear,' said Maddy. 'That was Emma, poor kid, ringing about the funeral. It's next Monday. She wants to come and stay with us later, which will be nice. They've had the Inquest already and it sounds like a verdict of Accidental Death.'

'I expected that verdict actually, didn't you?' said Ruth.

'No… I don't know what I expected. We've got to be at the house at 1.30.'

'Are you staying at Moorsend?' asked Ruth.

'No, it's full of Simon's relatives. Do you want to come?'

'Not really, I hate funerals. I'll stay here and do the horses. Anyway, you're going with Sally aren't you?'

'Yes,' replied Maddy. Then she sighed, putting her head in her hands. 'Oh Ruth, everything is so horrid at the moment.'

***

The next day at the dressage show Maddy met Louise Parkway, an old friend from Hampshire whom she hadn't seen for ages. Louise was a good horsewoman and Maddy liked and respected her. They soon started discussing Tamsin's accident, as well as the knife attacks on horses.

'We've had some assaults on horses as well as several road traffic accidents in our area,' said Louise.

'I know about the horse mutilators,' said Maddy. 'The police came round to warn me. I'm on the Horse Watch Committee.'

'Yes, of course you are. So am I.'

'What sort of attacks have you had near you?' Maddy asked.

'Some have been slashed with a knife, and one was blinded.'

'That's dreadful, that's what the police told me, but they said one had had its ear cut off.'

'Did they give you a website code?' asked Louise.

'No.'

'There's an organisation, some sort of gang who have a website. You can find them quite easily, I have their code. I'll give it to you.'

'Really. How did you get it?'

'Don't ask. Just say that I have friends in very odd places. Don't lose it and don't pass it on to anyone else; I'm giving it to you because you're on the committee. These people are very dangerous. Will you promise that you won't tell anyone, because it could cause a mass panic?'

'Of course.' Maddy felt bewildered.

'Look up their website when you get home. I can assure you it is most unpleasant. This is where you'll find it.' She wrote a name on a scrap of paper. 'When it comes up you enter this password and click on.' She showed Maddy a nine letter word.

'Thank you.' Maddy took the scrap of paper. 'I'll look it up tonight.'

'You might not thank me when you see what's on it. I think you have a right to know what is going on and, as I said, you are a sensible and responsible person.'

'You never know what is going to happen these days; things seem to get worse and worse,' replied Maddy.

'Except your riding, that seems to get better and better.' Louise smiled.

'Thank you. I'd better take Hyps home before he gets fed up. He's been so good.'

'Yes, you've got a good horse there. I expect I'll see you on Monday at the funeral.'

They said their goodbyes and Maddy walked back to her lorry. As she drove away she caught sight of Rhona marching towards her across the lorry park.

***

'It's Rhona again,' said Maddy to Ruth that evening as the phone rang.

'Answer it and get it over with. You know she'll persist.' Maddy grimaced and picked up the phone.

'Hello,' said the strident voice at the other end. 'I'm ringing about this funeral on Monday. I saw you today but you drove away. I need to know times and travelling arrangements.'

'I'm sorry, I didn't see you.' Maddy felt her hackles rise. 'I'm afraid I can't go with you and Jilly. I'm staying in the house and leaving tomorrow. I expect I'll see you there.' She put the phone down before Rhona could reply. She turned to Ruth. 'What a rude woman. I've told her now. Let's hope she stops ringing me.'

'Mmm,' replied Ruth. 'Except you told a porky.'

'She won't find out. I'm going to look up that website in a minute and see what's on it.'

'When you find it give me a shout. I'm going upstairs.'

Maddy went into her sitting room and sat at her computer. The room wasn't used very much. The big inglenook fireplace had a heap of cold ash in the grate and Maddy shivered as she brought up the internet. She found the website straight away and entered the word that Louise had given her. As she clicked on she sat riveted to the spot, cold with fear and anger.

She jumped up and ran up the main staircase, two steps at a time, stood at the foot of the stairs leading to Ruth's flat and yelled, 'Ruth! Come down'. Ruth came racing down the stairs, looking white faced.

'Whatever's the matter?'

'I've found the site.' Maddy headed back down to the sitting room. Ruth joined her and they both stared at the computer.

'I can't believe it.' Ruth gazed in horror as she saw a series of pictures of injured horses. All of them had been mutilated in one way or another. There were captions with each picture describing what had been done to the horse, and the name of the person or people who had done it. They all had names from characters in cartoon films.

Maddy scrolled down slowly and as she did so the pictures became worse.

'How could people do this?' asked Ruth.

'The horses all look old, poor things. They have trusted human beings all their lives and given of their best only to be treated like this. It's outrageous. I know what I would do to these people.'

'Click on that icon labelled "*Video*",' said Ruth.

'All right.' The two friends sat in stunned silence.

'This is worse. This is torture,' said Maddy. 'The horses look drugged but they're not anaesthetised. I've got to turn it off. I never knew that horses screamed in pain. I feel sick.'

'Me too.' Ruth jumped up. 'Let's go and check our horses.'

***

Maddy spent the Sunday before the funeral working in the yard. Ruth had gone out for the day and wouldn't be back until much later that evening. As most of the liveries came to ride their horses on a Sunday it was a busy day. Maddy gave a lesson to a young girl who kept her horse in the yard and helped Angela with Jupiter, who was being particularly difficult. Maddy rode him in the school and got him going quite well.

'Thank you,' said Angela begrudgingly. 'I think he hates me. He won't go like that for me.'

'Of course he doesn't hate you,' said Maddy. She wanted to say that it was because she was a more experienced rider, but thought that might offend.

'You're going to the funeral tomorrow, aren't you?' asked Angela.

'Yes.' Maddy tried not to snap. Everybody was asking her the same question and she was becoming tired of answering. Also she was worrying about the website as well as the funeral.

'When will you be back?'

'Tomorrow evening or Tuesday morning, I'm not sure yet. Why?' replied Maddy.

'I only wondered. Are Sally and Judith going with you?'

'No, just Sally. ' Maddy was surprised at the question because Judith was a new owner. She had only just come to the yard and Maddy didn't know her very well.

'I'll put Jupiter away now,' said Angela. Maddy watched her go and felt uneasy.

It had been a particularly long day and Maddy thankfully finished up in the yard with help from some of her liveries. Then she relaxed into a hot bath.

Sally arrived just as she was getting out.

'I've got loads of things to tell you,' said Maddy as they set off in Sally's little red Mini Cooper for dinner in a popular local pub.

They managed to get a table for two in the corner of the busy restaurant. While they ate Maddy told Sally about the visit from the police and her conversation with Louise Parkway. She mentioned the website and went on to say, 'I just wonder if the two things are connected'.

'What two things?'

'The website and Tamsin,' replied Maddy.

'I don't see how. You said the attacks were in Hampshire. Anyway, they're on horses in the field, not with riders on their backs.'

'I suppose so.'

'Are you going to say something to Simon?'

'Not tomorrow!'

'I didn't mean tomorrow,' replied Sally. 'I meant later, when things are back to normal'.

'I don't know... I suppose I'll have to tell him about that glove.'

'You've still got the glove then?'

'Oh yes, it's in the fridge,' replied Maddy. They chatted on about the yard and the liveries.

'Angela is being quite off-hand with me,' said Sally. 'I don't know what I've done to upset her.'

'Yes, she's being funny with me, too,' said Maddy. 'She asked if Judith was going with us tomorrow. You've met Judith, haven't you? She owns the black and white cob called Panda.'

'Yes, of course I have. She seems to be very nice.'

'She is. Well, Angela appears to be jealous of her for some reason, and envious of you come to that.'

'Look over there!' gasped Sally, changing the subject. Maddy turned round and saw Jilly Rich standing by the bar.

'I don't believe it,' said Maddy. 'They seem to be following me about, what's the matter with them?'

'Perhaps they're spying on us.'

'Don't be silly, it's just a coincidence. Rhona doesn't live all that far away and this is a good pub.'

'I think it's fishy, especially after Rhona's phone calls, which you did say were odd,' replied Sally.

'I can't see Rhona,' said Maddy. 'So you're wrong.'

'No, that's because she's right behind you,' whispered Sally and began to giggle. Maddy spun round in her chair. Her heart sank. Rhona was standing behind a square oak pillar which was the remnants of a door frame which had been left after the restaurant had been made into one room from two.

'I told her we were going to Moorsend today. Oh Lord!'

Rhona stared straight at them and Maddy, feeling that she had to say something, said rather feebly, 'Hello Rhona, what are you doing here?' Sally began to laugh helplessly.

'More to the point, what are you doing?' snapped Rhona. 'I thought you were going down to Devon tonight.'

'There was a last minute change of plan, too many relations in the house. We've to be there early tomorrow. I'm sorry, we could have gone with you after all.' She didn't dare look at Sally, who was making choking noises.

'What was Louise saying to you yesterday?' demanded Rhona.

Maddy was a little taken aback and she hesitated before replying, 'Nothing much... I can't remember. She said she thought Hyperion went well... That was all really. Why, should she have said something else?'

'No.' Then, as an afterthought, Rhona added: 'Did she mention my new horse?'

'No, she didn't.'

'I must say I can't wait to see this horse of yours,' Sally joined in the conversation. Rhona didn't bother to reply as Jilly sidled up to her carrying two drinks.

'I've ordered our food, Rhona,' said Jilly in her simpering voice. Then she said something in a very quiet voice. Rhona smiled and nodded.

Maddy could see that Sally was beginning to feel the effects of the wine and cringed as she opened her mouth to say, 'Talking about someone again, Jilly?'

'Oh no, I was just telling Rhona that our table will be ready in a minute,' tittered Jilly.

'I thought you were saying something really important,' said Sally.

'She was,' Rhona answered curtly. 'I'm hungry and I want to sit down.'

'Don't let us keep you,' said Sally. Then she added in a more friendly tone, 'The food is really good.'

'Yes, Rhona said the food is good here, that's why we came. I wanted to try it, I haven't been here before,' said Jilly. 'Here comes the waiter, Rhona; we're sitting over there.' They walked away in the direction of their table which was at the other end of the dining room.

'Thank goodness they've gone.' Maddy heaved a sigh of relief. 'You didn't have to giggle. I don't know how I kept a straight face. How long had she been standing there?'

'I don't know. They are peculiar.'

'Yes, and her blasted new horse is beginning to get on my nerves,' said Maddy.

'I'm curious. We'll have to make an effort to go and see it.'

'Yes, we definitely will,' agreed Maddy.

They finished their meal with no more interruptions, paid their bill and made their way to Sally's car.

'Are you all right to drive?' asked Maddy. 'Only you looked a little tight earlier on.'

'I'm absolutely fine. Get in.'

As the car turned in to the yard the security light flashed on, making the dogs bark.

'I thought you turned that thing off nowadays,' said Sally.

'I did, because the slightest thing triggers it, like a bat. It comes on and sets the dogs off.'

'Why turn it on then?'

'Because of the website.'

'Can I see this website?'

'No.'

'Why not?'

'Because it's horrible and it will give you nightmares. I'm not allowing you to watch it.' Sally subsided into sulky silence as they went indoors and found Ruth in the kitchen having a hot drink. Maddy told her about the meeting with Rhona and Jilly.

'That must have been embarrassing,' remarked Ruth.

'It was, and it didn't help with Sally openly giggling.'

Ruth turned to Sally and said, 'You're being very quiet'.

'Maddy won't show me this website,' complained Sally.

'Believe me you don't want to see it,' replied Ruth.

'Yes I do. You've seen it, so I want to see it.'

'All right, on your own head be it. Follow me.' Maddy marched into the sitting room and turned on the computer. 'Help yourself.' She put up the site and returned to the kitchen. 'Honestly,' she said to Ruth. 'I like Sally, but sometimes a little of her goes a very long way.'

Maddy and Ruth looked at each other and laughed as they heard shrieks coming from the sitting room.

'I'm going to throw up.' Sally ran into the kitchen. 'You shouldn't have let me see that.'

'I told you.' Maddy wondered how she was going to get through the next day with Sally as a companion. She decided that on no account was she going to let her have anything to drink.

***

They had an easy run down to Devon and arrived on the outskirts of Exmoor at mid-morning in time for coffee. They found some tea rooms in a picturesque village near Moorsend and were surprised to find it buzzing with people.

They spotted two women leaving a table and hurriedly sat down. The service was slow. However, when the waitress arrived she was very apologetic. 'We're usually shut on a Monday this time of year, but we opened for the funeral.' She looked them up and down. 'I take it you're going, seeing as how you're dressed in black. Dreadful thing to 'appen weren't it? 'Specially to a lovely lady like 'er. Still, when your time's up, I suppose.'

Maddy nodded and gave their order. As soon as the waitress had bustled away she said to Sally, 'We'll be here forever.'

'We've got masses of time to kill.' Sally looked around. 'I wonder if the person who owns the rubber glove is here.'

Maddy jumped. 'Don't be silly.'

'I'm not. They say that the murderer always goes to the funeral, that's why the police go too.'

'We haven't said that she was murdered,' whispered Maddy. She looked furtively around the room. 'And for goodness sake be careful with your choice of words.'

'We haven't actually said it, but we have inferred it and if our suspicions are right, then she was...' replied Sally.

Maddy suddenly slumped in her chair; she felt sad and frightened. 'You're right, I hadn't really thought of it like that. I think the... whoever did it, is one of those people on the website. Or it was a terrorist revenge killing.' She shuddered. She nearly said that the culprits would stand out like a sore thumb on Exmoor. Then she thought that any of those people would be able to merge perfectly into the background if they wanted to.

'Look over there.' Sally pointed to some people in the middle of the room. Maddy looked and saw two dressage judges, both of whom they knew, sitting with a couple of horse trials riders.

'Oh dear,' said Maddy. 'Let's pretend we haven't seen them. I don't feel like making polite conversation.'

'No', agreed Sally. 'I don't like them very much anyway.'

42

Maddy smiled. 'Only because one of them gave you low marks once.' Sally grinned too, and their mood lightened a little.

The waitress eventually arrived with their order. The coffee was lukewarm but the cakes were fresh. They ate in silence listening to the conversations of the people around them.

As they left the tea rooms they waved to the group of people at the middle table, who waved back and smiled. Several other people were leaving the little village and they found themselves following a stream of cars along the road to Moorsend. As they approached the lane to Simon's home the traffic slowed to walking pace. They were stopped by police at a T-junction. A few cars were allowed to turn right to Moorsend, but the majority were being directed left to the church.

Maddy presented her card and a young policeman waved them through.

'This is weird,' she said as she drove slowly down the lane towards Moorsend. Another policeman stopped them at the entrance to the long drive and checked her card again.

'Why is there so much security?' Sally asked him.

'Foreign royalty and VIPs coming. Class A security,' he replied briefly.

'Blimey!' remarked Sally. Maddy was very quiet as they continued down the drive. Two people, who Maddy recognised as grooms from Tamsin's yard, directed the 4 x 4 round to the stable yard.

'I'm glad you came with me,' said Maddy. 'This is very formal.'

'Yes,' replied Sally in a small voice.

Maddy parked the car. 'I think we'd better go in through the front door.' She saw two large security men blocking the way to the back of the house.

She kept her head down and hurried round to the front. Sally had to run to catch up with her. They arrived at the front door to be stopped by two more security guards who checked their names again and then let them in. Simon was standing in the hall welcoming the guests as they arrived. He looked immaculate and dignified in his well-cut, dark suit and black silk tie, although he appeared gaunt and drawn. Maddy blushed as she remembered their last meeting and the things that she had said to him.

He gave her a polite peck on the cheek and she shook his hand, but she couldn't look him in the face or say anything. She felt too close to tears. He shook Sally's hand politely and thanked them both for coming. Sally muttered a sentence that contained the word "condolences", but the rest was unintelligible. Simon then walked forward to greet the people who were coming in behind them.

Sally and Maddy made their way into the big drawing room. Some of the furniture had been removed from the room and the rest pushed to the sides. The room was rapidly filling up with people who were talking in hushed voices. Crisply dressed waiters and waitresses were handing out drinks and passing round large platters of canapés.

'Don't drink too much,' Maddy whispered to Sally, as she went to take a glass of wine that was being offered to her.

Maddy at last found Emma and they threw their arms around each other. Emma looked pale, drawn and thin. She didn't say very much but stood close to Maddy as people came to offer their condolences.

'I can't think of anything different to say,' she said to Maddy.

'You're doing very well,' replied Maddy. 'Just keep repeating yourself. What you're saying is exactly right.' Emma smiled a watery smile.

'What's that?' Maddy was startled by a distant thudding noise which was becoming louder and louder.

'The …' replied Emma, but the rest of her words were drowned as a helicopter hovered over the south lawn. The guests drifted over to the windows. An Arab Sheik and his wife stepped down from the aircraft, followed by a well-known business tycoon.

Simon walked out to greet them and ushered them across the lawn. He took them through the French windows and into Tamsin's sitting room. The rest of the guests started talking again, drifted away from the windows, sipped their drinks and picked at the canapés as if nothing had happened.

Richard came into the room to find Emma. He was wearing his military uniform which suited him very well. He looked exactly like Simon when he was that age. Maddy felt her stomach turn over.

After greeting her and Sally, he said to Emma, 'You're needed in mum's sitting room'.

Emma shot a startled look at Maddy saying, 'Oh Lord!' Richard put his arm around her and escorted her out of the room.

Maddy looked around and recognised several international riders. A member of the German horse trials team was talking to some Australian and New Zealand riders.

'It's like Who's Who in the eventing world,' muttered Sally.

'Yes.' replied Maddy. 'I wonder when it's going to start. You know we're following the hearse on foot to the church?'

'Yes, you have told me several times, that's why I am wearing flat shoes.'

Just then there was a hush, and someone announced: 'My lords, ladies and gentlemen, would you like to proceed into the hall?'

'Lords!' repeated Sally under her breath.

People began to walk slowly out into the hall. The front door was wide open and Maddy caught her breath as she suddenly saw the hearse. It was drawn by four black horses with plumes on their heads. White flowers surrounded the coffin. Two male grooms dressed in frock coats and top hats were holding the horses' heads and the driver perched on the box seat holding the reins.

Maddy caught sight of a black Rolls Royce sweeping majestically down the drive carrying the VIPs slowly towards the church. The hearse set off, followed by Simon and Richard with Emma walking between them. Behind them Monica led Mr. Darcy, Tamsin's medal winning horse. The rest of the mourners followed on. Maddy estimated there must have been well over a hundred, if not two hundred people. Everybody walked in silence.

As they approached the church they could see that the road had been cordoned off. Cars were parked in a field and a crowd of people stood in the churchyard behind a temporary fence. Maddy shivered as she wondered if the murderer was somewhere amongst them.

They filed into the church, most people making for the front, and to Maddy's disgust, some were almost pushing. She and Sally found two seats near the back. A lot of people had to stand. Maddy felt as if she was in a daze. When the service started she stood up and sat down when required, like an automaton.

A well-known international rider stood up and went to the lectern to give an address.

'We all knew and loved Tamsin,' he started. 'She was an inspiration to every team she was in, and thankfully she was often in the team.' People smiled. 'She had time for everyone. I have seen her stop and help the most novice of riders, as well as the more experienced ones. I can honestly say that I have never heard a bad word said against her. There are not many people who can boast that.' Again people smiled. Maddy's mind drifted away as she began to think about Jonathan's funeral. She jerked herself back to the present when the speaker's voice broke as he said, 'God bless you Tamsin. We'll all miss you so much'. He stepped down and returned to his seat, his face set and his eyes moist.

They stood up to sing another hymn. Maddy managed to open and shut her mouth but no words came out.

When the hymn finished Simon took his place behind the lectern. He stood tall and upright, his face looked gaunt; however, he was completely in control of his emotions. Maddy suddenly thought he looked lonely and vulnerable and her heart went out to him, in spite of everything. He waited until everyone had settled down in their seats before he spoke. His cultured voice rang out loud and clear.

'My children and I would like to thank you all for coming here today, and I would like to thank our friend for his moving words. My wife was one of the most truly good people I have ever known. She had an inner light that shone out and she lit the way for so many people. She lit the path for me on many occasions; without her patience and guidance I would long ago have fallen by the wayside. Not only was she my beloved wife, but she was also my best friend. She listened to my problems and quandaries and helped me find the answers to my dilemmas.

'She was a perfectionist in everything she did. You have all seen it in her riding, but she was the same in the home and as a mother. While I was in the army I was frequently away from home. She never complained and I have always thanked her for that. In fact there are so many things that I thank her for.' Simon suddenly stopped reading from his notes. He stared at the coffin and started to speak from his heart. The congregation sat very still. As the words were relayed outside a hush fell over the crowded churchyard, even the birds seemed to stop singing. It was as if everything and everyone were holding their breath.

'I thank God I met her and fell in love with her. I thank her for her deep understanding and treasure the loyal and tireless love that she gave to me. I will always remember her beauty and her goodness, her gentleness and her tremendous inner strength. She was kind and had a wonderful sense of humour. Her expertise and dedication to her sport were an inspiration to everyone. I thank her for her remarkable sense of right and wrong and for her courage in never wavering from doing what she believed in, however hard that was. I know I was privileged to be her husband and I thank her for allowing me to be so. Goodbye, my beloved Tamsin. God bless you.' Simon stepped down and returned to his seat.

He seemed to have an air of inner tranquillity and relief, as if he had unburdened his soul and received some sort of atonement. Maddy stared at him, struggling with her emotions. She had never seen a look like that on his face before. *He loved her,* she thought. *He really loved her. How could I have said those things to him? Tamsin, please forgive me. I don't blame him for hating me.*

At last the service was over and the coffin was carried out to the churchyard. Maddy and Sally found themselves right at the back of the group around the graveside. They could hear what was being said, but they couldn't see what was going on.

The Rolls Royce slipped away down the road as they walked silently back towards the house. Maddy felt drained and tired and glad that it was over. Soon they heard the helicopter as it circled above them and headed back towards London. As they approached the front door Maddy said quietly, 'I suppose we shall have to go in. I just want to go home'.

'Me too,' said Sally. 'That was the most emotional thing I've ever been through. I feel exhausted.'

'We'll have to say goodbye to Simon, Emma and Richard. Then we'll go home.' They made their way into the house and found Simon. Maddy took his hand and looked him straight in the eye saying, 'I'm so sorry, Simon.' He squeezed her hand and gave a ghost of a smile. She felt he knew what she meant.

Emma looked dreadful and Maddy wished they could take her back home with them. They stayed for a short while talking to her but other people soon wanted her attention so Maddy gave her a long hug. 'We have to go now. Tell me when you want to come and stay.'

'Yes, I will.'

Maddy and Sally drove away in silence. It wasn't until they were driving up the motorway nearly an hour later that Maddy broke the silence. 'What a terribly sad, but strangely uplifting experience. I feel in awe of it. But most of all I want to find the person who killed her.'

CHAPTER FOUR

On the day after the funeral life went on as usual. The new livery, Judith, arrived for a lesson. She was a lady in her sixties who had been a good rider in her youth but she hadn't ridden for several years.

Maddy greeted her by saying, 'How do you feel about coming for a hack today with Ruth, Sally and me?'

'I would love to, if you think I'm up to it. As you know, I am a little out of practice.'

'Of course you're ready for a hack in the woods. You'll soon be back to riding as you used to.'

'You're very kind,' Judith smiled, 'but I doubt that.'

Angela was standing close by. Maddy felt she had to ask, 'Why don't you come too?'

'No, I don't think so.' Angela walked away.

It was a lovely day. Maddy felt happy and free; it was a welcome break after the emotional experiences of the last few days. She chatted to Judith while Ruth and Sally followed behind, deep in conversation.

'Let's canter on,' said Maddy. She smelt the damp earth beginning to respond to the warmth of the sun and listened to the muffled hoof beats and the steady breathing of the horses. She felt the power from the horse beneath her as he strode effortlessly along the woodland ride. She hoped that it would be a long time before she had to give all this up.

As they approached the end of the track she held up her hand and dropped back to a walk. Turning to Judith she asked, 'Did you enjoy that?'

'Oh yes,' replied Judith laughing and patting Panda, her black and white cob. 'It's ages since I've enjoyed a ride like this. My children say I should join the Women's Institute instead of taking up riding again, but nothing beats the freedom of being on a horse.'

'No.' Maddy laughed, 'The Women's Institute indeed!'

All four riders felt elated as they rode back into the yard. Maddy saw Angela standing in the drive and asked, 'How's Jupiter?'

'All right.' Angela got into her car and drove away.

'What's wrong with her?' asked Maddy, but the others were engrossed in their conversation and didn't hear.

'The dogs are being very quiet,' remarked Maddy. 'They're usually going mad by now. Perhaps they haven't heard us.'

Sally was the first to finish settling her horse into its stable. Saying,

'I'll go and make some coffee', she walked to the house.

Seconds later she came flying back yelling, 'Maddy. Come here. Quick'.

Maddy ran into the kitchen followed by Judith and Ruth. She stopped in horror. The dogs lay lifeless on the floor. Zippy was just inside the door and Jock was under the table.

'What's the matter with them,' exclaimed Maddy. 'Are they breathing?'

'Zippy is.' Ruth was close to tears.

Maddy pulled the other one out from under the table. 'Yes, Jock's breathing too. Put them in their baskets. Keep them warm, I'll ring the vet.'

'What did he say?' asked Ruth as Maddy came off the phone.

'Mike said to keep them warm, which we've done. He... he told me what to do if they started fitting. He said it could be poison... Oh goodness. What are we going to do?'

'Keep calm,' said Judith. 'Wait until he comes. He won't be long.'

'You've left the fridge door open,' said Sally, 'and there's a hell of a mess in there.'

'What are you talking about?' Maddy grew cold. She glanced inside the fridge. 'Oh no!' She stood up looking pale and frightened.

'Whatever's the matter?' asked Sally.

'The glove. It's gone.'

'Are you sure?' gasped Ruth.

'Yes, of course I'm sure. It was here in the corner at the back. I put a jug of soup in front of it. That's fallen over and the glove is missing.'

'Oh Lord,' exclaimed Sally. 'You know what that means?'

'Of course I know what it means.'

'What does it mean?' Judith was bewildered. Maddy looked at Sally and Ruth.

'You'd better tell her,' said Ruth.

'Tell me what?' asked Judith.

Maddy took a deep breath. 'It's a long story.' She told Judith all about the events of the last two weeks. When she finished Judith looked appalled and frightened.

'Do you think they poisoned the dogs?' asked Ruth, who was sitting on the floor in between the two beds with a hand on each dog. She had tears in her eyes.

'I don't know,' said Maddy. 'They must have ... How could I have been so stupid?'

'How could anyone just walk in here?' asked Judith.

'Well, we never lock the kitchen door,' replied Ruth.

'I think it's time I spoke to Simon,' said Maddy. 'This is getting beyond a joke. I'll ring him this evening when I know what's wrong with the dogs.'

'Who was here while we were out?' asked Judith.

'Angela,' said Maddy. 'Anyone else?'

'I don't think so,' replied Ruth.

'She must have seen someone,' said Sally.

'Not necessarily, not if she was in the school or in Jupiter's stable,' said Ruth.

Judith looked at her watch. 'It's after 12 o'clock. I'm sorry but I have an appointment. I've got to go. I'll ring you later.'

'I'm so sorry to involve you in all this, Judith,' said Maddy.

'Don't worry about that,' said Judith smiling. 'Perhaps you'd better check the house to see if anything else has been stolen.'

'I hadn't thought of that.' Maddy did a tour of the house. Nothing else was missing. Then she paced up and down waiting for the vet.

He drove up the gravel drive in a cloud of dust and walked hurriedly into the kitchen. After carefully examining the dogs, he said, 'I think they may have been drugged. I can't tell for sure. I'll take blood samples and I want urine and faeces samples when they come round. Keep a very close eye on them and let me know of any change in their behaviour. Have you put rat poison down in the yard?'

'We never put poison down here.'

'Has anything been taken from the house?'

'No,' replied Maddy. He went on to ask some more searching questions. How long had they been out riding, who was there at the time, had they seen anyone suspicious lurking about? Maddy was pleased that he was busy taking blood samples from the dogs, and not looking at her as she replied.

'I've got to send these bloods away. It'll take at least five days for the results to come back. So I won't have the answer for you until the middle of next week.'

Maddy felt despondent.

Sally, who had been staring at the floor suddenly shouted, 'Look!' Maddy jumped. Behind the door lay a chunk of raw steak.

'Ah,' said Mike. 'I'll take that. This might give us a clue. Don't worry too much. I think that if it was poison we would be seeing adverse reactions from the dogs by now.'

Maddy gave him a piece of clingfilm to wrap around the meat, when a big black cat came sauntering into the kitchen.

'Thank goodness you're all right,' exclaimed Maddy, gathering him up and holding him very tight.

Mike picked up his bag, saying, 'It seems as if the meat was brought in here and given specifically to the dogs. I think you should call the police'.

'Yes.' Maddy tried to sound as if she meant it.

'Let me know of any changes.' The vet hurried out of the kitchen.

When he had gone Sally and Maddy stared at each other.

'Oh God! What have I done?' Maddy was becoming distraught. 'If Zippy and Jock die I'll never forgive myself.' She sat staring at the dogs lying in their baskets, then she sat up and exclaimed, 'And what about the horses - are they in danger too?'

Ruth jumped up. 'I'm going out to the yard.'

'Who on earth knew that I had the glove?' Maddy asked.

'I don't know,' replied Sally. 'Whoever it was is a killer or his accomplice.' She shivered. 'I hate to leave you on your own, but I've got to go home. I'm expecting an important call.'

'You go. Ruth is here; besides, now that they have what they want maybe they won't come back.'

'Okay. I'll ring you later.' Sally walked out to her car. She instantly flew back into the kitchen. 'Maddy!' she shouted.

'What now?' Maddy sighed.

'Simon!'

'What about him?'

'He's here! He's just arrived. Here.'

'I don't believe you.' Maddy walked to the back door. She froze as she saw him getting out of his car. 'I don't believe it. What does he want? He's probably after the glove. Is the kitchen tidy?' She looked round panicking. 'No it's a mess. Don't go, stay here.' She picked up the dirty coffee mugs and put them down again in the same place.

'Calm down,' said Sally. 'He can't eat you.'

'Yes,' Maddy violently nodded her head, 'he can.'

'Well, I'll stay to protect you. I think he's gorgeous. He's coming up the path towards the back door. You'd better go and say hello.'

'Do I look calm and in control?' asked Maddy. Sally didn't answer. Maddy managed to pull herself together and walked calmly out of the back door to greet him. She thought he looked good dressed in a cream cashmere jumper which he wore over an open necked, pale blue silk shirt. He had on light coloured slacks and wore a pair of very shiny brown brogues. He strolled towards the two women. Maddy felt like a guilty schoolgirl.

'Hello,' he said, in his deep cultured voice. 'Are you busy? I hope I'm not putting you out.'

'We are rather busy,' replied Maddy quickly.

'No, not at all.' Sally smiled at him under her eyelashes. 'Please come in.'

Maddy glared at her, but replied, 'Yes, come in.' She stood aside to let him walk into the kitchen and said in a slightly sarcastic tone, 'This is very unexpected. To what do we owe the pleasure of this visit?'

'I'll make some coffee.' Sally busily put the kettle on and cleared up the dirty mugs.

'Your dogs are very quiet.' Simon sat at the table and looked at the two sleeping canines. 'If I didn't know otherwise, I would think they were under an anaesthetic.'

'Yes.' Maddy offered no explanation and hoped that he was right.

'Black or white?' Sally smiled flirtatiously.

'Black no sugar, thank you,' replied Simon at his most charming.

Maddy heaved a sigh, thinking, *that's all I need, Simon and Sally having an affair.*

Simon said abruptly, 'I need to talk to you in private.'

Maddy thought, *you're not going to waste any time then.* She was trying not to look at the dogs so she stared out of the window. 'Maddy, did you hear?' said Simon. 'I need to speak to you.' She jumped and said; 'Why? I thought you were talking to Sally.'

'You know why,' he replied.

Maddy shot an anxious glance at Sally who nearly spilt the coffee that she was handing to him.

'Thank you.' He pretended not to notice that he had narrowly escaped a mug of scalding coffee in his lap.

'I was just on my way out,' said Sally.

'No, stay,' said Maddy.

Simon turned to Sally and said, 'Yes, I think that would be a good idea. I would hate to keep you'. Sally fled. Maddy stared after her, thinking how quickly she had given in. She turned to Simon, her eyes blazing. 'How dare you tell my friends what to do in my house.'

'So sorry,' he replied urbanely. 'But I need to ask you some questions.'

'What questions?' Maddy was belligerent. 'You walk in here out of the blue ordering people about. Who do you think you are?'

Simon ignored her outburst and, looking her straight in the eye, said in a soft voice, 'When you were at Southways Cross the other day, what were you doing?' Maddy sat open mouthed, staring at him. 'What were you doing, Maddy?' he repeated with an edge to his voice.

'I wasn't...'

'Don't lie.'

'How do you know?' she gasped.

'Because I saw you.'

'Nobody was there. You were out. You went to Barnstaple.'

'No, I followed you. I knew you would be up to something. Asking Monica questions, rushing off before lunch,' he replied, almost smiling. Maddy blushed and looked away, feeling mortified.

'You wanted me to go. You were furious because I was there in the first place.'

'I don't deny that.'

'Well then,' said Maddy, stung by the truth and now infuriated. 'I was embarrassed by what I said to you. Now I re-instate it.'

'Reinstate it?' He laughed. 'What's that supposed to mean?' Maddy looked away as she tried to think of something to say. He repeated, 'So what were you doing there?'

'Nothing,' she replied, glaring at him.

'I'm not playing games, Maddy.' His voice hardened and she began to feel frightened. 'You might as well tell me, I'll stay here all night if I have to.' He spoke unpleasantly, his eyes bored straight through her.

'You tell me,' she said facetiously. 'You seem to know everything.' He leant over and grabbed hold of her wrist. 'Let go,' she said angrily.

'Not until you tell me.'

He was hurting her but she looked him straight in the face and said, 'I didn't know you were into beating up women. Screwing them, yes, abusing them, no'. He let go of her arm as if it was red hot.

'You always have to harp back to that don't you?' he flew back at her. 'Just because I dumped you all those years ago. I don't know how anyone can be so sad and vindictive.'

'What do you mean? *You* dumped me?' she asked, surprised.

'Don't tell me you've forgotten,' he said sneering at her. 'I dropped you for Tamsin and you have never forgiven me.'

Maddy started laughing and he stared at her, a little taken aback.

'You thought for all this time that you had dumped me?' she said, still laughing. 'That's the funniest thing I have heard in ages.'

'What do you mean?' His eyes were like steel. 'I went out with Tamsin and then you went out with Jonathan.'

'No, sweetheart,' replied Maddy; this time she was sneering at him. 'You introduced me to Jonathan. I fell in love with him. I introduced you to Tamsin, and I let nature take its course. It worked, which left me free to go out with Jonathan, which was what I wanted all along. I knew you'd make a fuss if I told you I wanted to end our relationship. But you were far too up yourself to realise that it was me who called a halt to everything. And you haven't changed either, have you?'

He stared at her and said, 'I don't believe you.'

'Well, you wouldn't would you? Your head is so far up your own backside that I am surprised you can see anything at all.'

'There's no need to be crude. You are making all this up. You always had to be right. I remember how nasty you became if you didn't get your own way. Well, that just proves what a conniving bitch you are. I had a lucky escape!'

'Huh. You had a lucky escape? I had the Great Escape, the greatest escape of the century.'

'Now you're being childish.'

Maddy suddenly started giggling and said, 'You have to see the funny side to it, Simon'.

'I can't see anything funny at all.'

'Oh come on. You can't have been that disappointed, you married Tamsin very quickly.'

'Yes, I did,' he said, suddenly looking sad. 'I thought you went out with Jonathan pretty speedily too. I couldn't understand why you held a grudge.'

'I didn't hold a grudge.'

'No? Well if you didn't, why did you hound me with the Sonia thing then? You were as jealous as hell.'

'Jealous! You thought I was jealous? Come out of the dark ages, Simon.' She laughed.

Simon looked away. 'I don't mean jealous,' he said rather feebly.

'Well, what do you mean?'

His face hardened as he remembered the trouble she had caused and he snapped at her, 'Why did you do it?'

'Because everybody knew what you were doing. It was only going to be a matter of time before Tamsin knew anyway. You were making her look stupid.'

'I wasn't. You nearly lost me my marriage,' he snarled at her.

'No, *you* nearly lost your marriage, all by yourself. As I just said, somebody would have told her.'

'So you saved them the trouble,' he said sarcastically. 'How thoughtful of you.'

'Anyway, you carried on with a vengeance after Sonia. Tamsin always made excuses for you. I despised you.'

'I know what you thought of me, even after she told you the reason. You're just a vindictive bitch.'

'What reason?'

'Don't pretend she didn't tell you.'

'Tell me what?'

'The reason.'

'What reason? What are you talking about?'

'Oh, if you don't know, then I can't tell you.' He spoke slowly.

'You're making this up. What reason?'

'I'm not making it up. I wish I was.' He looked sad and pensive.

Maddy began to believe him and asked softly, 'What reason, Simon?'

He sighed and said, 'I can see why you thought so badly of me'. Maddy stared at him. 'You see Tamsin… Didn't you wonder why we got married so quickly?' He began fiddling with some papers that were lying on the table.

'No, I thought you loved each other.'

'So did I.' He looked miserable.

Maddy began to feel uneasy. 'What do you mean?' She had never seen Simon look so unsure of himself and embarrassed like this before. She didn't like it.

'Tamsin…' he paused, searching for words. 'Tamsin had had a bad experience.' He got up and walked over to the back door. Maddy didn't take her eyes off him and waited for him to continue.

'She did… she did love me… In her own way, as much as she could love any man.'

'You mean she was a lesbian.' Maddy was incredulous.

'Don't be so stupid,' he snapped back.

'What do you mean, then?' Maddy asked more gently.

'She had to leave home, because of her father.' As he said the word father his face became hard, and he continued; 'I didn't know it at the time. I didn't know until the Sonia incident.'

'Oh my God,' said Maddy, putting two and two together. 'You mean her father…?'

'Yes.' Simon looked at the floor. 'Yes… He made her life hell. The bastard. She would never let me sort him out.' He clenched his teeth.

'I never knew,' said Maddy quietly. 'She never said. Poor Tamsin. No wonder she adored you, and stuck up for you. I'm so sorry.'

'She hated talking about it but I did think that she had told you.' Maddy shook her head. He walked to the Aga and stood holding on to the rail as if it gave him support. He had never told anyone. Suddenly it was a relief to be able to talk about it. It was as if now he had started telling the story he couldn't stop.

'As I said,' he continued, 'she never mentioned it, only the once, when things came to a head. Our marriage had become a sham, in the physical sense, after Emma was born.' His face looked tragic but he managed a weak smile as he said, 'I think she thought it was her duty to provide me with an heir and a spare.' Maddy stared at him.

'She didn't like being touched, you see. But we loved each other in different ways. She needed me and I needed her. She was my best friend and the mother of my children, and now she's gone.' Maddy had never seen him look so vulnerable.

'Simon, I'm so sorry,' she said. She paused, remembering how good he was in bed. The sex between them had been brilliant; that was why she had found it impossible to break with him until she had met Jonathan. Simon was never too tired for sex, even after army exercises when he was completely shattered. *And his wife wouldn't let him touch her. Poor Simon,* thought Maddy as she sat at the table, dumbstruck. She wanted to get up and put her arms round him, but she didn't. She broke the silence, saying, 'So she didn't mind about your affairs'. He shook his head and Maddy added, 'Because of what came out after the Sonia incident?'

'Yes.'

'So I helped your marriage, then?' she said a little belligerently.

'I suppose so.'

'Well then there was no need for you to be so nasty to me,' she retorted. He didn't reply.

Maddy sat thinking of the mad things they used to get up to together, the intense pleasure that they gave each other, and the crazy places that they used to make love in. She smiled as she remembered.

'I'm glad you find it so funny,' he said sarcastically.

Maddy jumped and said, 'I don't think it's funny'.

'You're laughing.'

'I'm not. I was just remembering…' She blushed. 'Us.'

'Oh,' he said. Maddy caught sight of his smile as he turned away.

'Sit down and finish your coffee,' she said.

'Why are your dogs asleep,' he asked, changing the subject. 'They didn't bark when I came in and they haven't moved since.'

'They're… just tired.'

Simon gave her a long look. He had his emotions firmly under control as he said, 'To get back to the reason why I came here.' Maddy sighed, and looked away. 'What were you doing on the ridge? And don't give me any bullshit.'

Maddy took a deep breath. 'I was looking for clues. I don't think Tamsin's death was an accident.'

Simon's face hardened. 'Looking for clues? You think you are some sort of bloody detective?'

'No.'

'What were you playing at? And why don't you think it was an accident?'

'I'm surprised you thought it was an accident,' she retorted. He went quiet. 'Well?' she said. 'You don't do you?' He still said nothing. 'So why did you let the Coroner bring in a verdict of Accidental Death?' Simon still said nothing. 'Well I think that is even fishier.' Maddy stared at him. 'In fact I'm going to call the police.' She reached for her phone.

He grabbed her wrist. 'Don't you dare.'

Maddy grew frightened again. 'You…' she looked at him in horror. 'I can't believe it. Sally knows you're here if anything happens to me. And she knows the whole story. Or will you go and kill her too?'

Simon let go of her wrist. 'Don't be so stupid. You thought I killed Tamsin? You go too far Maddy! Your imagination runs away with itself. Of course I didn't kill her.'

'Well someone did and you are trying to cover it up.'

'I am not covering it up.'

'So why the verdict of Accidental Death, then?' she asked belligerently.

Simon walked over to the back door and stared out at the untidy back garden, as if mulling something over in his mind. He made a decision and turned back towards Maddy, saying, 'There was no real evidence. I couldn't find anything up on the ridge. I could see the horse had stopped by the thicket and then taken off and galloped down the field and on to the road. I couldn't find out the reason why. I didn't want the paparazzi camped out on my doorstep or every weirdo in the country coming up with their own theories'.

'You could have gone to the police.'

'They wouldn't find out any more than I could.'

Maddy stared at him and said, 'Why?'

'My job,' he said.

'You're a civil servant, aren't you?'

'Yes,' he said smiling. 'You could say that. Anyway that's not the point, the point is I *will* find her killer.'

'So you do believe someone killed her.' Maddy shivered.

'Yes.' Silence fell. 'Are you going to tell me if you found anything on the ridge?' he asked more kindly.

'All right,' said Maddy, 'I suppose so.'

'Good.' He nearly smiled. 'Well what?'

Maddy took a deep breath and said quietly, 'I found a latex glove.'

'You found what?' he barked at her.

'A latex glove.'

'You found a glove. And you took it away. You bloody little fool. Give it to me.' He looked furious.

'No… I can't.'

'I'm not playing games Maddy, give me the glove,' he repeated; his voice had a steel edge.

'I can't. It's been stolen.'

Simon's face looked thunderous as he barked, 'What do you mean?'

'I mean that when we were out riding this morning someone came in here, drugged the dogs and took the glove out of the fridge,' snapped Maddy. 'Don't you know you were tampering with evidence and destroying a crime scene? You could be prosecuted.'

'Don't be so ridiculous. That wasn't a crime scene, you just said so. Anyway you had been up there yourself before me.'

'That's different.'

'No it isn't,' she retorted.

'I'm not going to argue with you. Where did you find the glove? I couldn't find anything.'

'In the thicket. I dropped my phone in the gorse. I had a hell of a job to get it out. I had to shake the gorse bush for ages until it dropped to the ground. I must have dislodged the glove.'

'Then you brought it home and put it in your fridge. For God's sake Maddy, what were you thinking of? Why didn't you give it to me?'

Maddy glared at him and replied, 'You weren't being very approachable, were you?' He smiled grimly as he remembered, and Maddy continued, 'Also what I said to you the night before... Well, I couldn't face you'.

'You should control your temper then.'

Maddy smiled and said, 'You shouldn't have been so horrible'.

'Okay, okay, I'm sorry I was so rude.' Simon was becoming exasperated.

Maddy looked at him. 'Are you?'

'Yes,' he said wearily. 'Look, stop arguing, we're wasting time.' Maddy opened her mouth to say something, saw the look on his face and shut her mouth again. He continued: 'What do you mean it's been stolen?'

'Exactly that,' replied Maddy. 'That's why the dogs are asleep. They've been drugged.'

'When did this happen?'

'This morning when we were out riding.'

'I was just too late. Damn it, if I had got here sooner we would have the glove. What did it look like?'

'Just like a latex glove, like doctors use'.

'Or vets?'

'Yes.'

'Was there anything on it?'

'Like what?'

'Marks. Any substance? Was it sticky? Anything?'

'No, not that I was aware of, I didn't touch it. I was going to tell you. I told Sally and Judith that I was going to tell you. Then it was stolen.' Maddy felt a little foolish.

'Who the hell is Judith?'

'Only a livery.'

'How many people have you told?'

'Only Sally, Ruth and Judith.'

'Good God Maddy, half the county probably knows by now.'

'Don't exaggerate. What are you going to do?' Maddy was suddenly pleased that Simon was there and that she could hand the responsibility over to him.

'Who else have you told?' he asked.

'No one.'

'Have you discussed it anywhere?' Maddy blushed and he barked, 'You have, haven't you? Where?'

Maddy thought before she answered. 'Only in the local pub, and in a tea shop near Moorsend before the funeral.'

'Obviously you were overheard.'

Maddy fell silent. She was beginning to feel frightened. 'Do you think I am in danger?' she asked.

'You could be.'

Maddy thought he was trying to frighten her for some reason. She thought for a while and then said, 'You had a post mortem done on the horse. What did that show?'

Simon was a taken aback. 'How do you know about the post mortem?'

'Because I overheard your conversation on your mobile. What did it show?'

Simon sighed and shook his head. 'I knew you would poke your nose in. There was nothing found which would have made him bolt. The vet said there isn't really a drug guaranteed to make a horse bolt. There is something that could have been injected intravenously, but that wasn't found in his blood stream. However, they did find Ketamine in his blood, and that, on its own, wouldn't have made him bolt. Andy didn't find anything else, except that the horse had eaten some bread before he died. We presume the bread had been soaked in Ketamine.'

'So we might have found Ketamine on the glove?' Maddy felt deflated. 'And possibly something else?'

'Yes.'

'I'm sorry I took it. I can see now that it was a really silly thing to do.' She added wearily, 'Would you like some more coffee?'

'No thank you,' he replied. 'But I'll have a whisky. I'm sure you have a bottle somewhere.'

'Yes, in the dining room, in the cabinet, help yourself.' Simon went into the dining room to fetch the whisky. Maddy hardly ever used the room these days; it was dusty and unkempt. Simon came out carrying a bottle of Grouse and said, 'Why do you need such a big house? Your dining room looks like something out of a Dickens novel. It's covered in dust and cobwebs'.

'Don't exaggerate.' Maddy rose to the bait. 'And don't start criticising my home.'

'I'm not criticising. Just making an observation.'

'Well keep your observations to yourself. I didn't invite you here.'

'I'm sorry.' He sounded contrite. The tone of his voice made Maddy look up. He smiled down at her and she relaxed a little. 'Have you any ideas as to who could have done it?'

'It could be some people from a website, or terrorists or... I don't know.'

'A website? What website?'

'Louise Parkway, you know her don't you?'

'Not really, she's a dressage judge isn't she? Go on.'

'Well, she gave me the name of this site. I looked it up and it's horrible, it's about people mutilating horses.'

'Have you got a computer? Can I have a look?'

'Of course I've got a computer. It's in the sitting room.'

Maddy showed him the way. As he entered the room he looked round. 'Good God, Maddy, this is a tip as well.'

'Do you want to look at my computer, or would you rather go home?' she snapped.

He ignored her remark and said, 'Could you turn it on please and put up the site'. Maddy did as he said and gave him the password.

'Was anyone in the yard when you went out for your ride this morning?' asked Simon as he waited for the computer to warm up.

'Only Angela Tidebrook, a livery,' replied Maddy.

'Can I have her address please?'

'I suppose so, I'll write it down.' Maddy wrote the address on a piece of paper and gave it to him.

She went back into the kitchen and sat down at the table staring into space. Ruth and Sally came up the path laughing and talking.

'Where's the lovely Simon?' asked Sally as she bounced in.

'He's in the sitting room, looking at the website.' Maddy felt suddenly irritated and snapped, 'I thought you wanted to go home'.

'No, I decided to stay. What did he want?'

'He wanted to know what I was doing on the ridge. He saw me up there.'

'Blimey!' said Sally. 'I'm going to see what he is up to.'

'No, don't...' Maddy started, but Sally was already tiptoeing up the passage towards the sitting room door which was slightly ajar.

'He'll know she's there and he won't like it,' Maddy said to Ruth.

'Mmm,' said Ruth who was making a sandwich and watching the dogs.

A few minutes later Sally came back into the kitchen and whispered, 'He's on his mobile. He's very bossy, isn't he?'

'What's he saying?' asked Ruth.

'Something about like, *check it out*. He's barking orders at people. I don't understand half of what he's saying.'

'Just leave it,' snapped Maddy as Sally tiptoed down the passage again. She annoyed Maddy by staying outside the sitting room door for quite a while.

She came dancing back, saying, 'He's calling someone darling now.' Maddy stiffened. 'He said something about being late back and tell Anna. Who's Anna?'

'His housekeeper.' Maddy almost smiled. 'He'll know someone was listening to him and he won't be pleased. He thinks we could be in danger.'

'Well, I gathered that,' said Ruth.

Sally jumped as Simon came back into the kitchen. 'Hello ladies,' he said, cheerfully. 'You're looking very well Ruth. I hope Maddy isn't overworking you? Who was in the yard while you were all out riding?'

'Angela,' replied Maddy. 'I have already told you.'

'And she was the only person in the yard, no one else?' Simon looked at the others.

'No,' said Ruth. 'No one that I know of.' Simon looked at Sally, she shook her head.

'You're being very quiet,' he said to Sally. 'Perhaps you're a better listener than talker. I thought you might be good at creeping about and might have seen someone.'

Sally blushed and stammered, 'I... I...' Simon's mobile rang. He went outside before he answered it.

'Talk about being saved by the bell,' Ruth laughed.

'You could have warned me,' Sally said to Maddy.

'I did.'

'He makes me nervous,' said Sally, 'I don't know what to say to him.'

'He does that to a lot of people,' replied Maddy.

'But you're not frightened of him,' continued Sally. 'You answer him back.'

'I've known him for a long time. I knew him when he was a young Subaltern in the army. But I wouldn't say that I am never frightened of him,' remarked Maddy, thinking of her earlier conversation with him.

'I can't imagine him as a young Subaltern,' Sally shuddered. 'He's coming back in now.'

'I must say goodbye to you ladies. I have to get back.' Simon turned to Maddy and asked, 'Would you come out to the yard with me please.' She got up and obediently followed him outside. 'I've made some arrangements.' Maddy opened her mouth to speak but he carried on, 'I want you to install CCTV cameras. I would like to find the best sites for them. Please show me the layout of your yard'. Maddy meekly took him round the stables.

Her stable yard was originally a farm, but it hadn't been modernised like Moorsend. She had made use of the existing buildings and barns, so there were stables tucked away in odd corners. Also several small unused sheds dotted about, such as the old pig pens, a pump house and an old generator shed.

'It's not the easiest place to cover,' said Simon as he walked around, drawing rough plans in a small note book. 'Right, I want a camera here to cover this area.' He stopped and pointed to the corner of a barn. 'One up here.' He pointed to a telegraph pole that stood at the end of the row of old disused pig pens. He turned to look at Maddy. 'Are you listening? You need to tell the man who is coming tomorrow where to put them.'

'What man?'

'Didn't I say?'

'No. You didn't. Look I can't afford all this, is it really necessary?'

He ignored her question. 'I have arranged for someone to install them tomorrow because I'm pretty sure you'll be all right for tonight. The perpetrator has what he came for at the moment. But he could come back, so make sure you keep the cameras on all the time. Do you understand? I mean *all* the time.' Maddy nodded, not knowing what to say.

'Now this area,' he said, walking round a corner and pointing to the eves of the old Sussex cart shed that Maddy used for storing hay. 'The third camera can go here and another one here.' He walked to the feed shed. Then he stopped outside Hyperion's box which used to be the old bull pen. 'The fifth camera can go here.' He pointed to the roof of the building. He patted the stallion, who nuzzled his hand, and remarked, 'He looks well. I hear he's going well too'.

'Yes.' Maddy was taken aback. She wondered why animals always seemed to like Simon. 'How much are these cameras going to cost?' she asked again.

'Don't worry about that. They're only temporary. Also I have arranged for someone to keep watch.'

'What?' she exclaimed aghast. 'You mean watch the tapes?'

'No, I mean to watch your yard.'

'I don't understand. Aren't you going just a little over the top?'

'No, I'm not going over the top.' His face hardened. 'I'm not entirely sure who we're dealing with yet.'

Maddy grew cold and remarked, 'How can you possibly arrange all this, just like that?' She clicked her fingers. 'And who are these people doing it for you?'

'Don't you know what my job is?' He smiled at her.

'I thought you were a civil servant and you work for the Home Office.'

'Good.'

'What is your job then?'

'I'm a civil servant and I work for the Home Office,' he answered grinning. 'If you catch sight of my people let me know.'

'Why?'

'Because they're not supposed to be seen.'

'So if I see them and tell you, you'll have them sacked?'

'Something like that. It depends on the circumstances, but they're good men.'

'Shouldn't we give them cups of tea?' asked Maddy.

'Certainly not. They're here to do a job of work, not to socialize.'

'Should I tell the others, Sally and Ruth, and the liveries?' asked Maddy.

Simon thought for a moment and answered, 'Tell Ruth, but not the others. But tell everyone about the cameras.' He looked up as a car pulled into the yard, and asked, 'Who is this?'

'It's Judith, one of my liveries,' replied Maddy.

Simon watched her get out of her car and said, 'She looks familiar, but I can't quite place her.'

'You wouldn't know her,' said Maddy as they walked over to greet her.

'I was a little worried, so I came to see how you were,' said Judith, looking steadily at Simon.

'I'm fine. This is Simon Coulson.' Maddy introduced them.

'Simon, this is Judith Floyd-Williams.'

'How do you do, ma'am,' said Simon urbanely.

'How do you do,' replied Judith. 'You must be Colonel Coulson.'

'That's correct.'

'I believe you knew my husband, Brigadier Floyd-Williams.'

'Indeed I did,' replied Simon. 'And may I thank you for your card and kind words.'

'The least one could do.' Judith smiled. 'How clever of you to remember, you must have had so many cards.' Maddy was flabbergasted.

'How could I not remember your husband, ma'am? He taught me a lot; I owe him a great deal.' Maddy's mouth was wide open by now; she didn't know of Judith's military connections.

'Maddy, you look rather surprised,' said Judith. 'I think I owe you an explanation. Shall I go in?'

'Yes, please do,' Maddy managed to say.

'Such a small world,' Judith said and, turning to Simon, she continued, 'I'm very lucky to have found Maddy. She looks after my horse so beautifully.'

'Yes, quite,' replied Simon.

'Are the dogs all right?' asked Judith, turning to Maddy.

'No. But do go in. Ruth and Sally are in the kitchen, I'll be with you in a minute.'

'I'll say goodbye for now, Colonel Coulson.' Judith held out her hand. Simon took it and made a slight bow.

'Good bye,' he said. Maddy and Simon walked back to his car.

'How did you know her husband?' Maddy asked.

'He was my C.O. Jonathan would have known him too.'

'Well I never knew that.' Maddy was astonished. 'Judith is a lovely person. She hasn't been here very long.'

'Yes, what a piece of good luck… her being in your yard,' said Simon cheerfully.

'Really? Why?'

'Now you know where I want the CCTV cameras?' he said, ignoring her question and giving her the piece of paper torn from his note book. Maddy nodded.

'Do you want me to put marks on the buildings?' he asked.

'No, I'm not stupid.'

'You can confide in Mrs Floyd-Williams, in fact it would be a good thing if you did.'

'This is becoming unreal.'

'Well perhaps it'll teach you not to meddle in other people's affairs,' he said as they reached his car.

'I'm sorry Simon,' Maddy said, feeling remorseful. He was about to get into his car but he stopped and took her hand.

'Don't worry. You did well to find the glove. I couldn't find anything up there. Although we can't get the forensics from it, it has narrowed down the field. We can't bring Tamsin back but we can find her killer.' He gave her a quick hug and a peck on the cheek. She was surprised by the hug.

'By the way,' he said as he sat in his car. 'I have put someone on to that website. We should easily ferret out the horse mutilators.' He drove off, and then he stopped, reversed back and called out, 'And for goodness sake lock your back door in future'. Then he drove away.

'I didn't know you knew Simon,' Maddy said to Judith as she walked in.

'Well, I don't really know him. My husband was his Commanding Officer, and I remember being introduced to him and Tamsin at a Summer Ball. They stuck in my mind because she looked so fragile and nervous, rather like a startled deer. He was very protective of her and I wondered how she would cope with army life. Then she turned into Tamsin Coulson, the international rider. Simon did very well in the army, his name cropped up from time to time and I remembered it. Also when my husband was killed, he sent me a most charming letter. I felt I had to do the same when he lost his wife.'

'You must have met me and Jonathan then, as well,' said Maddy.

'I'm sorry Maddy, I have racked my brains and to be honest I can't remember. I met so many people you see.'

'No, of course,' replied Maddy, a little disappointed. 'But you certainly made an impression on Simon. I thought he was going to click his heels and kiss your hand. He treated you like royalty.'

'Yes, he does have beautiful manners,' replied Judith. Sally and Ruth stared at her in awe.

'You could have come with us to the funeral if we'd known,' said Maddy. 'You should have told me.'

'I'm not one to name drop. As I said, I wasn't a friend of theirs, not like you.'

'No, I suppose not,' replied Maddy. She was silent for a moment and then she demanded, 'Who told him that we never lock the back door?' Nobody spoke.

CHAPTER FIVE

Maddy, Ruth and Judith sat round the big kitchen table while Maddy told them about the CCTV cameras. Sally had gone home.

'Maddy dear, you couldn't have anyone better to look after you than Simon Coulson,' said Judith cheerfully.

'I'm sorry I've put you all in danger,' said Maddy. 'Simon says that now they have the glove, they probably won't come back.'

'Yes,' said Judith calmly. 'What other reason would they have for coming back?'

'I don't know,' replied Maddy.

They all fell silent. Ruth said, 'We're supposed to be going to Eastleigh Farm Horse Trials on Saturday'.

'So we are,' said Maddy. 'Do you think we should go?'

'Yes, definitely,' replied Judith, standing up. 'You mustn't give in to these people.'

'What people?' asked Ruth.

'Whoever it is who is doing these things. You mustn't let them win; that would never do. Thank you so much for the coffee, Maddy. I really must go home now. I was so pleased to meet Simon, such a charming man.'

'Before you go I have something to say.' Maddy smiled a little self-consciously. 'Simon is putting two undercover people in the yard to keep watch.'

'Oh, excellent,' said Judith enthusiastically. 'I thought he would.' Maddy and Ruth stared at her in astonishment. 'Well of course he should,' continued Judith. 'It's the procedure.'

'Oh, right.' Ruth nodded and looked at Maddy, who shrugged her shoulders.

'Simon told me that I should tell you and Ruth. Also I was to confide in Judith.'

'I'm flattered,' said Judith, 'and pleased.'

'Pleased,' exclaimed Maddy. 'You've only just arrived in my yard and all this happens. I wouldn't be surprised if you took your horse away and put it somewhere else.'

'I wouldn't miss this for the world. I lived with danger for years you know. I miss it.' The others stared at her again. 'Please don't think I'm wishing this on you, quite the opposite. But the situation exists and we have to get through it as best we can. Now, when are these people arriving?'

'I don't know,' replied Maddy.

Judith looked at her watch and did some calculations in her head. 'They could be here already.' Maddy and Ruth were startled and both looked out of the window.

'You won't see them.' Judith laughed. 'At least you shouldn't, if they are doing their job properly.'

'That's just what Simon said,' exclaimed Maddy. 'He also told me not to feed them.'

Judith chuckled. 'You're so funny Maddy. Don't worry, just do as Simon says, like the game.' Maddy didn't find that funny. 'When is he coming back?' added Judith.

'I don't know.'

'Well, his men will definitely be here before it gets dark.'

'It'll be very spooky having someone prowling around and I don't think I am going to like it. By the way, he took Angela's name and address. Do you think he'll go and see her?'

'Yes, of course he will,' replied Judith.

'Oh Lord, she's been very peculiar just lately. I don't know what the matter is and I wouldn't be surprised if she took her horse away. Actually I don't mind if she does.' Then Maddy looked at her watch and got up, saying, 'I must go and ride Hyps'.

'When is Gerhardt coming again?' asked Ruth. Gerhardt was Maddy's German dressage trainer.

'Oh goodness, on Monday, I nearly forgot.'

'You ought to come and watch her lesson, Judith. He's very good, you'll enjoy it.'

'That's an excellent idea. I'll certainly try to, if that's all right with you, Maddy,' replied Judith.

'Perfectly, I don't mind a bit.'

***

As Maddy was preparing the supper that evening Zippy stirred and licked his lips. Maddy ran out of the kitchen and half way up the stairs yelling, 'Ruth, Ruth!' Then she hurried back into the kitchen.

Ruth came tearing downstairs wearing a towelling dressing gown and a towel wrapped around her head like a turban. 'What is it?' she asked anxiously as she ran into the kitchen.

'Look!' Maddy was kneeling down beside Zippy's bed. 'He's

waking up.' The dog lifted his head and tried to wag his tail.

'Thank goodness. You lie still for a bit.' Ruth talked to him while she stroked his head. He settled back and heaved a sigh, then he tried to get up again but fell back down.

'What shall we do?' asked Ruth.

'I'll ask Mike.' Maddy dialled his number.

The vet answered straight away. 'Keep him warm and treat him as if he was recovering from an anaesthetic. I'm pretty sure your dogs were drugged, especially as both of them are having the same symptoms. If there is any change give me a ring. They probably had the same dose, and as Jock is smaller he might take longer to come round. Have you informed the police?'

Maddy hesitated before replying, 'That's all in hand'. She looked at Ruth and made a face.

'Okay, as I said, let me know if there are any significant changes. Goodbye.' He rang off.

Just then Zippy made an effort and managed to stand up. He wobbled his way across the kitchen floor and then flopped down. Within a few minutes Jock moved and tried to get up but fell back on to his cushion.

Much to Maddy's relief, by the time the Ten O'clock News came on to the television both dogs had fully recovered.

Maddy looked at Ruth. 'We'll have to go out and do the late night feeds.'

'I know.' Ruth looked nervous. 'Those people might be there.'

'According to Judith they'll definitely be here.'

'I'm not looking forward to going out.'

'Neither am I. We'll stay together all the time,' replied Maddy.

'Okay. Don't have a pee in a loose box.'

'I never do.' Maddy was affronted.

'Yes you do.'

'Only very occasionally. Come on, no point in delaying it any longer.' They reluctantly got up and went outside to the back lawn where both dogs managed to lift their legs without falling over.

'Well, they're not going to protect us,' said Maddy as they went back into the kitchen to lie down. She shut and locked the kitchen door and put the key in her pocket.

She and Ruth walked stealthily into the yard looking anxiously around. 'Don't leave me,' said Maddy.

'Ditto,' replied Ruth. There was a rattling noise. They both jumped.

'What's that,' exclaimed Ruth, looking into the dark yard. 'I wish the dogs were here.'

'It's Jupiter. He always rattles his door when we come out.'

'Oh yes, so he does. Come on let's do this as quickly as we can and then we can get back indoors,' said Ruth. They hurried round together. It didn't take them very long. Everything looked peaceful. The horses continued munching their hay; they seemed completely unconcerned about any strangers in the yard.

Ruth and Maddy were relieved to be back inside the kitchen behind the locked door. Ruth flopped down on to a chair while Maddy put the kettle on.

The phone rang. Maddy picked it up quickly, saying to Ruth, 'It's Simon'.

'Are you all right?' he asked.

'Yes, we've just been out to do the late night feeds.'

'I heard,' he said. 'I also heard you have a fabulous horse.'

'How…? Your men are in place then?'

'Yes.'

'Does one of them ride?'

'I believe so.'

'I take it you saw Angela?' asked Maddy.

'Yes, I spoke to her.'

'I suppose you upset her. She rang Ruth to say she's not coming for a few days. I wouldn't be surprised if she took her horse away.'

'I told her to be careful, certainly. She's obviously taken my advice.'

'Oh, I see… Simon, we can't cope with these invisible people lurking about in the yard.'

'They're not lurking. They're on surveillance.'

'Don't split hairs. I can't handle it and neither can Ruth. We can't do the work properly. We don't like it.'

After a pause Simon said, 'All right. Would it help if you met them?' Maddy turned to Ruth and repeated his words.

'Yes… I think so,' Ruth replied slowly. 'Let's try. I would like to see what they look like, wouldn't you?'

Maddy nodded and turned back to Simon. 'Yes, we would like to meet them.'

'Fair enough; both of you stand just outside your kitchen door and they'll come and introduce themselves.'

70

'You're joking,' replied Maddy, but he had rung off. 'We're ordered to stand by the kitchen door.'

'Then jump to it,' said Ruth. They started laughing.

They both stood obediently outside the door, trying unsuccessfully not to giggle and peering into the darkness. They didn't have long to wait before a human form emerged silently out of the shadows.

'Bloody hell!' Ruth muttered under her breath. The man was over six feet tall; his black woolly hat hid his short dark hair and framed his good-looking face.

'Good evening, ma'am,' he addressed Maddy. 'I'm John.'

'G..good evening. I'm Maddy and this is Ruth.' The man gave Ruth a long look.

'Hi,' he said.

Ruth stared back into his big round blue eyes and said, 'Hello.'

'We're here to look after you. If you need anything, shout. This is my mobile number.' He handed Maddy a piece of paper in a black gloved hand. It had two numbers on it. 'Mine and Sarah's,' he explained.

'Sarah?' asked Maddy.

'Yes, my partner. You'll meet her in a minute.' He had a slight Geordie accent.

'I'll take your mobile number, Miss,' he said to Ruth.

'Don't you want mine?' asked Maddy.

'I have it and your landline.'

'Oh.'

'The boss gave them to me. Orders to ring if need be.'

'Oh.' Maddy was lost for words. Ruth couldn't keep her eyes off the tall rugged-looking man; he glanced at her and gave her a quick smile. The smile transformed his face. He had very white even teeth and his eyes sparkled. He nodded to Maddy and then disappeared silently into the night.

'Blimey!' exclaimed Ruth, staring at the space where he had been standing.

'A man of few words,' remarked Maddy.

'Mmmm.' Ruth still stared at the shadows.

'What do we do now?' asked Maddy.

'Don't know.' They stood still. Maddy noticed a slight movement at the side of the house.

'What...' Ruth started to say. Then she saw another human form appearing from out of nowhere; as it came closer they could see it was a girl. She was tall and slim and looked to be in her twenties. She was dressed in combat gear, like the man, and she too kept in the shadows.

'I'm Sarah.' She smiled. Her face was long and she had a pointed nose. She spoke with a Scottish accent. 'Don't worry about us,' she continued turning to Maddy. 'We're here to protect you. May I say you have a fantastic horse, Ma'am.'

'D... do you ride?' Maddy asked.

'Yes, a little, but I don't get much time now.'

'You could ride one of ours...' Maddy paused.

'I don't think the boss would allow that.' She smiled.

'No, of course not.'

'Nice meeting you ma'am.' She too melted into the shadows and disappeared.

'Well,' gasped Maddy. 'I don't believe this is happening.' She and Ruth went inside and locked the kitchen door behind them.

'No.' Ruth stared into space. Simon rang, startling them both again.

'You've met them?' he said.

'Yes,' answered Maddy. 'We're still recovering.'

'Why? What happened? Did they do anything wrong? Were they rude?'

'No, not at all. On the contrary, they were very polite. You didn't say one of them was a girl. The thing is, Simon, we're not used to this cloak and dagger stuff, like you.'

Simon laughed. 'Do you feel happier now that you have met them?' Maddy repeated the question to Ruth who replied, 'Definitely'.

'Can you work with them?' asked Simon. Maddy relayed his message again.

'Oh yes,' replied Ruth, still staring into space.

Maddy turned back to the phone. 'Ruth's happy with the situation... And so am I. I certainly feel safer.'

'That's good. Just ring me if you are at all uneasy, or if you need anything.'

'Yes, thank you, Simon.' He rang off. Maddy looked at Ruth. 'Gosh, he is being nice. Let's hope it lasts.'

***

The next morning Ruth had nearly finished her mucking out by the time Maddy arrived out on the yard.

'You're up early this morning,' said Maddy. 'What now?' she

asked, looking up as a white van drove into the yard.

'CCTV cameras,' said Ruth. 'You can tell by the way it has "CCTV CAMERAS FOR YOU" written on the side.'

Maddy smiled. 'Thank you Ruth, I can read. I'd better show them around I suppose. I still don't know who's going to pay for all this.' She showed the men round the yard and gave them Simon's note.

When they finished, she asked, 'Where are you going to send the bill? Do you need my name?'

'That's all taken care of, madam.'

Maddy stared after them as they drove away. She jumped as another car drove up the drive and stopped beside her. 'Did I startle you? You seemed to be in a daze.'

'Oh it's you, Sally. Yes, my mind was on something else. Can you see our cameras?' Maddy asked.

'No. But I did see the sign at the end of the drive.'

'What sign?'

'A big sign saying CCTV cameras in operation here.'

'I didn't know they were going to put that up, although Simon did say to tell people.'

'Well, anyone who passes the bottom of the drive will certainly know. The sign's big enough.'

Maddy looked closely at Sally and said, 'You're looking peaky'.

'I went out last night. I've got a bit of a hangover. I'll park the car and tell you all about it.'

'So what happened?' asked Maddy as Sally joined her again. 'I... we went to The Royal Oak at Beckfield. And you'll never guess who was there.' She perked up suddenly.

'Who?' asked Maddy.

'Rhona and Jilly, and guess who was there too?'

'I've no idea,' said Maddy.

'Angela!'

'Good Lord! Whatever is she doing with those two? Did you speak to them? What did Angela say when she saw you?'

'They pretended not to see me, because they turned away when we arrived.'

'Who's *we*?' Maddy was intrigued. 'You didn't say you were going out.'

'It was a blind date. Well, a sort of a blind date.'

'Really. Who is he?'

73

'He's the husband of a friend of a friend.'

'Husband! You're not going out with a married man?' Maddy was aghast.

'No, ex-husband. His wife went off with somebody else. He's really nice and we got on very well.'

'Are you seeing him again, and has he got a name?'

'Nigel. And yes I think so. Anyway, when we walked into the pub Angela, Rhona and Jilly were all in the bar. Then we went into the restaurant and I didn't see them again. I must say Angela looked embarrassed and pretended to be deep in conversation with the others.'

'I wouldn't be surprised if she takes her horse to Rhona's stables,' said Maddy. 'She's not happy here anymore.'

'No, you're right.' Ruth walked up to say hello to Sally. 'She's been making snide remarks for a while now.'

'Well, she can take her horse away for all I care,' said Maddy. 'I don't like people whinging all the time. We work hard to look after her horrible horse, and that's all the thanks we get. She's creating an atmosphere in the yard and I don't like it.'

'Yes, she is,' agreed Sally. 'I always check to see if her car's here when I come up the drive. When it is, it puts a dampener on the day because you know she's going to make some nasty remark. She makes one feel awkward.'

'So when are you going to see this man again?' Maddy changed the subject.

'I don't know. He's going to ring.'

'What's he like?'

'Nice,' said Sally nonchalantly.

'Are you coming with us to the horse trials on Saturday?' Maddy asked.

'Yes, I think so.'

'Actually Maddy, do you mind if I stay here?' Ruth interrupted. 'There's a lot to do and I think someone should stay in the yard.'

Maddy was surprised. 'Yes, I suppose so. If Sally and Judith come with me I'll be fine.'

Sally looked down at the ground and said quietly, 'Well, I think I can come.' Ruth and Maddy looked at each other.

'When will you know?' Maddy felt let down. It made sense Ruth staying in the yard, but she was a little annoyed with Sally whom she had been counting on.

'I don't know,' said Sally. 'I would like to come, it just depends…'

'On this man I suppose.'

'Well, yes.' She looked sheepish.

Maddy heaved a sigh and walked towards the tack room, saying, 'We had better get going, it's ten o'clock already. I'm going to ride Highwayman in the school.'

'I'll come and join you. I could put up some jumps for you if you like.' Sally could see Maddy was irritated, but she wasn't going to miss a day out with her new man. He was supposed to be ringing her that evening to make arrangements for Saturday and she was determined to make herself available. However, he was being a bit vague and difficult to pin down to any definite time.

Maddy rode her grey event horse, Highwayman, while Sally rode Poppy at the same time. Maddy could see that Sally's mind wasn't on her riding and when Judith turned up to ride Panda, Sally announced, 'Good heavens, I've got to go. You don't mind, do you? Judith you could help Maddy with the jumps.'

Maddy stood and watched as Sally put her horse away. 'She didn't ride for long,' she remarked to Judith.

'What would you like me to?' asked Judith.

'Nothing thank you. Let's go out in the wood with Hyperion and Panda.'

***

Ruth was wondering where John was; she had spent all morning looking over her shoulder but she hadn't caught sight of him or heard him. He, on the other hand had been closely watching her. He wanted to speak to her but he didn't dare approach her while Maddy was around.

He had his chance when Maddy and Judith rode out of the yard and Ruth brought Jupiter out of his loose box, tied him up and started to groom him. John began to throw small stones at the horse, hitting him on his flank. The horse swished his tail and fidgeted, becoming annoyed and agitated.

Ruth said crossly, 'For goodness sake stand still.' John threw another stone, harder this time and it caught Jupiter on his stomach, making him kick out sideways. Ruth hadn't noticed the stones and she walked round behind him to see if he had a fly annoying him. John threw another one just as Ruth was right behind the horse, and he lashed out, but this time backwards at Ruth. He caught her half way up her thigh. She let out a cry of surprise and pain. The force of the blow sent her flying backwards. She tripped over a bucket and fell heavily on to the concrete yard. She lay still for a moment, winded.

'Are you all right?' asked a Geordie accent. Ruth looked up into a pair of big blue eyes smiling down at her, and she smiled back.

'Just lie still,' said John grinning. 'You'll be fine in a minute. I'll give you mouth to mouth resuscitation.'

'That won't be necessary.' Ruth caught her breath and sat up. She tried to stand up but her leg was too painful and she couldn't get to her feet. His strong arms lifted her up.

'I can manage,' she said.

'It's okay. I've got you.'

'Thank you.'

'No problem.' His white teeth flashed and his eyes twinkled. 'All in a day's work. You worried me. Thought it was serious.' Ruth looked white, the blood had drained from her face and she felt dizzy. John felt her sway, so he tightened his grip and carried her the short distance to a plastic mounting block. 'Sit down,' he said. 'Does that horse normally behave like that?'

'Sometimes. He doesn't like people very much. But something was bothering him. I don't know what it was. Did you see anything?'

'No.' John kept a dead pan face.

'Oh well, never mind. All in a day's work, like you said. He's nasty, like his bloody owner.' The dizziness was passing over. 'You bastard,' she suddenly yelled at Jupiter.

'Sorry,' he said, squatting down beside her. 'I thought I was helping.'

'Not you, the horse. Sorry to be such a wimp. It was the shock.'

'What do you mean, like his owner? Who's his owner?'

'Angela. Maddy thinks she's going to move him from here. The sooner the better I say, then he can kick Rhona.' She laughed.

'Who's Rhona?'

'A large woman. Quite tall. Bossy with no manners. Dark bushy hair. Posh voice.'

'She sounds very pleasant. I can't wait to meet her.' John smiled.

'You can't meet anyone. You're supposed to be invisible. She goes around with a pasty faced, smaller woman called Jilly. She sidles up to people and simpers. She has a South London accent.'

'They sound like Little and Large.'

Ruth started laughing. 'Yes, you could say that.'

'You all right now? Can you walk?'

Ruth painfully took a couple of steps and said, 'I don't know.'

'I'll help you,' he said, putting his arm round her.

'As I just said, you are supposed to be invisible. You're not supposed to be talking to me, what are you doing?'

'I'm allowed to rescue you from vicious horses.'

Ruth laughed and took a few more steps saying, 'I can walk now, thank you. I'm going to make a cup of tea. Do you want one?'

'That would be nice, and some biscuits. Bring it in there.' He pointed to the barn.

'Okay,' said Ruth, taking some more painful steps. She turned and asked, 'Chocolate digestives all right?' But he had vanished. Smiling to herself, she limped over to the horse, untied him and put him back in his stable. She patted him and quietly said, 'Thanks mate.' Surprised that someone was being kind to him for once, he nuzzled her hand. Ruth patted him again and limped back to the kitchen to make the tea.

***

Maddy and Judith were enjoying their quiet hack in the wood.

'I'm surprised at Sally.' Maddy was talking about the man Sally had been out with the previous night. 'She's never mentioned him before. I find it a bit odd.'

'Yes, so do I. Who is he?'

'Well, that's just it, she was very cagey. She wouldn't really say. In fact she didn't say much about him at all. I mean, where did she meet him? And why didn't she tell us she was going out on a date?' Maddy paused for a moment. 'You don't think its Simon do you?'

'I don't think so. Would you mind if it was?'

'No,' Maddy quickly replied. 'It's nothing to do with me. He rang at about 11 o'clock last night.' She went on to tell Judith about the meeting with John and Sarah. 'Then he rang back. He had obviously spoken to them in between.' She laughed. 'So the dinner would have been a little disturbed. He rang off very quickly, but I didn't hear any background noise over the phone, only that humming noise you get when someone is in a car. Mind you, I think he thinks Sally is an airhead. But he would still sha... go to bed with her.'

'I think it's extremely unlikely that he was with her.' Judith sounded positive. 'I think you under-estimate him. I don't think he's quite as promiscuous as you think he is. Also I really don't think he would be interested in Sally.'

Unless he had some ulterior motive, of course, Maddy thought to herself. She said, 'Ruth isn't coming with me on Saturday. Sally might be going out with this man. Would you mind coming to the horse trials?'

'I would love to come, if you think I'll be of any use.'

'Of course you will,' replied Maddy smiling. 'I need someone sensible around me at the moment.'

'I couldn't agree more. Does Simon know you are going to these horse trials?'

'I don't know.'

'Well, I think you should tell him.'

'Why?' asked Maddy.

'Because he needs to know where you are.'

'I expect I'll tell him,' she replied.

Judith shook her head and sighed, but Maddy didn't notice because just at that moment Hyperion decided that a piece of dead wood lying on the track was a poisonous snake. He stopped and snorted, his eyes standing out on stalks and his nostrils flaring. Panda came to the rescue by walking past the piece of wood with a superior look on his face.

'What was that noise?' asked Maddy, startled.

'I didn't hear anything,' replied Judith.

Hyperion suddenly spooked and shot forwards. 'There it is again,' said Maddy.

This time Judith heard it. 'It sounded like a twig snapping and someone brushing through the undergrowth.'

'That's what I thought.' Maddy looked behind her. 'Come on. Let's get out of here.'

'I think we should go home. Let's take this little path, cut through there and go back as quickly as possible.'

Maddy shivered. 'Good idea.' They speeded up and left the main track. The path they were following narrowed and they had to slow down to a walk.

'Perhaps this wasn't such a good idea,' said Judith as she glanced over her shoulder. 'I think I heard that noise again. Someone's following us.'

'I can't go any faster. Mind your head on that branch,' Maddy turned in her saddle as Judith ducked under the overhanging tree. Hyperion shot forwards and suddenly Maddy's hands were full. 'Look out, there's a fallen tree trunk here. Can you jump it?'

'Yes, I think so.'

Maddy's horse leapt over the log, she turned to watch Judith hanging on to the saddle as Panda jumped it too. 'Well done,' she said. 'We're nearly at the road now. I can trot on now. Are you all right?'

'Yes, hurry.' Judith started grinning. 'I never thought I would be jumping again at my age. I'm fine.'

Both women were laughing as they reached the comparative safety of the road.

'I don't know what possessed me to take that little path,' said Maddy.

'Actually it was my idea, but we're back safe and sound now.'

As they rode back into the yard they saw Ruth limping across to the hay barn.

'Whatever has happened?' asked Maddy.

'Jupiter kicked me.'

'That's it. I've had enough,' said Maddy, as she helped Judith to settle her horse in his stable in the barn. 'I'm going to tell Angela to take her horse away.'

'Do you think that's wise?' asked Judith.

'Definitely,' replied Maddy. Then she saw the two empty mugs and a plate of biscuit crumbs standing on a shelf in the barn.

'What are these doing?' she asked Ruth.

'A long story,' replied Ruth. 'Tell you later.' Judith had also seen the mugs, but she said nothing.

'So what happened?' asked Maddy after Judith had gone home. Ruth told Maddy how Jupiter had kicked her and how John had picked her up.

'At least they're making themselves useful.' Maddy laughed. 'Judith is coming with me to the horse trials, so you can stay here if you like. What do you make of Sally's boyfriend?'

'I don't know. It's all very sudden. I'm surprised she kept it so quiet.'

'I know. I wonder who he is,' said Maddy. 'Nigel? Do you know any Nigels?'

'No, and who is the friend of the friend?'

'I don't know all her friends. Do you think she got him off the internet?'

'Goodness knows. I hope not,' replied Ruth.

That afternoon Maddy went shopping, leaving Ruth alone on the yard again. She was in the feed shed tidying up when John materialised from out of nowhere. Frightened, she snapped at him, 'I'll be glad when you've buggered off and left us in peace'.

He smiled, and she turned away, hoping that he wouldn't notice how pleased she was to see him.

'You'll miss us when we go,' he said.

'No, I won't,' retorted Ruth and sat down on a feed bin.

John sat beside her. 'Liar! How's your leg?' he asked, putting his hand on her knee.

'Get off.' She hit out at his hand but he quickly took it away and she hit her own leg instead.

'Ouch!' she cried. 'You stupid bastard, I suppose you think that's funny.'

He put his arm around her and gave her a quick hug. 'No,' he said laughing. 'Perhaps you will let me massage it now.'

Ruth smiled, but she got up and said, 'I can't sit here all day talking nonsense with you'.

'No, sit down, I'm sorry. I'll behave myself.'

'All right.' She sat down again.

'I hear your boss is going out with her horse on Saturday.'

'Yes, that's right.'

'Has she told the Colonel?'

'I don't know, I haven't asked her. Why?'

'Mmm,' said John. 'He thinks a lot of your boss, does the Colonel.'

'How do you know?' asked Ruth surprised. 'I bet he doesn't discuss her with you.'

'No, but I can tell by his attitude.'

'Oh, yeah.'

'Straight up. He'll have our guts for garters if anything happens to her. I can tell you that.'

'He probably will, but that doesn't mean anything.'

'I know the Colonel. Known him for a while now. Definitely keen on your boss. I know the signs.'

Ruth shook her head and retorted, 'So why aren't you following her to the supermarket then?'

'We are,' he replied.

Ruth couldn't find an answer to that. So she said, 'This new boyfriend of Sally's is a bit odd'.

'What new boyfriend?'

Ruth told him about Sally's blind date. 'She's being very cagey. She won't tell us anything about him, which is unlike her. She usually gives us a blow by blow account of anything like that.'

'What's his name?'

'Nigel.'

'Has he got a surname?'

'I expect so.' Ruth sighed, and spoke as if to a small child, 'but I don't know what it is.'

'I don't suppose your Maddy has told the Colonel about this *Nigel*,' asked John, pronouncing the name in a posh accent.

'I don't know…'

'You haven't asked her.' John finished the sentence.

'Right,' said Ruth.

John thought for a moment. 'You can't describe him in any way can you?'

'No. I told you. She's being very secretive.'

'Well,' John suddenly stood up, 'Back to work.'

'Will you tell Simon then, about the horse trials?' asked Ruth.

'Yes.' He gave her a quick hug and a kiss on her cheek, and before she could say anything he vanished.

She stood up and shook her head. She thought he was getting very familiar and she wasn't sure if she liked it.

When Maddy returned with the shopping Ruth didn't like to ask her if she thought that she had been followed.

***

As soon as the Ten O'clock News came on the television, Ruth said, 'I don't mind doing the horses on my own tonight'. She tried to stand up but her leg had stiffened and she was having difficulty in getting to her feet.

'No, I won't hear of it,' said Maddy. 'Anyway, you seem to have seized up.'

'I'll be all right when I start moving.' Ruth hobbled to the door.

They went outside together and the dogs, who had fully recovered, went with them.

Ruth was doing the horses in the barn when a woolly hat popped up over the door. She jumped and said crossly, 'There you go again, creeping up on people. Haven't you got anything better to do?'

'No,' replied John, grinning. 'It's our job. Any chance of a bacon butty?'

'You are joking, aren't you?'

'No, I'm starving, so is Sarah.' John smiled. 'How's your leg?'

'Changing colour and looking like a horse shoe.'

'Want me to check it out?' He grinned. 'The offer of a massage still stands.'

'I don't think that's funny.' Ruth turned away and hung up a hay net.

'What did you say?' asked Maddy. 'Are you talking to yourself?' Ruth jumped and looked round. John had disappeared and Maddy was standing at the door.

'I...I was talking to the horse,' she said.

'Oh, I see,' smiled Maddy. 'Your leg looks a little less stiff.'

'Yes, it's okay, you go in. I'll finish up, you look tired.'

'All right. If you're sure you don't mind. I think I'll go up, have a bath and go to bed. I feel shattered.'

'Good night, then.' Ruth smiled.

After Maddy had gone, John appeared again and said, 'I'll help you finish'.

Ruth looked at him in amazement. 'Do you know anything about horses?'

'Yes, a bit. My sister is horse mad.' He made himself useful carrying some hay nets and then he swept up after her.

Ruth was impressed. 'Aren't you supposed to be working?'

'I am working. What do you call this?'

'I meant...' started Ruth.

John flashed his white teeth at her and said, 'I'm earning my bacon butty'.

'Yes, I suppose you are,' Ruth laughed. 'I'll go and do it.'

'Bring them in here. Don't forget one for Sarah,' ordered John.

'What happened to the magic word? We are not at home to Mr. Rude.' Ruth spoke again as if to a child.

John made a face. 'Please Ruth.' Putting on a posh voice, he added,

'One would be ever so grateful'.

'That's better.' She laughed and went indoors.

While Maddy was in the bath Ruth cooked some bacon, made the sandwiches and then took them outside. She obediently went into the barn where John was waiting for her. He took Sarah's sandwiches, disappeared and then came back for his own.

'Much appreciated,' he said and stayed chatting to her, munching as they sat on two wobbly hay bales. He asked her questions about the liveries, who they were, and which were their horses.

'Most of them come at the weekend, apart from the ones you already know. That Warm Blood,' she said pointing to a horse, 'belongs to…'

'Only warm, I'm a hot blood.' John put his arm around her and pulled her towards him. She looked up at him. He bent down to kiss her lips. She panicked, pulled away and he nearly dropped his sandwich.

'You've got butter and grease all round your mouth,' she said, feeling disgusted.

He wiped his mouth with the back of his hand and asked, 'That better?'

'No.' Ruth pulled a face and drew back from him. John made another attempt to put his arm round her, and the bales, which were stacked one on top of the other, nearly fell over. 'You'll lose your sarnie,' she said. 'And I'm not going to make you another one. I don't know why I am telling you all about the liveries, you're not listening, you obviously only have a one-track mind.'

'When I am around a pretty, sexy girl like you I can't help it.'

Ruth blushed and got up off the hay bales saying, 'I'm going in now. Maddy will wonder what I'm doing'.

He also got up, speaking more seriously. 'Thank you. As I said, we did appreciate the sandwiches. I hope I didn't offend you just now.'

'You're a creep.' Ruth got up and walked away without turning round, leaving John staring after her.

'Not one of your easy lays eh, John?' said a voice in his ear. 'She's not a scrubber. You'll have to improve your technique.'

'Shut up Sarah,' said John.

When Maddy got out of the bath, she could smell cooked bacon. She smiled to herself, guessing what Ruth was up to. She went to bed, but she lay awake thinking of the things that Simon had said to her the day before. She didn't know if she believed him or not. Also why hadn't he been in touch? Typical, she thought, just leaving his men and cluttering off. She thought of Tamsin and her marriage and then Emma, who was supposed to be coming to stay. Maddy didn't think Simon would let her come now, not at the moment anyway. She lay tossing and turning until she heard Ruth go up to bed.

Eventually she was dropping off when the phone rang. 'Yes,' she barked. It was Simon. 'It's after midnight. What do you want?'

'Are you asleep?'

'Not now,' she replied. 'What is it?'

'I'm sorry to ring you so late. I have been rather busy. Is everything all right? Are you happy with my men?'

'Yes.' Maddy smiled.

'I hear you're going to Eastleigh Farm on Saturday?'

'Yes I am.' Maddy was suddenly not surprised that he knew exactly what she was doing.

'Right you are. I'll let you get back to sleep now.' Then he continued in a softer tone, 'Please ring me if you have a problem. You know that I am only at the end of a phone, don't you?'

'Yes,' she suddenly felt tearful, 'Simon...'

'What is it?' he enquired quietly.

'Thank you.'

'You're welcome.' He rang off.

CHAPTER SIX

Maddy woke up in a better mood. It was a lovely day and the weather forecast for the next few days was good too.

'Do you know what you're doing tomorrow, for the horse trials?' Maddy asked Sally when she came to ride.

'I'm not sure yet. Can we meet you there?'

'Yes, of course,' said Maddy. 'Actually, I was going to ask you if I can use your lorry as I've only got one horse.' Sally readily agreed. 'Thank you,' continued Maddy. 'So will we get to meet Nigel tomorrow?'

'Yes, I suppose so.'

'You don't sound very sure,' said Maddy.

'I am. It's just that… Well, I don't know. He's… a bit vague sometimes. He answers a question with another question.'

'Do you like him?'

'Oh yes, he's ever so good looking,' replied Sally. 'He dresses well, and he flashes his money about. We had a lovely meal, nothing was too much trouble. We're going to Brinkley Manor for dinner tomorrow.'

'Wow!' Maddy was impressed. 'It's expensive there, and very good.'

'I know. ' Sally smiled. 'Do you know your times for tomorrow?'

'Yes. My dressage is at 3.50, show jumping 4.30, and the cross country must be 5.20.'

***

Maddy took Judith to walk the cross country course that afternoon. When they arrived at Eastleigh Farm several competitors were doing the same thing. They hadn't got very far when they saw Louise Parkway in front of them.

'Hello,' called out Maddy.

Louise, who was studying the obstacle called The Duck Pond, turned and smiled. 'I was hoping I might see you here. Have you heard about the ponies near the junction on the M25?'

'No, I've been a bit tied up just lately.'

'It was dreadful. A pony was found mutilated in a field shelter. He had been shot with a bolt from a cross bow, and another pony from the same paddock was found on the motorway.'

'No, I hadn't heard.' Maddy was shocked. 'Who would do such a thing? I mean what sort of mentality? Was there an accident on the motorway?'

'No. Luckily the pony was just grazing on the side of the hard shoulder, quite oblivious of the traffic. The other one had to be put down.' Judith looked stunned and Maddy asked, 'You mean it was that bad?'

'Yes, and that's not the worst. Someone had written *BOLTED!* on the side of the shed.'

Maddy stared at Louise in horror. 'Oh my God,' she whispered. 'Tamsin!'

Louise nodded grimly. 'Makes you think, doesn't it?'

'Oh God, here comes Rhona,' Maddy abruptly changed the subject.

'Such an unpleasant woman,' said Louise. 'I had a run in with her the other day over her new horse. Have a good look at it tomorrow; I'll be interested to hear what you say about it.'

'Why?' asked Maddy.

'I'm not saying any more. I'll let you make up your own mind first.' Louise smiled. 'I'll talk to you later; I'm going before she catches up with us, 'bye.' She walked quickly away to the next fence.

'Hello, fancy meeting you here,' gasped Rhona, out of breath. 'What was Louise saying to you?'

'Nothing very much, why?' queried Maddy.

'No reason.' Rhona looked tight lipped. 'Are you competing tomorrow?'

'Yes, in the novice.'

'So am I. What are your times?' Maddy told her. 'My dressage is at 2.40,' Rhona continued. 'Which horse are you bringing tomorrow? Your black horse?'

'No, a grey, Highwayman. I don't think you've seen him before.'

'I'll look out for you.'

'Actually, I'm glad I've seen you Rhona,' said Maddy. 'Have you got room for another livery?' Judith, who had been quietly waiting for Maddy, looked up in surprise.

'I will have in two weeks' time, why?'

'Well, it's for Angela Tidebrook. I don't think she's happy in my yard anymore.'

'Oh,' said Rhona. 'I haven't seen her for ages so I wouldn't know. But she's welcome to come to my yard if she wants to.'

'Thank you,' said Maddy. 'Don't let me keep you. I need to pace this fence out again. I've forgotten what the strides are now.'

Rhona gave the combination of The Duck Pond a cursory look and walked on.

'Fancy her lying about not seeing Angela,' said Judith.

'She lies all the time, so does Jilly. I never believe a word they say, not until I've checked it out first. But what is worse is that poor pony.' Maddy felt cold.

'Yes,' Judith shuddered, 'and not all that far from us.'

***

Ruth hadn't been impressed by John's behaviour the night before. So when he popped up from behind a stable door she carried on mucking out.

'Good morning.' He grinned at her.

She gave him a brief glance and said, 'Haven't you anything better to do?'

'No, I would rather talk to you.'

'Well I'm busy.' She pushed the half-empty wheelbarrow out through the open loose box door. John had to jump out of the way.

'Look out,' he exclaimed.

'No, you look out,' she retorted. 'That's if you value your job.' He stared after her as she made her way to the muck heap. He wasn't used to girls treating him like that. He was very aware of his good looks and his fit muscled body. As Sarah had pointed out, he usually went for the girls who were ready to fall into bed with him. He found it too much trouble to run after them, so he let them chase him. When he was bored he dropped them and, because of his job, that was easy.

On her way back from the muck heap, Ruth said, 'If you stand there Maddy will see you, and she has orders to tell Simon if she does'.

John didn't know what to say, so he disappeared again.

'Told you,' said a voice in his ear.

'All right Miss Know-all. You've made your point.'

That afternoon, while Maddy was out walking the course, John decided to talk to Ruth again. Highwayman was tied up in the covered area that they used for washing down the horses and Ruth was shampooing his silver mane and tail. John appeared suddenly from around the side and frightened the horse who jumped back, pulling on his lead rope. He would have broken his head collar but, as Ruth had tied him to a piece of orange baler twine which was attached to the ring, he broke that instead.

'For God's sake,' she yelled at John. 'Go away! I've had enough. You're frightening the bloody horses now.' He fled. He knew that if Ruth told Simon, Simon would move him elsewhere and he certainly didn't want to get on the wrong side of the colonel.

Although she was cross with John, Ruth still felt attracted to him. She liked his smile and his fit healthy body. He was different from the boys that she had been out with before; he reminded her of a wild animal and it might be fun to tame him. He was a challenge. She smiled to herself as she finished washing the horse.

When Maddy and Judith arrived back at October Farm they discussed what time they needed to leave the next day. 'I'll just check my dressage times, before you go.' Maddy went into the house and quickly came out with a piece of paper in her hand.

'I've given everyone the wrong times,' she said. 'My dressage is at 2.50 not 3.50, and everything else is an hour earlier. A good thing I looked at them again. Can you make it earlier?'

Yes, of course. I'll be here at about 1 o'clock.'

'Thank you Judith, you're a star.'

***

As they were driving to the horse trials, Judith asked Maddy, 'Why did you mention Angela and her horse to Rhona yesterday?'

'Well, when I ask Angela to take her horse away, I now know that she will have somewhere to take it. Why? Don't you think I should have mentioned it?'

'I don't know. Like you, I don't trust Rhona. She could stir up trouble. There's something about her... I don't know what it is.'

'I know what you mean. I've known her for a long time. I think she's quite harmless, just bombastic, arrogant and ambitious. She's trying to become someone important in British Dressage or British Eventing.'

'What do you mean by something important?'

'Well, she's half way to becoming a List 1 judge, that's the top list. Then she wants to become an International judge, only I think she might be too old, but that wouldn't occur to her. She always seems to be able to do whatever she has set her mind on doing. I'm pretty sure she wants to become a Director of British Dressage.'

'Oh. Poor British Dressage.'

'Quite,' Maddy laughed.

'Has Simon been in touch?' asked Judith, changing the subject.

'Yes, very briefly the night before last, in the middle of the night. I wasn't very polite to start with; I couldn't get to sleep and just as I dropped off he rang and woke me up.'

'Oh dear,' said Judith smiling. 'What did you say?'

'I can't remember, but the call ended amicably.'

'Oh good. What about his operatives, are they all right?'

'Yes, I suppose so. I don't see or hear them. In fact I've forgotten they are there, most of the time.'

'That's all right then, as long as you aren't fraternizing with them.'

'Good lord, no.'

When they arrived at the venue the lorry park was very full but Maddy managed to find a place tucked away in a corner next to a hedge.

Highwayman looked well, his darker grey dapples standing out in contrast to his flowing white tail. As Maddy rode off to the dressage arenas Judith said, 'He looks lovely. Ruth has certainly done a good job in turning him out so beautifully.'

Once back at the lorry again, Maddy said, 'I think I'll go straight to the show jumping while he's warm. Do you want to follow me up there?'

They were leaving the lorry park when Maddy turned to Judith and said, 'Oh, sorry, I forgot his rug, would you mind fetching it. The light weight blue one please?'

'Not at all, I'll see you up there.'

Maddy arrived at the show jumping ring just in time for a lull in the competition, giving the riders time to walk the course. Fortunately she saw someone she knew, and asked her to hold Highwayman. When she returned from walking the course she found Judith talking to her.

'This is Jane,' Maddy introduced them.

Jane helped Maddy warm up over the practice fence. Once in the ring Highwayman jumped well until he turned back towards the exit to an upright of planks. He lost his concentration and knocked the fence down. He finished by sailing over the more difficult fences at the end of the course.

Maddy smiled as she came out. 'I'm really pleased with him, just one down, stupid flimsy planks. Good boy.'

Jane came running up. 'Well done.' She searched in her pocket and brought out a titbit for the horse.

Judith rushed forwards and knocked Jane's hand just as she was about to give something to Highwayman. 'No!' she cried. Jane and Maddy looked at her in surprise as something small and white fell to the ground.

'Sorry,' said Judith, looking at Maddy. 'But he can't have titbits.'

'No, that's right,' replied Maddy, feeling shaken. She had never seen Judith move so fast or be so forceful. She turned to Jane and said, 'Thank you so much for your help.'

'That's all right.' Jane looked a bit bewildered. As soon as she left, Judith picked up the white object, wrapped it in a tissue and put it in her handbag.

Maddy was a little subdued when she arrived back at the lorry. She didn't say anything about the incident with the titbit and neither did Judith.

'I think I'll change into my cross-country gear and go down to the start. You never know, they might let me go early, it's worth a try. Can you hold Highwayman?'

'Of course.' Judith took hold of the horse.

'Don't let him eat any grass,' called out Maddy.

'No,' replied Judith. 'Where are Sally and Nigel?'

'Oh my God!' cried Maddy, leaning out of the lorry and feeling mortified. 'I told her the wrong times, and I forgot to give her the right ones. She'll miss me.'

'Oh dear,' replied Judith. 'Never mind, she could get here at any time if she wanted to. There are lots of good people to watch, even I have recognised some riders and I don't know all that much about eventing. There are some big names in your section too.'

'I know,' called Maddy from the lorry. 'I had noticed, so if we do well I shall be really pleased. I would be happy to finish in the first ten.'

'I'll go down to The Duck Pond and watch you through there,' said Judith as Maddy mounted Highwayman once more.

Judith was enjoying herself. She hurried off to the water complex and sat on a log. She found it interesting watching the different riders tackle the water. Most of them just took it in their stride but some had no end of problems.

She heard Maddy's name announced over the PA system, her dressage score was given as 27. It didn't mean anything to Judith, who was used to dressage scores given in percentages, but it sounded very low because everybody else's score was higher.

Maddy came flying over a brush fence, steadied her horse and jumped neatly down into the water. Highwayman cantered through and up the step on to the grass; he met the timber upright that followed on a perfect stride, galloped away across the field and sailed over the next fence.

Judith was just starting to walk back to the finish when she heard a commotion behind her. She turned round and saw a horse refusing at the water. The rider, who was a large ungainly woman, was shouting and hitting the horse until eventually it took off from a standstill, leapt into the water, landed on all four legs and stopped dead. The rider was hanging on to the reins in order to stop herself from falling off. She pulled herself back into the saddle, kicked the horse forward and they clambered up out of the water. They didn't have enough momentum to jump the next fence. The rider turned a circle, while all the time swearing at the horse, but it still didn't have enough impulsion to jump the obstacle.

The fence judge asked her to leave the course, but the woman took no notice, missed out the fence and carried on to the next one. As Judith walked back she heard an announcement saying Rhona Whitehaven had been eliminated at The Duck Pond.

Judith found Maddy walking Highwayman back to the lorry.

'Your dressage score was 27, isn't that rather low?' asked Judith.

'Are you sure?' Maddy was delighted.

'Yes, positive.'

'That's brilliant. It's supposed to be low, the score is worked out in penalties, 27 is very good.'

'Oh,' said Judith. 'Thank goodness, because everyone else's scores were higher. I thought you were last.'

Maddy laughed and said, 'I am so pleased with him; he jumped clear around the cross country but I don't know if I got time faults'.

'I shouldn't think so, he went like the wind,' said Judith. She helped Maddy take his tack off and stow it in the lorry. They washed him down and threw a rug over him. Maddy tipped out the sweaty water and fetched some fresh from inside the lorry in order to give him a drink.

'We'll walk towards the score board and that'll help cool him off a bit,' said Maddy. Judith told Maddy about Rhona. 'I know, isn't she an idiot?' Maddy laughed. 'I saw her in the dressage warm up. She's got a very nice horse. He looks familiar but I can't think where I've seen him before. He's a big bay thoroughbred with a round white star on his forehead. The way he moves rings a bell but I can't think why. He'd go much better with a different rider.'

'Well, she got eliminated on the cross country and she wouldn't leave the course. The fence judge was furious.'

'Stupid woman,' said Maddy. They arrived near the score board, but it was roped off and horses weren't allowed in that area.

'Could you walk him round while I go and have a look?' asked Maddy.

'Yes, of course.' Judith took the horse. She turned around and saw Sally's irate face coming towards her.

'There you are, we've been looking all over for you,' said Sally petulantly. 'We found the lorry, but you weren't in it. Shouldn't Maddy be show jumping?'

'Hello Sally,' said Judith. 'Unfortunately she gave everyone the wrong times; she was so annoyed with herself. She's finished now. Didn't you see her?'

'No, we didn't. We arrived too late,' snapped Sally. She turned to her uninterested companion. 'We've missed her. I knew we should have got here earlier.' Judith looked at the seedy man by her side. 'This is Nigel by the way,' said Sally, suddenly remembering her manners, 'and this is Judith Floyd-Williams.'

Nigel politely stepped forward to shake hands, but at that moment Highwayman swung his hind quarters round and knocked into him. Nigel looked furious. He brushed his tweed jacket with a neatly gloved hand where the horse had touched it. He was a slightly built man, about the same height as Sally. His limp dark hair was neatly cut with the front flopping over his forehead. Judith thought he might have been good looking when he was younger, but now his face was lined and his skin was sallow. He didn't quite fit in with the rest of the horsey spectators and she had the impression that he was trying to be someone he wasn't.

Both he and Sally were annoyed at missing Maddy and the conversation became rather strained. Judith was relieved to see Maddy coming back looking very pleased.

'We're second. The section hasn't finished yet,' she said to Judith. 'I did get 27 for dressage plus 4 jumping penalties, which makes my score 31. Someone got a dressage score of 30 but had no jumping penalties. The rest, whose scores aren't up yet, have higher dressage scores, so they can't beat me even if they go clear. I had the best dressage. I'm so pleased.'

'Hello!' snapped Sally.

'Oh, Sally, I didn't see you there,' said Maddy. 'I'm so sorry about the times. What a mix up.'

'Never mind.' Sally was slightly mollified. 'This is Nigel Warrington.'

'How do you do.' He smiled and came forward. 'I've heard so much about you. I'm delighted to meet you. Such a pity we missed your performance, especially as you did so well. You must be very good, coming second,' he continued. 'It all looks very complicated to me. Sally has done her best to explain the sport to me, but I'm still at a loss.' Maddy smiled and took hold of Highwayman.

'It was nice meeting you, Nigel,' she said. 'I expect we'll see you again sometime.'

'Oh, yes indeed,' he replied. 'Would you like to join Sally and me for dinner tonight?' Maddy was rather taken aback and glanced at Sally, who looked furious, and then at Judith, who looked surprised.

Maddy winked at Judith and replied, 'That's very kind of you to invite us, but Judith and I are doing something already, aren't we?' Sally looked relieved.

'Well, both of you could come with us.' Nigel seemed determined not to give up.

'No, we really couldn't,' said Judith, stepping in. 'We're meeting friends of mine, but thanks so much anyway.'

'Oh, what a pity. I would really like to take all you lovely ladies out for dinner,' he tittered. 'Are you sure you can't alter your plans? Here's my card if you change your mind. I'm sure your friends wouldn't mind.' He leered at Maddy and gave her his card.

'I'm sure they would, Mr. Warrington,' replied Judith, firmly. 'Goodbye to you.' Maddy wanted to giggle and had to turn away. Sally looked livid, Judith swept off towards the lorry and Maddy followed her leading Highwayman, stuffing the card into her pocket. Nigel stood watching them go with a fatuous grin on his face.

As soon as they were out of earshot, Maddy started laughing, and said, 'What a little toad. You were brilliant. I didn't think we were ever going to get rid of him. Well done. Sally didn't look very pleased, did she? Whatever is she doing with him? Thank you for coming to my rescue.'

Judith laughed. 'No problem, I enjoyed it. I got used to getting rid of toadies when my husband was in the army.'

'I'm looking forward to a quiet evening. Imagine going out with him.' Maddy shuddered.

When they got back to the lorry, Maddy gave Highwayman another drink of water. Then she bandaged his legs for the return journey and loaded him onto the lorry. She and Judith were clearing up the gear that had accumulated on the ground when Maddy suddenly gasped, 'Look! Come here'. Judith, alarmed at her tone of voice, dropped what she was carrying and ran round the lorry.

'What?' she said.

'That footprint.'

'What about it?'

'It's the same. It's the same as the one on my phone. I took a photo of it.' Judith looked bewildered. Maddy got out her phone and frantically pushed buttons saying, 'Where the hell is it? Don't say I've lost it. No, here it is.' She showed the picture to Judith. 'I took it up at Southways Cross, on the ridge, where Tamsin…'

'Good lord!' exclaimed Judith. She stared at the soggy, earthy patch of ground where Maddy had tipped the water after she had sponged Highwayman down, and then back at the phone. On the ground lay the exact replica of the footprint.

Judith said sharply, 'Ring Simon.' Maddy hesitated. 'Now!' ordered Judith. Maddy stared at her but she did as she was told.

He answered straight away. 'Hello, Maddy, what's wrong?'

'Judith told me to ring you,' replied Maddy, with a catch in her voice. 'I've seen the footprint. Here… I have it on my phone and now it's here.'

'What footprint?'

'The one I took on Exmoor,' Maddy spoke faster and faster. 'On the ridge, in the hide. I told you I thought that someone was waiting for Tamsin.'

'Where are you?'

'At Eastleigh.'

'I know, but where at Eastleigh?'

'By my lorry.'

'Now take a deep breath,' said Simon calmly, 'and start again. You have a picture of a footprint on your phone. Where did you take it?'

'On Southways Ridge.'

'In the hide?'

'Yes, and now it's here.'

'Are you sure it's the same one?' Simon asked. Maddy could hear him talking to someone else, but she couldn't hear what he was saying.

'Yes, absolutely, isn't it Judith? The same.'

'Yes.' Judith spoke loudly. 'It's exactly the same one.'

'All right,' said Simon, speaking slowly and clearly. 'How's your horse?'

Maddy jumped. 'He's fine. He's eating his hay.' She looked into the lorry and added, 'He's as right as rain. Why?'

'Good. Have you finished competing?'

'Yes. I came second.'

'Well done. Have you any idea when that footprint was made?'

'I do actually. It was after I had finished competing, because it's on the wet patch where I tipped a bucket of water. Then we went up to look at the score board and take my number back. Someone must have come to my lorry, because my lorry... or rather Sally's lorry, because we've got Sally's lorry not mine, anyway the lorry is parked in a corner. Nobody would just be walking past.'

'Did you leave the horse alone in the lorry?'

'No, we took him with us.'

'Good. Has anyone given him anything to eat?'

'No. Only his hay net.'

'Where had you left that?'

'Tied on the side of the lorry.'

'Take it away.'

Maddy hesitated. 'Do you think...?'

'Now Maddy,' ordered Simon.

'Okay, I'm giving the phone to Judith.' Maddy climbed up beside her horse and untied the hay net. Highwayman wasn't very pleased.

'She's right,' said Judith to Simon. 'It's the same footprint. It's most distinctive.'

'Stay with her. I'll get her horsebox taken away,' said Simon grimly.

'All right,' said Judith. Maddy came back and took the phone.

'Is your own lorry in working order?' asked Simon.

'Yes. I only used Sally's because it's smaller than mine.'

'Good. Is Ruth at home?'

'Yes.'

'Ring her and tell her to come and pick you up in your lorry. Tell anyone who asks that Sally's has broken down. I'm sending some people to pick it up. Now unload the horse and preserve the footprint. You haven't walked all over it?'

'No, of course not,' replied Maddy. She could hear Simon talking again to someone else.

'Did you lock the lorry when you left it?' Simon asked.

'Umm, yes and no,' answered Maddy.

'What do you mean, yes and no?'

'I locked the cab and I can't remember if I locked the living compartment. But it's very small... I probably did.' Simon sighed quietly. Maddy continued, 'I locked the tack away in the locker on the side'.

'Good. What about the water? You gave your horse a drink I expect? Did you bring the water with you?'

'Yes.'

'Was it locked away?'

Maddy thought for a moment. 'I don't know. It was in the living bit.'

'Don't use it, and don't touch it,' said Simon. 'Now take the horse out and wait until you're picked up by Ruth. Don't forget, if anyone, and I mean *anyone*, asks what is wrong, including Sally, you say the lorry won't start and the garage is coming out. Do you understand? Do not let them in or near the horsebox, leave it exactly as it is.'

'What about my tack?'

'Leave it in there.'

'Simon...'

'You'll get it back. You must have other tack at home.'

'Yes, but...'

'Maddy the most important thing is that you and your horse are still in one piece. I, for one want to keep it like that. You're a pain in the arse but I am very fond of you, and so is my daughter. So stop worrying about your tack, and put Judith on the phone.'

'Yes,' said Maddy meekly. She suddenly felt deflated, and handed the phone to Judith who said, 'Yes... Yes... That's right...' She looked at Highwayman as Maddy led him down the ramp. 'He seems to be fine. All right, will do,' she said into the phone. 'Straight away... any signs... Don't worry I'll see her off... Yes Sally and her boyfriend... Nigel Warrington... Probably from the internet, nobody would introduce her to that weasel except her worst enemy... Don't worry. See you later... Goodbye Simon.' She was laughing when she came off the phone. She told Maddy most of what he had said. She left out that he had told her to call the vet immediately if the horse showed any signs of distress.

'You'd better ring Ruth.' Judith handed Maddy back her phone.

***

Ruth was in the tack room; it was after five o'clock and nearly time to do the evening feeds. John startled her as he appeared in the doorway.

'What do you want?' she asked abruptly, and then turned back to her work.

'The shit has hit the fan,' he said. Ruth spun round. He looked deadly serious, even a little frightening, as he ordered, 'Get Maddy's lorry!'

'What?' Ruth was suddenly alarmed. 'What's happened?'

'Not sure yet. Maddy's okay, horse okay, lorry u.s. You've got to go and pick them up.' Ruth stood and stared at him.

'It's all right,' he said more gently, realising that he had frightened her. 'Where are the lorry keys?'

'In the house and I'm not going anywhere until I hear from Maddy,' answered Ruth, digging her toes in.

'Please don't get stroppy.' John became unsympathetic again. 'I'm not joking.'

Ruth watched him walking fast towards the house, then she saw Sarah who said, 'It's all right Ruth, this is genuine. They need you to pick them up, but they're all right.' Ruth ran into the house, overtaking John. She grabbed the lorry keys, then rushed back to the lorry and sat in the cab shaking.

'Please start, please start.' She fumbled with the key. She turned it in the ignition and the lorry obligingly roared into life. 'Thank you,' she said quietly. She sat letting the engine tick over, waiting for the air pressure to build up in the brake pipes and, just as the lorry went '*pssss,*' telling her that it had, her phone rang. It was Maddy.

'Thank Goodness,' said Ruth, 'are you all right?'

'Yes, can you pick us up?'

'I'm on my way.'

'Bring some hay,' said Maddy.

Ruth turned and yelled at John, 'I need a hay net, that one will do'. He picked up the hay that was waiting to be given to a horse. 'Bung it in the back,' Ruth shouted and then, 'Thanks,' as he obeyed her order.

'What's happened?' Ruth frantically asked Maddy, 'Are you all right?'

'Yes, we're fine,' replied Maddy. 'I saw the footprint beside the lorry.'

Ruth knew exactly what she meant. 'Oh, my God! I'm on my way.' She lifted her foot off the clutch and backed the lorry out of its parking place. John jumped on to the step outside the cab and leant through the window. He put his hand over Ruth's as she held the steering wheel. Ruth looked into his face; she thought he was going to kiss her again but he didn't. He smiled and said gently, 'Take care and drive safely, everything will be fine. I want you back in one piece.'

Ruth smiled and suddenly felt reassured.

***

Maddy was letting Highwayman eat grass while she stood talking to Judith. She felt surprisingly relaxed; the competition was over and the lorries were steadily leaving the field. She saw Louise Parkway walking in their direction so she waved and called out.

Louise came over. 'Hello, what are you doing?'

'The lorry won't start,' replied Maddy, lying convincingly. 'Ruth is coming to pick us up and the garage is coming to collect the lorry.'

'What a nuisance for you,' Louise commiserated. 'Well done, you came second in your section. That's a very nice horse.' She looked at Highwayman. 'I wouldn't mind him myself. I suppose he's not for sale?'

'Only at the right price,' Maddy laughed.

'Yes, he would be expensive.' Louise sighed.

'I saw Rhona,' said Maddy. 'What a waste of a good horse. He reminds me of someone's horse, but I can't think whose.'

'Yes, that's just it, I tackled her about it. A most unpleasant woman, as I've said before. The horse is the spitting image of...' Just then her phone rang. 'Sorry,' she said to Maddy and then into her phone, 'Hello. All right, I'm coming now.' She turned to Maddy and explained, 'Problems. I've got to go. See you soon'. She turned and walked away.

'I hope Sally doesn't come down here,' said Maddy to Judith. 'I don't know what we're going to say to her, do you?'

'Don't worry,' replied Judith. 'I don't think she'll let that boyfriend of hers near you again.'

Maddy laughed. 'No, probably not, she wasn't very pleased when he invited us out to dinner.'

'No,' said Judith. 'He asked you, not me. I was only asked because we were supposed to be doing something together.'

'What a creep.'

'I don't think he was enjoying himself very much. I think he found the whole thing a bore. I was so pleased when you came back; the conversation was getting very strained.'

'What am I going to tell Sally about her lorry?' asked Maddy.

'The truth of course.'

'Shall I unload some of my gear?'

'No,' said Judith firmly, and then she added, 'Do you need it?'

'Well, not really. Luckily I was using an old dressage saddle, not the one I use for Hyps. I've got a spare bridle for Highwayman and another jumping saddle if I need to ride him. How long will they keep the lorry?'

'I don't know.'

'The tack was secure in that locker', said Maddy, pointing to a compartment on the side of the lorry. 'Surely I can take it out.'

'No,' said Judith, obeying Simon's orders. He had told her not to let Maddy touch anything.

'I wish they would hurry up. This is not what we need at the end of a competition. I want to go home.' A few people came up to congratulate Maddy and to sympathize about the lorry.

One of them was Jilly Rich. 'Hello,' she said. 'What are you doing?'

'The lorry won't start.' Maddy was fed up with repeating herself.

'Why not?'

'I don't know. If I knew then I could start it.'

'Shall I look?' asked Jilly.

'Are you a mechanic?'

'No.'

'Well then, no thank you,' snapped Maddy.

'Thank you for trying to help.' Judith stepped in and smiled at Jilly. 'How did your friend Rhona get on today?'

'Very well. She got 37 for dressage and then no jumping penalties, I think.' Maddy and Judith looked at each other.

'I thought she had a stop on the cross country,' said Maddy.

'N... no, I don't think so. Oh yes, she had a run out at the water, somebody walked in front of the fence and she had to circle to avoid running into them.'

'How annoying for her,' said Judith.

'Yes it was. It unsettled the horse and lost her the competition.'

'Yes... yes, I suppose it must have.' Judith kept a deadpan face.

Maddy had a job to keep a straight face too and said, 'Nice horse though'.

'Yes, and only seven.'

'He reminds me of another horse, but I can't think which one,' said Maddy.

'Yes, other people have said that. But he's quite ordinary; I mean a bright bay thoroughbred, there are lots of them about.'

'I wouldn't call him ordinary,' said Maddy. 'Lots of bright bay thoroughbreds about though.'

'How are you getting home?' asked Jilly.

'Ruth's coming with my lorry.' Jilly muttered something and then, much to Maddy's relief, wandered away.

'Rhona's horse's age varies every time they talk about it.' Maddy laughed.

'Yes, I noticed that too,' replied Judith.

At last they saw Ruth arrive. She stopped in the middle of the fast emptying field looking for Maddy.

'Thank goodness.' Maddy waved madly. Ruth saw her and began to drive towards them.

'Hi,' said Ruth, as she jumped out of the cab. 'Are you all right?'

'Yes, we're fine, only fed up with hanging around and everybody asking questions,' replied Maddy.

'Where's the footprint?' asked Ruth.

'Over there, under my back protector.'

Ruth walked over and carefully lifted up the back protector, 'Oh yes, bloody hell!' she exclaimed, looking around as if the owner of the print was still there.

'Come on, let's load this horse, I'm fed up with holding him,' said Maddy. 'Although he's been a very good boy.' She patted him. 'We came second.'

'That's brilliant,' exclaimed Ruth. 'Well done.'

'Is there any water for him in the lorry?' asked Maddy.

'Yes I think so.' Ruth looked in the living compartment. She brought out a large plastic can and a bucket. They gave Highwayman another drink and loaded him into Maddy's lorry. He stood contentedly munching his hay.

'He looks fine,' remarked Ruth.

'Yes, hopefully,' said Maddy.

'What do we do now?'

'We'll have to wait for the people coming to collect Sally's lorry,' Judith told her.

'What people?' asked Ruth.

'Forensics I imagine,' replied Judith.

'I wish they would hurry up,' said Maddy and, turning to Ruth, she asked, 'Did you bring any food? I'm starving'.

'No, you didn't say. Anyway I didn't have time.'

'I think this must be them now.' Judith pointed to a recovery truck that was coming across the field.

'About time,' exclaimed Maddy, going to meet them. Her phone rang at that moment and she stopped to answer it.

'The recovery vehicle is arriving,' said Simon without any preamble. 'Two men in green overalls.' He gave Maddy the name that was written on the side of the truck and the registration number.

'Yes, I can see them.'

'Good, let them take the lorry. Is everything still inside and nothing been removed?'

'Yes... no... correct,' replied Maddy.

'Give them the keys.'

'Yes.' Maddy became irritated, feeling that she was supposed to add 'sir' at the end of each sentence.

'See you later.' Simon rang off before she could reply.

'Typical,' she said to Ruth and Judith, while looking at her phone and waving it in the air. 'He hung up, just as I was going to say something.'

'What were you going to say?' asked Judith.

'I don't know. He said something about see you later.' Then she laughed. 'I could have said we were going out with Nigel and wouldn't be in.' Maddy and Judith laughed.

Ruth looked confused and asked, 'Am I missing something? Have you met Nigel? What's he like?'

'He's creepy,' replied Maddy. 'And he invited Judith and me out to dinner with them.'

'No!' said Ruth. 'Are you going?'

'No fear.'

'Excuse me.' One of the men in green overalls had got out of the truck and was standing waiting. 'Is this the lorry?'

'It's all yours,' replied Maddy.

The driver manoeuvred the recovery truck into position and winched the horsebox onto the back; then they drove off across the field with the rear wheels of Sally's lorry bumping over the uneven ground.

'What shall we do about this footprint?' asked Maddy. Nobody replied. 'Judith,' repeated Maddy, 'what shall we do?'

'Take another photo, I suppose,' replied Judith. 'I think you should ask Simon.'

'Well I could have asked him, if he hadn't rung off so rudely.'

'He is busy,' replied Judith.

'Don't make excuses for him,' said Maddy.

'Well, you can ask him now, because here he is,' said Ruth.

'What,' exclaimed Maddy. She spun round and saw Simon's silver Mercedes coming across the field towards them.

CHAPTER SEVEN

Simon pulled up beside Maddy, Judith and Ruth, who were all standing staring at the back protector lying on the ground.

'Hello,' he said, smiling.

'Hi.' Maddy smiled back. She thought he looked more relaxed than the last time they had met. 'You always seem to arrive on cue.'

'I was planning on getting here earlier.' He got out of his car. 'Congratulations on coming second. Who won?' Maddy told him; it was a well-known rider on an experienced horse.

'Even better, that horse is almost out of novice.'

'Yes, and there were a lot of good people in the section, too.' Maddy mentioned the names of some of the other competitors.

'Well done, said Simon. 'You must be very pleased.'

'I am.'

'Where's the footprint?'

'Under that.' Simon examined the footmark, then went back to his car and took out a tape measure. He compared the footprint with Maddy's photo and then he measured it.

'It looks to be the same one. Why didn't you tell me you had this photo on your phone?'

'I forgot, what with the dogs and everything. I'm sorry. It might still be there, up in the thicket. I've got other photos of the hide.'

Simon looked at her mobile. 'We'll download those on to your computer when we get home.' He spoke on his phone as he climbed into Maddy's lorry to look at Highwayman, who was happily munching his hay. Abruptly ending the conversation, he ran a hand down the horse's neck and felt his ears, saying, 'He's dry and warm and he looks fine, thank goodness'.

'Shall I take him home now?' asked Ruth.

'Yes. Simon turned to Maddy. 'Will it be all right if Ruth takes him by herself? I need to talk to you and Judith, and I want to wait until the field clears a little more before I have my people come in to look at this site. I don't want to draw attention to them. I can take you home later.'

'Isn't illegal to transport a horse on your own? I thought the driver had to have an attendant with them nowadays?'

'Technically, yes, but it's not very far to October Farm. Ruth can always ring if something happens. I'll take full responsibility if anything goes wrong.'

'In that case...' Maddy looked at Ruth.

'Maddy, for heaven's sake, I've been driving horses around the countryside for ages on my own,' said Ruth.

'I'm only joking,' replied Maddy. 'I know you're perfectly capable.'

'I'm glad we've cleared that up.' Simon closed the lorry ramp. Ruth climbed into the cab smiling and drove away.

'Shall we sit in my car?' Simon asked Maddy and Judith, as he walked round and held the front passenger door open. Judith hesitated.

'You sit in the front.' Maddy stood back. 'I'm starving. I don't suppose you've got anything to eat, Simon?' She expected him to say no.

'In the boot. Anna made me some sandwiches.'

'Good Lord, why?' asked Maddy.

'Anna usually gives me something. I don't always have time to stop and eat. It depends where I am and what I'm doing.'

'You talk to Judith, I'll get them,' said Maddy. Simon pushed a button on the dashboard and the boot opened. Maddy found a big plastic cold box which she brought into the back of the car.

'I don't believe it,' exclaimed Maddy, opening the box. 'There's everything in here. Do you always carry this with you?' she asked in awe.

Simon was listening intently to Judith, and writing down what she was saying. 'Yes, I think so,' he replied distractedly.

'Gosh. There's a veritable feast in here; all sorts of sandwiches, smoked salmon and cucumber, pate, chicken and some ripe Brie. And... wow, my favourite wine, a bottle of Chateau Margaux.'

'Maddy, we don't want a running commentary,' said Simon, who was trying to concentrate on what Judith was telling him. 'Just take what you want.'

'Judith,' asked Maddy, ignoring him. 'What would you like?'

'Some smoked salmon would be lovely, thank you.' Judith smiled

'Here you are. Would you like a glass of wine?'

'Yes please.'

'What would you like, Simon?' asked Maddy.

'A chicken sandwich please.'

'Do you mean to say Anna gives you all this every day?' asked Maddy incredulously.

'I think she put in something extra for you. I told her I was coming here. She thought you wouldn't have much with you.'

'How kind of her,' said Maddy. 'Please thank her. I'll write a little note and put it in the box. I'm going to have some Brie and crusty bread.' Maddy fell silent as she cut the bread and spread it with the cheese.

'Thank goodness for that.' Simon smiled. 'Now we can get on.'

Judith carried on from where she had left off. 'When I reached Maddy at the show jumping ring, she was walking the course and a girl was holding Highwayman. Then when Maddy finished jumping, this same girl tried to give the horse this.' Judith produced the tissue containing the white object from her handbag. 'It might be a mint, but it might be something else.'

'Well done.' Simon took the tissue and put it into a small plastic bag that he got out of the glove compartment. 'Who was this girl?' he asked Maddy.

'I was a bit surprised when you knocked it out of her hand, but I didn't realise that you had picked it up,' said Maddy. 'She's okay, she wouldn't do anything.'

'Yes,' Simon persisted. 'But what's her name?'

'Jane something, I can't remember her surname. She used to come for lessons with me. She had a nice little horse called...'

'Never mind her horse's name. What's her name?' Simon butted in with an air of controlled frustration.

'Well, I'm trying to remember. The horse's name was connected to hers. Patrick, that's the name of the horse. Got it... Down.'

'What has Down got to do with Patrick?' asked Simon, trying not to laugh.

'Down Patrick... racecourse in Northern Ireland. Jane Down. Told you,' said Maddy proudly. 'Haven't seen her for ages, but she's okay.' Simon wrote down the name.

'Would it be too difficult for you to remember her address? Maddy was struggling to open the bottle of wine. 'I'll do that.' Simon took the bottle and the corkscrew. 'The address, please?'

'Umm. Now, let me see...'

'No more word puzzles, please.' Simon expertly pulled the cork and handed the bottle back to Maddy.

'Mill Farm, Rushy Lane, Rushy Green,' replied Maddy quickly. 'What if you find out it's only a mint? Thanks,' she said as he passed back the open bottle of wine.

'Nothing. I'll tear up her address. We have to check everything.'

'Okay... Here.' She passed a glass of wine to Judith and one to Simon. He put their glasses on a little shelf that he had pulled out from under the dashboard.

'You'll find a tray in the back somewhere,' he said to Maddy.

'Oh yes, here it is,' she said. *I could get used to this,* she thought, as she leaned back into the comfortable leather seats, sipping her wine and starting on the paté sandwiches.

Judith told Simon about Rhona's behaviour on the cross country course. 'She got eliminated, but she wouldn't leave the course. She was swearing at the horse, it was most embarrassing.'

'Yes, remarked Maddy. 'It would be funny if she wasn't a judge. There's something very odd about that horse of hers though, but I don't know what it is. I can't quite put my finger on it.'

'Yes, I think there is,' said Simon. 'I haven't seen it yet, but when I do I'll tell you. Don't mention this to any one.'

'I already have… to Rhona,' replied Maddy, unconcernedly taking another sip of her wine 'Actually, Louise Parkway mentioned it too.' Maddy sat up, surprised as she caught sight of the look on Simon's face in the driving mirror, but it had gone in a flash before she had time to say anything.

'Never mind, but don't talk about it again.'

'All right,' replied Maddy.

Judith went on to say how they had come back to the lorry after the cross country and then returned to the score board with the horse where she met Sally and Nigel.

'They were annoyed because Maddy had given them the wrong times and they had missed her,' said Judith.

'What do you mean, the wrong times?' asked Simon sharply.

'Well, I told everyone my dressage time was 3.50 by mistake, but it was 2.50. So they came an hour too late; Sally was furious, then that cretin Nigel invited me and Judith out to dinner with them and she got even crosser.

'And you accuse me of upsetting people, retorted Simon. 'Who else did you give the wrong times to?'

'Rhona, Louise Parkway, I can't remember; probably anyone else who asked me when we were walking the course the day before. It was only when we got back and I checked my times that I realised I had made a mistake. I forgot to tell Sally.'

'Did you meet several people while you were walking the course?' asked Simon.

'Yes, quite a few.'

'So the owner of the footprint might not have realised that you had finished riding?' said Simon. 'They might have thought that you still had your cross country to do.'

'Yes, I suppose so,' replied Maddy, who was looking inside the cold box. 'There's a Banoffee Pie in here. My favourite pudding. Judith, do you want some?'

'Yes, please,' replied Judith, smiling as Simon heaved a sigh of exasperation.

'Simon?' asked Maddy.

'No thank you.' Maddy passed a slice of pie to Judith and slowly ate her own, savouring every mouthful. 'This is so good. Simon, you could have got here earlier before we were dying of starvation.'

'Well, I do beg your pardon,' he said with a straight face. Judith was in fits of laughter. 'I was a little tied up in a meeting in Downing Street this morning. I should have told the P.M. that I was needed urgently elsewhere.'

'Oh very funny,' said Maddy. 'I had an appointment with the Queen this morning at Buck House, but I cancelled it.'

'Getting back to reality then,' said Simon, 'what's this Nigel like?'

'A creep,' replied Maddy.

'Seedy,' said Judith.

'He sounds charming. What is his surname?' asked Simon.

'Warrington,' replied Judith. 'Maddy has got his card.'

'Can I see it?'

'You can have it with pleasure.' Maddy got it out of her pocket.

'Why did he give you his card?'

'Because he asked Judith and me out to dinner with him and Sally tonight. We both said no; we said that we were meeting friends of Judith's in order to get out of going with him. Then Judith snubbed him and stalked off, so he gave me his card in case we changed our minds.'

'Excellent.' Simon looked at the card. 'We'll all go out to dinner with them tonight. Ring him and tell him you've changed your minds.'

'You are joking? I'd rather have teeth pulled', said Maddy.

'It might be quite good fun,' Judith added, smiling.

'Fun!' exclaimed Maddy. 'Can you imagine Nigel and Simon together? It would be like trying to mix oil and water ending up with a curdled mayonnaise.'

'I think you're mixing your metaphors.' Simon smiled urbanely.

'And Sally simpering and flirting with both men,' Maddy

shuddered. 'I'd throw up.'

'After all you've just eaten,' remarked Simon, grinning, 'I expect you'll throw up anyway.'

'Yes,' Judith replied to Maddy's question. 'I can imagine them together. It could be a most interesting evening, unless of course you would rather I didn't come. I wouldn't want to play gooseberry.'

'Don't be so silly, play gooseberry indeed. I wouldn't go without you, that's if I go at all.'

'Judith and I can go together,' said Simon.

'Oh no you won't,' retorted Maddy. 'If Judith goes, I go.'

Judith looked at Simon, who winked at her and smiled, saying, 'Stop eating. You won't have any appetite left for dinner'. He leant over and tried to take away the remains of the Banoffee Pie.

'Get off,' said Maddy, hanging on to her bowl. 'You'll make a mess in the car. He let go of the bowl and she fell back into the seat, laughing, 'All right, I'll ring the little squirt. Where's my phone?'

'Use this one. Simon took a mobile phone out of the glove compartment and handed it to her. 'He won't be able to get the number, it comes up withheld.'

'What shall I say? I hope he doesn't answer.'

Simon thought for a moment. 'Say that only one of Judith's friends has turned up, and that you would like to go out to dinner with him and Sally after all, and does the offer of dinner still stand? Then when he says yes...'

'He might not say yes,' Maddy butted in.

'He will,' said Judith.

'How do you know?' asked Maddy.

'Because he's more interested in you than Sally.'

Maddy opened her mouth to ask why, when Simon added quickly, 'When he says *Yes*, ask him to pick us up at your house as Judith's friend has offered to drive everyone... because he doesn't drink'.

'Well that's a joke,' retorted Maddy. 'You drink like a fish.'

'No more than you,' replied Simon 'You're half cut already.'

'I am not. I've only had two glasses of wine.'

'Two?' said Simon. 'We've only had one each.'

'Well, I'm sorry,' said Maddy, picking up the bottle of wine and dropping the phone. 'Please have some more.'

'Children! children!' Judith laughed. 'The job in hand, please.'

'You mean the glove.' Maddy giggled.

'Oh God,' said Simon, wearily. 'Perhaps you'd better ring him, Judith.'

'I'm quite capable of making a phone call,' retorted Maddy, putting down the wine bottle and picking up the phone. 'What's the number?' Simon read out the number as Maddy dialled it.

'I hope he doesn't answer,' she said again, but Nigel answered fairly quickly.

'Smile,' whispered Simon.

Maddy obediently smiled and said, 'Hello Nigel, its Maddy here'.

'Hello Maddy.' Nigel sounded pleased.

'Does your offer of dinner still stand?' she asked, still smiling.

'By all means,' he replied. 'Do you mean you can come after all?'

'Yes. The thing is that only one of Judith's friends has turned up. He's a little difficult to please and we thought he would prefer the company of another male. Two females might overpower him and bore him rather. Actually, to tell you the truth,' Maddy was getting well into the swing of it, 'he's a bit of a bore and the thought of spending the evening with him… Well….' Judith caught sight of the look on Simon's face and couldn't contain her laughter.

'I understand,' said Nigel, in a tone that made Maddy cringe. 'That would be fine.' Maddy could feel him preening himself.

'Would you like to come to my house? Judith's friend would be prepared to drive us all. He doesn't…' Maddy couldn't get the words out as she saw Judith shaking.

'Yes, of course,' replied Nigel. 'That would be a good idea because my car is rather small. It's a Porsche…' He paused, waiting for Maddy to make a remark. Simon turned and mouthed, *say something.* Maddy understood what Simon meant and tittered, 'Oh, a Porsche! I've never been in a Porsche before'.

'I would be delighted to take you out in mine.'

Maddy made a face and said, 'Another time, perhaps?'

'Definitely,' he said. 'In any case we'll come to your house this evening, at about 7.30?' Simon looked at his watch and shook his head. It was already after six. 'Eight o'clock,' he mouthed.

'Oh,' said Maddy. 'You know us girls. I don't think we would be ready by then. Where are we going?'

'Brinkley Manor. Do you know it?'

'Oh yes.' Maddy sounded suitably impressed. 'That's very posh, we really will have to look our best. Could you pick us up at eight?'

'No problem,' said Nigel. 'See you and your friends later then. We'll be five in all?'

'Yes,' said Maddy, taking her time as if counting the people on her fingers, 'that's right, looking forward to seeing you at eight. Goodbye.'

'You were brilliant,' Judith laughed

'You made me out to be an idiot,' said Simon.

'Yes,' said Judith. 'Isn't Nigel going to have a shock when he meets you?'

'Sally's going to be furious,' said Maddy. 'She'll wonder who this friend of Judith's is.'

'Well, she'll soon find out,' said Simon, taking something out of his ear.

'You were listening in,' said Maddy indignantly.

'Yes,' replied Simon blandly. 'Excuse me; I have to make a phone call.' He got out of the car and said something brief into his phone and a white transit van which had been parked near the entrance to the field drove slowly towards them.

'You two are so funny together,' said Judith, while Simon was out of the car. 'I've never seen him so relaxed.'

'Huh,' said Maddy. 'He's probably drunk.'

'Don't be silly. You heard him say we had only had one glass of wine.'

'Oh Judith.' Maddy was mortified. 'Have some more, I don't want to hog it all. Actually I need a little more after that experience on the phone. Isn't Nigel awful?'

'Yes, I can't wait to see his face when Simon turns up.'

'But what about Sally? What is she going to say?' Maddy picked up the wine bottle and poured some into Judith's glass and some more into her own.

'Thank you,' said Judith. 'Don't worry about her, she fancies Simon. Tell him to flirt with her; she'll love it.'

'She'll flirt with him anyway,' said Maddy. 'It gets on my nerves.'

Does it? thought Judith, smiling to herself. She continued out loud, 'I think Simon knows what he's doing. I mean he's not interested in her, don't worry about her.'

'I'm not worried about her,' replied Maddy airily

The white van drew up close to the car and two men got out. Simon showed them the spot where Sally's lorry had been parked and the footprint. They nodded and spoke to Simon while they changed into white overalls. All the other lorries had now left the park.

'We're not going to have much time to change before we go out,' said Maddy to Judith. 'Shall we stop at your house and you can collect something to wear? Then you could change at my house.'

'Yes, that would be a good idea,' replied Judith. When Simon came back they told him of their plans.

'Where to?' asked Simon, as he drove out of the field. Judith directed him to her pretty tile hung house, which wasn't very far from Maddy's yard. Simon drove down the gravel drive lined with daffodils. Well-kept lawns lay on each side of the house and neat flower beds were placed on either side of the front door.

'I won't be long.' Judith got out of the car. 'I know what I'm going to wear.'

'I bet your house is neat and tidy, everything is in its place and you can put your hand on anything you want without having to search for it', said Maddy.

'Well...' replied Judith.

'I knew it,' said Maddy.

'You see I would never have made a colonel's wife,' said Maddy to Simon. 'Poor Jonathan, he would never have been promoted while he was married to me.'

'Johnnie was a good officer and a good soldier. I wish I had him working with me now,' said Simon. Then he added quietly, looking down, 'Sometimes I envied him his marriage.' Maddy felt close to tears; neither of them spoke for a few moments.

'How's Emma?' Maddy broke the silence. 'I meant to ask earlier but I forgot.'

'She's well enough, given the circumstances. Monica is being marvellous. I don't know what I would do without her just now. Emma seems to have thrown herself into the horses.'

'That's the great thing about horses. They help you get through so much, and they help you cope with things. They're such a comfort in all sorts of ways.'

'Yes.' Simon turned in his seat and looked at her. 'You've managed so well. I do admire the way you've picked up your life.' Maddy blushed, and her tears felt very close to overflowing. She looked out of the car window at the flowering wisteria growing up the front of Judith's house. *I can't handle all these compliments*, she thought.

'Emma wanted to come and stay with you.' Simon lightened the tone of the conversation.

'I know. But it's not a good idea at the moment.'

'No. I fobbed her off for the time being, I told her that you would have her a little later in the year. Would that be all right?'

'Yes, absolutely.'

'She wants to come up here and do some competing.'

'That would be great,' replied Maddy.

Simon smiled. 'She's riding some of her mother's horses and riding them very well too.'

'That's good,' replied Maddy, remembering Emma's remark about feeling her mother was with her when she was riding.

'She reminds me of Tamsin when she's riding. It's uncanny. She needs to polish up her dressage though; I'm sure you could help her.'

'Of course I would,' replied Maddy. 'How many horses does she want to bring?'

'I've no idea.'

'Do I need to build more stables?' asked Maddy.

'Probably.' Simon laughed.

Judith came out of her house and smiled to herself as she saw them looking so comfortable together.

'That was quick,' remarked Maddy.

'It's now a quarter to seven,' said Simon. 'Are you both going to be ready by eight?'

'No problem. Drive on,' said Maddy

'Yes, ma'am,' he replied.

As soon as they arrived back at Maddy's yard Simon went into the barn to call a meeting with John and Sarah. Then he found Ruth and asked her to move Maddy's lorry while he parked his car behind it, out of sight at the back of the yard.

'Do your usual ten o'clock feeds,' Simon smiled at Ruth. 'Take no notice of what you might see going on in the yard.' Ruth looked enquiringly at him and nodded, but he said no more.

Both Maddy and Judith changed quickly and arrived downstairs more or less together. Judith looked smart in a pale green silk dress and jacket. Maddy was wearing very high heels with a figure hugging black dress. She draped a long blue chiffon stole around her shoulders which made her blue eyes look big and vibrant. Her dark hair was piled on top of her head. The sun had caught her face while she had been riding that day, giving her a healthy glow. She looked stunning.

Simon stared at her as he came into the kitchen. He had changed his shirt for a plain white one and wore his navy and burgundy striped regimental tie.

'What are we going to tell Sally about her lorry?' asked Maddy before Simon had time to compliment her on her appearance.

'Nothing,' replied Simon. 'We have put your lorry at an angle, hiding my car and the space where Sally's lorry usually goes. She won't notice unless she goes round the back.'

'Suppose she wants to show Nigel her horse? She would have to go round the back then,' said Maddy.

'Then we'll have to distract her,' replied Simon.

'He won't want to look at her horse,' said Judith. 'That's the last thing he'll want to look at. Anyway, there won't be time.'

'I hope you're right. Does anyone want a drink?' asked Maddy. 'I know I do.'

'Good idea,' agreed Simon. 'Judith?'

'G & T please. Have you got one?' she asked Maddy.

'Yes, gin and whisky in the dining room,' said Maddy to Simon, who was heading in that direction. She added, 'Mind the cobwebs.'

He grinned and came back with a bottle of each. While they waited in the kitchen, Maddy took a large gulp of whisky.

'Steady on,' said Simon, smiling at her. 'I want my troops sober.'

Maddy smiled. 'I'm just a little agitated.'

'Don't worry, we'll nail the little bastard if he's done anything wrong,' said Simon calmly. Maddy began to sip her drink slowly and sat twiddling the fringe of her stole between her fingers. She noticed Judith sat upright, poised and calm.

At eight o'clock a red Porsche came down the drive with Nigel at the wheel.

'He can only just see over the steering wheel,' Maddy laughed.

'I'm glad he's brought his car,' said Simon, 'that will make things quicker and easier.' Maddy looked at him enquiringly, but he said no more.

'Where shall I park?' Nigel asked Sally as he drove up the drive.

'Just here,' said Sally, looking around for another car. She saw Judith's car, which had been there since the morning, and hoped that her friend, whoever he was, wasn't coming

Nigel left his car and walked towards the house, leaving Sally to struggle out of the low seat while the big heavy car door swung shut on her legs. As he walked his eyes were everywhere, taking in the yard, the stables and size of the house. Sally eventually managed to extricate herself from the Porsche and caught up with him.

'Where do we go?' he asked, looking for the front door.

'In here,' replied Sally, heading for the kitchen. She was wearing a yellow linen suit and looked very elegant, but not stunning like Maddy.

Maddy came out of the kitchen door to welcome them; Nigel stared up at her. She now towered above him in her high heels.

'Hello,' said Maddy. 'Come in.'

'May I say you look dazzling,' said Nigel. Maddy gave him a weak smile and led them into the kitchen.

'Who are these friends of Judith's?' Sally asked Maddy waspishly. At that moment Simon stepped forward and the look on Sally's face was one of combined horror, shock and fury.

'Good evening,' said Simon courteously. 'Lovely to see you again so soon, and looking so beautiful.' Sally blushed and simpered, the look of fury vanishing fast.

'Yes.' She smiled up at him.

'Do you know this person?' Nigel sounded annoyed. 'You said that you didn't.' The fact that Sally was appalled to see Simon had escaped his notice.

'This is Simon Coulson,' said Sally. 'Simon, Nigel Warrington.' As Maddy had predicted, the two men disliked each other on sight. Simon shook Nigel's limp, damp hand. He needed all his self-discipline to stop himself from getting out his handkerchief and wiping his own hand.

Sally took Maddy to one side and asked, 'What's going on? Why is he here?'

'Not my idea,' replied Maddy. 'I'll explain later.'

Judith was watching Nigel, who was looking around Maddy's kitchen, taking in the Crown Derby china and the cut glass on the dresser.

'Perhaps we should go.' Maddy felt uneasy, also noticing Nigel's wandering eyes.

'I'll get my car.' Simon went outside

'If I'd seen his car here we would have driven away, said Sally. Nobody replied to that. Judith was trying to make polite conversation with Nigel, but he was either staring at Maddy or her possessions and wasn't listening.

Simon eventually brought his car round. Nigel didn't look pleased when he saw the top-of-the-range, powerful silver Mercedes. Judith got in the front, Maddy and Sally sat either side of Nigel in the back.

It only took a short while to get to Brinkley Manor, but to Maddy it seemed to take forever. Nigel sat very close to her and pressed his thigh against hers. She was wedged up against the door, not able get away from him. His hand lay loosely half way down his thigh, almost touching her leg.

'May I say you have a lovely property?' he said.

'Thank you,' said Maddy, trying to catch Simon's eye in the mirror, but he appeared to be concentrating on the road ahead.

'A beautiful woman with a beautiful house,' said Nigel.

'She has a beautiful horse too,' said Simon, suddenly grinning at Maddy in the mirror.

'Yes, we caught sight of it,' said Nigel, 'but we missed seeing her ride it. He tried to make the word *ride* sound erotic, but instead he made Maddy cringe. He added, bending his head towards her, 'Such a pity, another time perhaps?' He spoke quite well but he mispronounced the vowels on certain words which made Maddy sure he was putting on an educated accent. She stared straight ahead and said, 'Sally has a very nice horse'.

'Oh,' replied Nigel and then lapsed into silence. Judith did her best to make conversation; Maddy responded but no one else bothered to join in.

Sally sat staring out of the window fuming, realising how Nigel had lost interest in her as soon as he had set eyes on Maddy. He had even talked of going home early until Maddy had called.

At last they arrived at Brinkley Manor, an imposing house built of local grey stone, surrounded by sweeping lawns and set at the end of a long drive. It had an unusual turreted facade with big bay windows on the front overlooking the drive. A large lawn at the back dropped away to a ha-ha, dividing the parkland from the gardens and allowing uninterrupted views across the rolling countryside to the South Downs beyond. Closer to the house fountains played in formal gardens.

Once the car was parked, Nigel walked on ahead with Sally, who was doing her best to keep up with him.

Maddy looked at Simon and raised her eyes to heaven saying, 'I knew this would be a disaster'.

He smiled warmly at her and replied quietly, 'You look nearly as beautiful as your property'.

She looked up at him and said, 'Very funny; your car went down well too. Sally is never going to forgive me for this.'

'She'll be thanking you before the evening is out. The Porsche is hired.'

'No!' Maddy turned to Judith and said, 'Simon says the Porsche is hired'.

'That doesn't surprise me.'

They caught up with Nigel and Sally in the reception area, and then they headed towards the dining room together.

The head waiter gave Nigel a cursory look and ushered them to a table in the corner of the restaurant close to the entrance to the kitchens. Nigel began to tell everyone where to sit.

'I don't think this will do at all,' said Simon, turning to the head waiter as he watched waitresses brushing past with plates from the kitchens. Maddy wanted to giggle, but she agreed with Simon it was a horrible table. The head waiter looked at Simon, who continued in his smooth upper crust accent: 'You must be mistaken, this can't be our table'. The waiter saw the Guards regimental tie, heard the accent and recognized the firm demeanour of a man who was used to giving orders and who expected to be obeyed.

'I beg your pardon, sir. What name was it?' asked the waiter.

'Colonel Coulson,' replied Simon, smiling.

'Of course, my mistake. I believe you would like a table in the bay window, Colonel?'

'Yes,' replied Simon. He turned to Judith and Maddy and said, 'Would that suit you ladies?'

'Yes, thank you,' replied Judith, 'that would be very nice.' Maddy nodded, and then she caught sight of Nigel; he looked livid. Sally refused to even look at Maddy, let alone speak to her.

They all sat down by the window overlooking the formal gardens: Simon sat next to Judith and Sally, and Maddy sat between Judith and Nigel, almost opposite Simon.

'Excuse me.' As soon as everyone was seated, Simon disappeared into the reception area. Nigel tried to see what he was doing but lost sight of him.

'This is very nice,' said Judith. Sally glared at her. Nigel was sitting closer to Maddy than to Sally. Maddy tried to move her chair closer to Judith, but the chairs were big and heavy and the carpet was thick. The chair wouldn't go where Maddy wanted it to, so she turned her upper body towards Judith instead. Nigel tried to talk to her, but she was engrossed in conversation with Judith.

'I know his sort,' said Nigel to Sally. 'He thinks he's important, but he is probably a nobody. His accent is obviously put on.'

Before Sally could answer, Simon came back to the table. Sally was sulking. Maddy continued to talk to Judith with her back turned towards Nigel, and he was still trying to attract her attention. Simon smiled to himself as he sat down. He turned to Sally and asked charmingly, 'How are you getting on with your horse?'

She responded, smiling and tossing her head, 'She's going very well. I've started jumping her'.

'Good.' He pretended to listen to her rattle on about Poppy. 'So you'll be out competing soon?'

'Oh yes.' Sally smiled and passed her tongue over her lips. Maddy watched her and Simon out of the corner of her eye.

There were no prices on the ladies' menus and Nigel had to control his reaction when he saw the prices on his menu but then quickly congratulated himself for making contingency plans where the payment of the bill was concerned. He even smiled to himself as they all chose some of the most expensive dishes. As soon as they were ready to order, a waiter appeared from nowhere, automatically going to Simon and ignoring Nigel. The wine waiter brought the wine list and also gave it to Simon, who ordered an expensive Chateau Neuf du Pape.

Simon turned to Nigel and asked, 'So what do you do for a living?'

'I'm an executive,' replied Nigel.

'Oh really,' said Simon, 'what for?'

'A chain of restaurants.'

'Where?' asked Simon, rather rudely Maddy thought, although she smiled to herself because Nigel was obviously beginning to squirm.

'Round about London,' replied Nigel airily.

Judith quickly said, 'That must be interesting,' before Simon had time to ask, *what restaurants*?

'Yes,' said Nigel. 'I get out and about and meet a lot of people.'

Pity you couldn't find us a better table then, thought Maddy.

'How are your dogs?' Simon asked Maddy, abruptly changing the subject while watching Nigel at the same time. 'I thought they looked very well just now.'

'Yes, they're absolutely fine.'

'Do you know what it was?' Simon asked.

'No. The vet said the results wouldn't be back until the middle of next week.'

'You will let me know what caused it, won't you?' asked Simon.

'Of course I will.'

Nigel appeared to be bored by the conversation and was talking to Sally, who answered him in an offhand manner.

Maddy suddenly felt Nigel's hand on her knee and jumped; she turned and glared at him. He hastily removed it. She noticed Simon's face harden. Sally said something and fluttered her eyelashes at him; he ignored her. *God, this is a nightmare*, thought Maddy.

The tension was nearly broken when the excellent starters arrived, and Maddy decided to enjoy hers in spite of the company. She chatted to Judith about the horse trials; however she noticed Simon was beginning to flirt with Sally again. She gave Nigel a quick glance and saw that he was sulking.

'Excuse me.' Simon rose from the table when they finished eating.

'Where's he going?' Nigel grumpily asked Judith.

'I don't know. He suffers from stomach trouble sometimes.' Maddy tried not to laugh.

Simon, his face looking hard, reappeared just before the main course arrived. Maddy shivered and glanced at Judith.

'Are you all right?' Judith asked Simon.

'Not really.' Maddy and Judith exchanged glances again. Simon smiled and replied, 'Nothing for you to worry about. Enjoy your meal'.

Maddy was enjoying the main course immensely until she felt a hand on her knee again. This time she pretended to drop her fork and very deftly used it to stab Nigel's hand. He quickly snatched it out of the way and winced in pain. Simon looked thunderous; Maddy looked at Judith and then had a desire to giggle.

Sally was smiling and tossing her head, trying to attract Simon's attention. But he got up from the table once more and went outside.

'There he goes again,' said Nigel.

'Yes,' said Judith, who was beginning to feel agitated. She glanced at Maddy, who was enjoying the last of her meal.

Maddy looked up and asked quietly, 'What is it?'

'I don't know,' replied Judith, equally quietly, 'but something has happened.' Maddy felt cold.

'Are you two sharing secrets again?' asked Sally.

'Not for much longer,' replied Judith, who could see Simon coming back. His face was as black as thunder.

'Right,' he said without any preamble, 'we're going home.'

'What?' exclaimed Maddy. Sally looked indignant and annoyed. Judith immediately picked up her hand bag, put her napkin on the table and prepared to stand up.

'Are you ready?' she asked Maddy quietly. Maddy nodded, gathered up her handbag and pushed her chair back too.

'The meal was lovely, but I can't stand any more of this company,' she replied quietly to Judith.

'How dare you,' said Nigel to Simon. 'You've ruined this evening right from the start. Who do you think you are, ordering us about? You go home if you're unwell, we'll return in a taxi.' Simon took a leather ID holder out of his pocket and flashed a card in Nigel's face. Nigel went pale.

'I think you'd better stand up, Mr. Fish,' said Simon in a voice of steel, staring grimly at Nigel. He had enunciated the words *Mister Fish* extremely clearly. Everybody stared at Simon and then at Nigel, who went white and then very red in the face.

'What are you talking about?' asked Sally. Everyone ignored her.

'I'm not going anywhere.' Nigel tried unsuccessfully to brazen things out: 'I don't know what you are talking about, that is not my name. You've clearly made a mistake'.

'I have made no mistake,' said Simon calmly, a stony look on his face. 'Your name is Kelvin Fish.' Maddy started giggling while Sally stared open mouthed at Nigel and Simon in turn, then glowered at Maddy. Nigel/Kelvin still remained seated, his face so red that Maddy thought he was going to suffer an apoplexy.

'Come on,' said Judith to Maddy. They left the restaurant together. Then they stood in the doorway watching the unfolding scene; some of the other diners had noticed the commotion and were beginning to turn and stare too. Nigel was refusing to get up and Sally had started to cry.

'I don't believe you,' she said to Simon.

'Oh yes, it's true enough. Will you please leave with us now, Mr. Fish,' said Simon in a very quiet but threatening voice, 'or I will have you removed.' Nigel looked up and saw two burly waiters approaching menacingly, so he stood up and meekly followed Simon outside to the car. Judith and Maddy had made their way there as soon as they saw Nigel give in. Sally followed in tears.

'I don't believe this is happening,' Sally said to Maddy and Judith when she caught up with them. 'You knew about this and you let Simon humiliate me... and Nigel.'

'We certainly did not know,' snapped Maddy.

'How could you do this to me? Sally continued railing at Maddy.

'It's not Maddy's fault,' said Judith.

'You can shut up, you old bitch.' Sally was becoming hysterical.

'No, you shut up,' said Maddy. 'You brought the little weasel down here. He doesn't even own that flash car of his. Where did you meet him?' Sally sulkily shut her mouth.

'Where?' repeated Maddy, towering above Sally and looking menacing.

'I...'

'Off the bloody internet.' Sally went quiet and blushed 'You did, didn't you?' Sally nodded and looked down at the ground.

By this time Simon had man-handled Nigel into the front seat of the car and locked the doors. Nigel tried to get out but found that he couldn't open the door from the inside. Simon went round to the driver's side and got into the car. He unlocked the back doors briefly while the women got in and then drove off.

'What's happening?' asked Nigel. 'Who are you?'

'You'll find out,' said Simon through gritted teeth. 'You saw my ID.'

'You bitch!' Nigel screamed at Sally. She burst into tears again.

'Don't you blame Sally,' said Simon, 'just keep quiet.' Sally perked up a little as Simon stuck up for her, but Nigel had no intention of keeping quiet. He started screaming and swearing, hurling threats and abuse at Sally. She shrank back into her seat looking frightened and started shaking.

Maddy suddenly felt sorry for her and shouted, 'Shut up, you little creep'. But that made him worse. Simon leant forward and jabbed him in his face with his elbow. Nigel gave a cry of pain and blood poured out of his nose.

'Find him a tissue someone.' said Simon. 'I don't want blood all over my car.' Judith pulled a wad of tissues out of her handbag and passed them to Nigel. He held them up to his face, muttering something. Maddy tried not to laugh; Sally was crying and Judith sat looking out of the window into the night as if nothing had happened.

'I'm really sorry about telling you the wrong times,' said Maddy to Sally, trying to make amends, 'it was a genuine mistake.'

'It spoilt everything,' sobbed Sally.

Simon was incensed by her remark and by her attitude and said grimly, 'Thank God she did. That mistake probably saved her life and the life of her horse. I shall want to know exactly what you mean by that statement when we get home.'

'I don't know what you are talking about,' sobbed Sally. 'I haven't done anything. You're just picking on me. Let me out, I want to go home.'

'Oh shut up, Sally,' said Maddy. 'Simon, what do you mean?'

'I'll explain when we get home and after I've dealt with this.' He gestured towards Nigel, who sat cowering in his seat.

Nigel tried to open his door again when they stopped at some traffic lights, but Simon gave him a grim smile and said, 'You'll get out when I say so.' Maddy flinched at his tone of voice.

They turned off the main road into Maddy's lane. Simon said, as if into thin air, 'ETA three minutes. John front passenger, Sarah driver's side rear.' Maddy looked at Judith and smiled; she suddenly felt safe. Nigel looked terrified.

As they pulled up, two figures came from out of the shadows and Sally gave a cry. 'Who are they?' she gasped.

'Our resident minders,' replied Maddy. Simon waited until John was at Nigel's door and Sarah was at Sally's door before he unlocked the car.

'Take him into the kitchen,' ordered Simon.

'Sir!' replied John, who flung open the door and man-handled Nigel out of the car.

'Who are you?' whimpered Nigel. 'What do you want?'

'Just go along quietly and you won't get hurt,' said Simon.

'I need the toilet,' said Nigel desperately.

'Take him,' ordered Simon.

'Sir!' John frogmarched Nigel into the house. Nobody except Judith thought it was odd that John knew exactly where to find the downstairs cloakroom in Maddy's house.

'Come with me ma'am. Sally had stopped crying and obediently let Sarah take hold of her arm. She felt dazed and was glad to have something to lean on. She stared at Simon.

'You've had a lucky escape,' Simon told her kindly. He turned to Sarah and said, 'Take her in.'

Sally, completely bemused, walked up the path to the kitchen with Sarah.

'I think you are being a bit hard on her,' said Maddy.

'I want to know why she is still so uptight about the times,' answered Simon grimly.

'You don't think…' started Maddy looking up at him anxiously.

Simon put his arm around her, gave her a hug and smiled. 'I don't exactly know what I think yet.' He turned to Judith and asked, 'Would you like someone to take you home?'

'Certainly not. I want to hear what the beastly little man has to say. Also I'm surprised at Sally's behaviour. She found him on the internet you know.'

'Yes, "*Datamate*",' replied Simon.

'Datamate,' repeated Maddy. 'What a name.'

'She's done it before,' said Simon.

'How do you know?' asked Maddy.

'We checked her computer,' Simon replied casually.

'How…?' asked Maddy.

'Don't ask.'

'I don't know why she has to go on the internet looking for men,' said Judith. 'She's attractive and well-spoken and not unintelligent.' She saw the look on Simon's face and added, 'Well maybe not all that intelligent, but very personable and likeable'.

'She's an airhead and far too desperate, puts people off,' replied Simon.

'Oh,' said Judith.

Ruth came round the corner of the yard and Maddy jumped.

'I've just finished the late night feeds,' she said.

'Is the grey horse all right?' asked Simon.

'Yes, quite normal; he's eaten up and he hasn't broken out in a cold sweat. No ill effects from anything.'

'Good,' said Simon smiling. 'I wouldn't mind that horse for Emma, but she probably has enough horses at the moment.'

'Will you sell him? I mean after he went so well today,' asked Judith, looking at Maddy.

'At the right price.'

'Come on,' said Simon. 'We have a man to see in the kitchen.'

CHAPTER EIGHT

Simon, followed by Maddy and Judith, went into the kitchen. Nigel was sitting at the table with blood stains on his face from his nose bleed. He sat glaring at Sally, while John was standing over him like a dog guarding a bone.

Maddy felt dreadful when she saw how exhausted Sally looked. She walked towards her and put her hand out and said, 'Sally…'

Sally looked up at her and snapped, 'You've lost another livery. I'm taking Poppy away from here.'

Maddy sighed and looked at Simon, who gave her a brief reassuring smile. Judith sat down and Maddy sat opposite her.

Simon asked Ruth, 'Perhaps some coffee might be a good idea?' She nodded and put the kettle on while trying not to look at John.

Simon sat down facing Nigel and Sally. 'Right, Mr. Fish, why did you go to Sally's lorry at the horse trials?'

Nigel winced when he heard his name and answered sullenly, 'I don't know what you are talking about.'

'Today at the horse trials you went with Sally to her horsebox,' Simon repeated slowly and deliberately. 'Why?' he barked, leaning forwards.

Nigel jumped and shuffled in his chair. 'I don't know.'

'You don't know. You mean you were following Sally around like a lap dog, two paces behind her and obeying her every command?' Simon sneered at him.

'No.'

'Well then, why did you go to Sally's lorry? Yes, of course, you wanted to value it… see how much Sally is worth. That was the reason, wasn't it?' Everybody sat very still. Ruth was rooted to the Aga, having taken the kettle off the hob. The mugs containing coffee granules stood waiting on the work surface.

'No,' replied Nigel sulkily. 'We went to find Maddy.'

'You went to find Maddy.' Simon leant back in his chair. 'What did you do when you saw that she wasn't there?'

'Nothing.'

'Nothing?' repeated Simon sarcastically, leaning forward again. 'You did and said nothing, like a robot waiting for your next command.'

'I… I can't remember,' answered Nigel, looking at Sally, who was staring at Simon. Simon paused and then leant forward again.

'Did you have a screw driver with you?' he bellowed, making everybody jump except John, who didn't move a muscle. Nigel nearly shot out of his chair. John put his hands on his shoulders and pressed him down uncomfortably into his seat.

'No…no,' he stuttered. Everyone, except Sarah who was watching Sally, stared at Simon.

'Did you tamper with the lorry?' thundered Simon.

'No…no…What do you mean?' Nigel was now genuinely terrified.

'Did you know Tamsin Coulson?' asked Simon with a tight, grim look on his face. Everybody froze and waited. The silence in the room was unbearable.

'Nn….nno…' replied Nigel trying to swallow. 'Who… who is she?'

'She was my wife,' snarled Simon. 'Someone killed her.' He paused and leant forward again. 'Was it you?' His tone was menacing.

'Nnno…nno…' repeated Nigel, shaking. 'I've never killed anyone. I don't know your wife.' He was becoming hysterical and twisted about in his chair, 'I didn't... I didn't...'

'Sir!' interrupted John.

'Yes?' snapped Simon.

'Sir, I think he needs the toilet again.'

Simon sat back in his seat and waved his hand as if brushing away an insect. 'Take him away,' he said airily, 'and you had better clean him up while you are there.' John marched Nigel off to Maddy's downstairs cloakroom once more.

'You could finish making the coffee,' Simon smiled at Ruth. She started and put the kettle back on the hob.

'Now then.' Simon turned to Sally. 'What did you do when you got to your lorry?'

Sally stared at him and asked belligerently, 'What are you accusing me of?'

'Was the lorry cab locked?' asked Simon, ignoring her question.

'Yes.'

'You tried the door?'

'Yes,' replied Sally.

'What about the living compartment?'

'Locked too.'

'Did you have the spare set of keys?' asked Simon.

'No,' she snapped.

'Where are they?'

'I don't know,' she said. 'What's this all about?'

'Come, come,' he said patronisingly. 'You must know where your spare set of keys is?'

'No,' she repeated. 'I think they're here, ask her.' Sally glared at Maddy.

'They are here,' said Maddy to Simon, 'and don't bully Sally.' Sally continued scowling at Maddy.

'I don't think she's appreciating your help,' said Simon with a hint of a smile.

'I don't care if she appreciates it or not. She's a friend and I won't have her bullied in my house.' Sally looked slightly mollified but continued to glower at Simon.

'Do you think,' said Simon to Maddy, 'you could possibly tell me where the spare keys are?'

'Of course, they are hanging on that hook in the cupboard behind you. It's where I keep all my keys. You only have to ask nicely.' Judith had to turn her head away so that Simon couldn't see her smile.

'Would you be so kind as to point them out to me, without touching them please?' He opened the cupboard door.

'Certainly,' replied Maddy, standing up and pointing to a small bunch of keys. 'There they are.'

'You're sure?' he asked.

'Of course I'm sure.'

'Good.' Simon smiled at her.

Ruth had made the coffee and put the mugs, milk and sugar on the table. 'Help yourselves,' she said.

Simon and Maddy sat down again. Simon faced Sally, who was stirring her coffee. He asked, kindly this time, 'What did you do when you went to your lorry?'

She shrugged her shoulders and replied sulkily, 'I looked inside the horse compartment; it was empty. All the other doors were locked. Maddy was obviously riding so we went to find her'.

'Did you see anyone else near the lorry?' asked Simon.

'No, only the people in the lorry next to mine.'

'Who were they?'

'I don't know. I've never seen them before.'

'Did you have a screwdriver with you?' asked Simon.

'What? Why would I have a screwdriver?' she queried, looking at Maddy for help, but Maddy was looking quizzically at Judith, who shrugged her shoulders.

'Did you?' barked Simon.

'No, of course not.'

'What about in the lorry? Is there one in the lorry?'

'Maybe in the toolbox,' she replied, again looking at Maddy for help. Simon sighed and lifted his eyes to heaven.

'Is there a toolbox in Sally's lorry and does it contain a screw driver?' He asked.

'Yes to the first question and I don't know to the second,' replied Maddy.

'Well, go and look,' said Sally to Simon. Maddy looked at Simon and raised her eyebrows.

'Yes, quite,' he replied.

'Have you got a copy of this week's "Horse and Hound"?' Simon asked, suddenly changing the subject.

Sally hesitated and replied, 'Yes, why?'

'Where is it?'

'At home I expect.'

'Did you have it with you today at the horse trials?'

'No, why?'

Simon didn't answer at first; he was studying her face and then he said, 'So it should be in your house?'

'Yes.'

'Good, we'll get it later,' he said as John came back into the kitchen with Nigel. The blood had gone but his face was bruised.

'Sit him down for the moment,' ordered Simon. 'He can go in a minute.' Nigel looked a little brighter.

'Has no one wondered who paid for the dinner tonight?' asked Simon.

'We forgot to pay,' said Maddy.

'No, we didn't, did we Mr. Fish?' Nigel looked uncomfortable and shrugged his shoulders.

'I think we've got Sally to thank, don't you?' said Simon.

'What?' exclaimed Sally, 'I didn't pay!'

'Oh yes you did,' stated Simon. Sally jumped and Nigel tried to get up but John pushed him back down. 'Sally rang the restaurant and gave them her card number and told them to charge everything to her.'

'I did not.' Sally was horrified.

'The Manor assured me that you did. I think you'll see that this number tallies with your card number.' Nigel looked increasingly uncomfortable, while Sally picked up her handbag and got out her credit card. She checked the numbers on her card with those that Simon had given her.

'Yes,' she said incredulously, 'that is my card number.'

'And this is the bill that you were expected to pay.' He handed her a copy. Sally went pale; it was for over £200. Simon continued, 'I think it's just as well we left when we did: I would hate to think what it would have cost after desserts, coffee, liqueurs and some more wine.'

Sally sat staring at the bill. 'I don't understand,' she said. Then she looked at Nigel. He had the good grace to squirm.

'You bastard,' she shouted. 'You bloody little creep.'

'Don't worry,' said Simon. 'I paid the bill. It won't come off your card.'

'Thank you,' replied Sally quietly.

Simon was dialling a number on his mobile. 'Coulson here,' he said into his phone. 'You can come and pick him up now.' Nigel made a serious attempt to get up; this time John slammed him back into his chair and he gave a cry of pain.

'I'll have you for assault. Both of you. You broke my nose,' he accused Simon.

'Did I?' asked Simon. 'Did anyone see me or anyone else assault Mr. Fish?' Everyone shook their heads.

'Mr. Fish isn't your only name, is it?' continued Simon. 'Apart from Nigel Warrington, you seem to have had several other names. Sarah, perhaps you would like to tell us some of them.'

Sarah took a piece of paper out of her pocket and started reading. 'Edward Carmichael, Robert Bonnington-Smythe, Richard Groombridge, the list goes on, sir,' said Sarah.

'Yes,' agreed Simon. 'I particularly like The Honourable Jeremy Carlyle.' Everybody stared at Nigel, who shrunk further down into his chair. 'I don't know what you're talking about,' he managed to say.

'Oh I think you do,' said Simon. 'You very obligingly left your laptop in the Porsche. My men have had a field day. Of course, the police will have more time to go through it all later, but for the moment they have enough to charge you with. They'll be here soon and I think they'll be delighted to have you in custody; quite a few petty crimes and frauds will be cleared up. Oh, by the way you were quite right; you do work for a chain of restaurants. I didn't realise that the drive-in operatives at McDonalds are called executives but we live and learn. Now, would you like me to inform your wife that you are to be arrested?' Nigel glared at Simon, but said nothing.

'His wife?' gasped Sally, 'He hasn't got one.'

'Yes, I'm afraid he has, and four children.' Sally lapsed into silence again.

'How did he use Sally's credit card?' asked Maddy.

'Sally's and several other women's cards,' said Simon. 'He probably took it out of her handbag when she was getting ready to go out. Apparently he does a very good impersonation of a woman over the phone. But count yourself lucky,' he turned to Sally, 'the woman who paid for the hire of the Porsche…' Simon looked at a name on a piece of paper. 'A Mrs Jennifer Ridley-Jones is going to have to pay quite a tidy sum, £150 per day, for seven days, amounting to just over £1,000. Also a £4,000 deposit which will eventually be returned if the car is unharmed. He hired it for a week over the Internet using her credit card. We contacted Mrs Ridley-Jones; she doesn't know anyone called Nigel Warrington or Kelvin Fish.' Simon turned to Nigel. 'You kindly left her telephone number and address on your laptop.' By now Nigel looked crumpled and broken. 'Before the police come to collect him, I need everybody's finger prints.'

'What!' exclaimed Maddy. Sally looked up, startled, but Simon was on his phone again.

'You can't do that,' said Maddy.

'I'm afraid I can,' replied Simon kindly.

'Show me that ID thing,' demanded Maddy.

'All right.' Simon handed her his card. Maddy stared at it.

'I don't believe you! You aren't anything to do with these people. They're… they're…'

'Yes, quite,' replied Simon taking his card back.

'Let me see,' said Sally. Her eyes nearly popped out of her head when she saw the card and she stared at Simon. Judith sat quietly sipping her coffee.

'Judith,' said Maddy. 'Look at the card. Look at who he works for.'

Judith laughed and said, 'My dear Maddy, didn't you know? He doesn't just work for them, he's very nearly the head of the department.' Simon grinned, looking almost embarrassed.

'You're joking! I don't believe you,' said Maddy. 'Someone could have told me.' Then she rounded on Simon, 'You said you were a civil servant.'

He laughed and replied, 'No, you told me I was a civil servant.'

'Well, he is a sort of civil servant,' said Judith, 'and he does work for the Home Office.'

'Well…' said Maddy.

'I did tell you there was no one better to look after you,' said Judith.

'I know you did.' Maddy shook her head. 'But I just thought… I don't know what I thought.' Then, as it dawned on her, she said incredulously, 'So this morning… all that about Downing Street?'

Judith nodded, saying, 'Probably true.'

Maddy looked at Simon. He was still grinning and looking sheepish.

'Well,' demanded Maddy, 'Was it true?' Simon nodded. 'What a name dropper!' said Maddy to Judith.

'You told me you were going to have tea with the Queen,' he retorted, 'so what do you call that?'

'That's different, you knew it wasn't true.' Maddy laughed.

Just then a man dressed in white overalls came into the kitchen carrying all the paraphernalia needed to take finger prints.

'Who's he and where did he spring from?' asked Maddy, who was beginning to think that nothing would surprise her any more.

'Only from your yard,' replied Simon, as if that explained everything. 'I'm sorry to have to ask everyone to do this, but we need them in order to eliminate all of you.'

'What from?' asked Maddy. Simon was saved from answering as a car came up the drive with a blue light swirling on the roof.

'Good, just in time,' said Simon and went out into the yard to meet the police. A few minutes later he came back in with two uniformed officers.

'That's your man,' said Simon.

'You look as if you've been in the wars, sir,' said one of the men to Nigel.

'Yes, I was assaulted by him.' Nigel pointed to Simon. 'And him.' He gestured at John.

'Did anyone see this man being attacked?' Simon asked again. Everyone shook their heads.

'No,' said Sally. 'He's lying, no one assaulted him.'

'You bitch,' Nigel shouted. 'You set me up. I'll get you for this.'

'Oh dear,' said Simon, 'threatening behaviour as well.'

'I'll get her, I'll get her!' yelled Nigel.

Simon walked up to Nigel, put his face very close to his and said very quietly and very menacingly, 'If you so much as touch one hair of her head, I'll have my friend John here to beat you to a pulp. Do you understand?'

'Did you hear that? Did you hear that?' Nigel frantically asked the police.

'No, sir, I'm afraid we missed it,' one of them answered as they both shook their heads. Nigel lapsed into a sulky, frightened silence.

'May we have his prints before you take him away?' asked Simon.

The police agreed, and the man in white painstakingly took Nigel's fingerprints; when he finished he gave Nigel a cloth to wipe his fingers. The police handcuffed the, now subdued, little fraudster, cautioned him and led him away.

Nigel didn't say a word to anyone as he stood up; they all watched him leave in silence. Sally stared down at the table and Simon signalled to John to go back out into the yard. John gave Ruth a tell-tale look as he went out, making her blush.

'Now that Nigel has gone,' said Simon, 'I'll explain the developments of this evening. First a drink: I think we all need one.' The whisky and gin bottles were still on the worktop. Ruth hastily got a can of lager from the fridge for herself, pleased to be able to turn away from Simon's gaze.

'We have examined Sally's lorry and...' he began.

'What!' exclaimed Sally. 'What do you mean?'

'I'm sorry,' said Simon. 'You don't know yet, do you?' She shook her head, staring at Simon.

He quickly explained about the footprint and the lorry being taken away. Sally opened her mouth and then shut it again; she looked first at Maddy, who was drinking her whisky, and then at Judith who was looking down at the table. 'I don't believe you...' she stared at Simon.

'That's up to you,' continued Simon. 'But we found that the grill covering the air vent to the heating system on the outside of the lorry had been unscrewed. Some newspaper had been stuffed into the outlet and then the grill had been screwed back on again. This means that the carbon monoxide from the heating system would back up and eventually fill the interior of the lorry. The windows had been crudely jammed shut and it wouldn't have been possible to open them from the inside. On a long journey those fumes would have asphyxiated the people in the lorry and, as you can imagine, the driver would have become unconscious, or worse. On your short journey of about half an hour or so things might not have been so bad, but at best you would both have had very nasty headaches.' There was a heavy silence. Judith studied her glass and Maddy stared at Simon. Sally looked horrified.

'If Maddy hadn't noticed the footprint, sooner or later someone driving that lorry could have had a very nasty accident,' remarked Simon. Nobody said a word. The man in white was still quietly going round the table taking everyone's finger prints.

Simon's phone rang, breaking the silence. As he listened to the caller his face clouded over and hardened.

'Yes,' he said at intervals. 'How… Where…. And the horses…' His face looked strained as he went out of the kitchen into the yard still talking. Maddy went cold.

'Whatever has happened?' she asked Judith.

'I don't know,' she replied.

'Please God it's not Emma,' said Maddy.

'Oh my Lord.' Judith was appalled. 'Don't even think about that.' They sat in worried silence waiting for Simon to come back in.

When he did, Maddy thought he looked haggard and suddenly very tired. He announced, 'I have some more bad news to tell you'.

'What?' Maddy felt numb.

'This evening Louise Parkway had a bad accident on her way home in her horsebox.'

'What happened?' gasped Maddy.

'The police don't know yet, but the lorry missed a bend in the road and carried straight on into a wood, hit a tree and turned over on to its side.'

'Oh my God,' said Maddy, 'Is she…?'

'Louise is badly hurt and in intensive care, which is bad enough, but unfortunately her groom is in a coma. The two horses that she was transporting had to be put down at the site of the accident. They were too badly injured to be saved.'

'Dear God!' said Judith.

'Given what we found in Sally's horsebox, I have informed the police and they'll be examining Louise's lorry. I think the two incidents are probably connected.'

'You think it was the same person who did it?' exclaimed Maddy.

'Yes, I do,' replied Simon grimly.

'Not Nigel?' asked Sally in a flat voice.

'No I don't think so. He's a nasty little fraudster who preys on women. He's into petty crimes but I don't think he's a murderer. Besides, I don't believe he knew Louise. No, I don't think it was him, unless you watched him unscrew the air vent on your lorry. Were you with him all the time?'

'Yes,' replied Sally.

'Well then,' said Simon, wanting to raise his eyes to heaven, though he didn't. He did give Maddy a look and she would have laughed if it hadn't been so tragic.

'Who on earth did it?' asked Maddy.

'I don't know, but rest assured when I know I'll nail them.' The look on Simon's face made Maddy shiver.

The tension mounted in the kitchen as everyone started talking at once.

'Calm down,' said Simon. He turned to Maddy. 'I want to send you a new livery. Have you got a free loosebox? I'm sure you have; as you rightly say, your liveries do seem to be deserting you at an alarming rate.'

Sally blushed. 'I want to stay if you'll still have me Maddy?'

'Of course I will.' Maddy turned to Simon and answered, 'Yes, I have got a free box as a matter of fact. Why are you sending me a livery when you have a huge yard in Devon? Are you feeling sorry for me?'

'No, I have a difficult horse which Tamsin rescued. I believe that you could get it going for me. Emma and Monica don't have the time and I feel a smaller yard would suit him better.'

Maddy nodded. 'All right, what's wrong with him?'

'I'll tell you when he arrives, which will be tomorrow, by the way.'

'You don't hang about, do you?' exclaimed Maddy.

'I have another operative who is due to arrive tomorrow morning as well: his name is Colin. He will stay in the house, if you don't mind?'

Maddy nodded, feeling bemused.

'Is your department taking over the investigation, Simon?' asked Judith.

Simon smiled sheepishly and replied, 'Not officially. I have been given a certain length of time by the powers that be to find my wife's killer. I'm allowed to use some of the department's resources, some things I'll be paying for myself.'

'Oh I see.' said Judith. Then she added, 'I ought to be getting home now, I can hardly keep my eyes open.'

'Why don't you stay the night?' suggested Maddy.

'No, no, I'll take Sally home too, if you like, it's on the way.'

'No,' said Simon. 'I want Sarah to take Sally home and pick up her "Horse and Hound", thank you all the same. I agree with Maddy; I think you should stay here for the night.'

'Very well.'

'Don't I get a say in the matter?' Sally asked. Simon didn't answer.

'You'd better get off,' he ordered Sarah. Then turning to Sally he asked kindly, 'Will you be all right? I am sure you're not the target. Nigel is safely tucked up in a police cell for the night, although I'm confident that he won't hurt you.'

'Yes,' replied Sally. 'I'll be fine. Nigel left some things in my house...'

'I think you'll find them gone.'

'What! How?'

'We collected them earlier,' replied Simon. Sally stared at him, opened her mouth to say something, changed her mind and stood up.

'I'm going to bed, if that's OK?' said Ruth.

'Yes, you get off,' replied Maddy and, turning to Simon, she added, 'Aren't you supposed to have some sort of warrant to take things from people's houses?'

'We were just collecting his belongings for him,' Simon replied airily.

'Does Nigel know that?' asked Maddy.

'He does now.' Simon grinned.

Sally got up to leave and Maddy stood up and gave her a hug saying, 'Take care.'

'And you.' Sally smiled and hugged her back. 'I'm sorry about everything.'

'Don't be daft,' said Maddy.

'Check the house,' Simon said quietly to Sarah while Sally was talking to Maddy.

'Why the "Horse and Hound"?' asked Maddy when they had gone.

'The middle pages of this week's edition were used to block up the air vent in the lorry.'

'You don't really think Sally did it, do you?'

'No, but I have to check. Don't forget our friend Mr. Fish.'

'Yes.' Maddy smiled. 'How could I ever forget?' She looked at Judith and added, 'When John said, "*I think he needs the toilet again,*" I thought I was going to crack up.'

'So did I.' Judith laughed. 'The odious little man!'

'Can you remember who was parked next to you at the horse trials?' Simon changed the subject.

'Yes, I think so,' replied Maddy. 'It was a blue and silver lorry. Now, the name reminded me of my bedside rug.' She paused. Simon looked at Judith, and raised his eyebrows. 'Sheeply Equestrian Centre was the name on the lorry and the name of the rider was on the driver's door… it was … Charlotte. I remembered that because of Charlotte's Web and you going on about cobwebs in my dining room.'

'Well done,' he said putting his hand over hers across the table. 'They might have seen something with a bit of luck. Can you remember who was on the other side?'

'There wasn't anyone, we were in the corner.'

'Of course you were.' He withdrew his hand and wrote down the name and address. He turned to Judith and said, 'Mind you, you'll have to put up with the cobwebs and the dust in your bedroom.'

'There's nothing wrong with Maddy's house,' said Judith.

'No, nothing that a mop and duster couldn't cure.' Simon grinned.

'It's a good job that you're not staying here then, isn't it?' retorted Maddy.

'Well, I was rather hoping that I could stay, actually,' he replied, laughing.

'Did you? There's always the spare loosebox, or the barn or wherever it is that John and Sarah sleep.'

'I asked for that, I apologise. Please can I stay, Maddy?'

'I suppose so,' she replied and, turning to Judith, said, 'He has arachnophobia, but don't tell his men, they'll call him a sissy'.

'All right, you've made your point,' said Simon. 'I won't mention the cobwebs again, except the website.' Maddy opened her mouth to say something, but he continued, 'We've tracked down the members of the horse-harming gang. We're going to round them up next week'.

'Oh, good,' said Maddy. 'You are clever!'

Simon looked rather self-satisfied and said, 'I think Tamsin would be pleased, don't you?'

'Yes, I do,' replied Maddy enthusiastically.

'So do I,' agreed Judith, smiling at him.

Simon looked almost embarrassed for a moment and then said grimly, 'After we have interrogated them we will hand them over to the police. Excuse me, I have to go and see my men'. He got up abruptly and left the kitchen.

'This is dreadful news about Louise Parkway,' said Judith.

'I know,' agreed Maddy. 'I'm trying to get my head round it. I'll find out how she is tomorrow.'

'You and Simon are getting on better.'

'Yes,' replied Maddy, smiling. 'He's very motivated, isn't he?'

'Yes, we always thought it was because his wife was so well known and at the top of her sport, and he had to be one step ahead of her.'

'He was always ambitious. When I first met him he was very intense and focused on his army career, which was before he had met Tamsin. Jonathan wasn't quite so hard and ruthless, and that's why I chose him.' Maddy smiled and looked up at the photo of Jonathan above the Aga.

'I don't know when Simon and Tamsin ever saw one another,' continued Judith, noticing Maddy's glance at Jonathan. 'He was hardly ever at home and when he was, she was off riding somewhere. She was so absorbed on her horses.'

'Oh yes, I know, I used to come away feeling exhausted when I stayed with her. She never stopped planning and working things out, deciding which horse to take where, and when. How to ride this horse, or that horse. After a competition she would analyse what she had done wrong if she didn't win. She never blamed the horse you know; she always said it was her fault for not riding properly, or that the training programme had been wrong. I do miss her though, she was such a help and quite inspiring, although I didn't see a lot of her latterly. She had an inner strength. She never talked much about Simon. I never really saw them together. He thought I was a bad influence, I think. He didn't like me very much, especially after Jonathan was killed. He avoided me like the plague.'

Judith smiled. 'I met them together at some Regimental re-union, not all that long ago, actually. I thought their relationship was very brittle; they both seemed to be on edge. I don't think she liked those social events, she looked so thin and tense. He was always very formal and correct. Quite starchy actually, not like he is with you.'

'She was thin,' agreed Maddy, 'but very fit. Simon told me he loved her, and I believe him.'

'Oh yes,' said Judith. 'I'm sure he loved her in his own way. She belonged to him. She was his wife. He was very proud of her, after all, she was his prize possession.'

'Judith, that sounds awful.'

'I suppose it does, but a man like Simon has to have everything just right. His wife, his children, his house…'

'Just as well he never married me then,' returned Maddy, laughing.

'As sad as it is, that side of things has come to an end now,' said Judith. 'I think his priorities will change and I think he will begin to value different things.'

'What do you mean?'

'Well, his children, for a start. I think he might begin to see them as people in their own right. Also he might spend more time with them; look at how he was talking about Emma today.'

'Yes, you're right. He said how well she was riding. There was more than just pride in his voice, he was almost emotional.'

'That's what I mean,' said Judith. 'True emotion is coming into his life. He may find it quite strange but it will be good for him.'

'Good for who?' asked Simon as he came back into the room.

'We were just talking about…. my horse,' replied Judith as if butter wouldn't melt. He gave her a long look and she smiled blandly back at him.

'This is Sally's "Horse and Hound",' Simon changed the subject, and opened the magazine in the middle. All the pages were there.

'Thank goodness for that,' said Judith. 'If you'll excuse me, I think I'll go up to bed now.' Maddy showed her the way to her bedroom.

Simon was still in the kitchen when Maddy came down again. 'May I take a whisky up to bed with me?' he asked.

'Of course,' replied Maddy. 'Can you turn off the lights?' She went back upstairs into the small bedroom that she had allocated for him. She was making up the bed when he joined her.

'I can do that,' he said. 'I'm not completely helpless.'

'I can manage.' Maddy was trying to put the duvet into its cover. Simon took off his jacket and his tie and undid the top button of his shirt. Maddy watched him, remembering that once she knew every inch of his body. She wondered if it still looked the same.

'Give it to me,' he said as he took hold of the duvet and very deftly put it into its cover.

'That was clever.'

'I'm not just a pretty face.'

'Who says you have a pretty face?' asked Maddy, laughing.

'Not as pretty as yours, I admit,' he replied and then added quickly, before she could answer, 'Thank you for your help and co-operation today.'

'That's all right. ' She looked up into his face. 'I'm glad we can be friends now.'

'Yes, so am I,' he agreed. 'Sit down for a minute.'

Maddy sat on the bedroom chair, feeling that it would be too dangerous to sit on the bed. She was beginning to admit to herself that she still found him very attractive. The old chemistry was still there.

He sat down on the bed opposite her. 'I want to set a trap: would you be willing to help me?'

'A trap for who?'

Simon took a sip of his whisky. 'I have a vague idea who may be behind all this, but I need proof.'

'Who?' repeated Maddy.

'I can't say.' He held up his hand. 'Don't ask me.'

'What will it entail?... This trap.'

'I'll tell you more nearer the time. It may be dangerous but I will have as much protection for you as I can. I'll be here too. It's only fair to warn you that these traps have been known to backfire, but I promise you that I will take every precaution.' His face hardened. 'I blame myself for letting Tamsin get killed and I'm not going to allow anyone else to get hurt. I couldn't even protect my own wife... what a failure.'

'Of course I'll help. I'm not a wimp,' Maddy replied, and then she added, 'What are you talking about? A failure?'

'I let her down. You know what my job is...'

'Don't talk rubbish.'

'It's not rubbish. It's the truth.' He looked miserable. Maddy leant forward and picked up his hand.

'That is complete nonsense,' she retorted. 'Did you know this person was out on the loose and after Tamsin?'

'No,' he replied in a hollow voice. 'No I didn't.'

'Well then. I won't have you talk like that... Or even think it.'

He smiled weakly and repeated, 'You know what my job is...'

'Don't beat yourself up over this. It was something that you had no control over. You can't be everywhere at once and know exactly what is going to happen next. You're not God.'

'Some people might disagree with you there,' he smiled faintly.

'I certainly don't think you're God,' Maddy laughed.

'I know you don't,' he said dismally and continued: 'No, you're right, I suppose. You know I loved her, don't you? Some people think I didn't, maybe with good reason. I just feel so awful, I hate feeling like this.'

Maddy thought of her conversation earlier with Judith and said, 'It's called emotion Simon, and love. That's what love is. I had it and I lost it. It's tough and it's hard, but it eases with time so they say, but it's always there in the background. It'll stay with you forever.'

'Well you have made me feel better,' he said. 'Are you saying I'm going to feel like this for the rest of my life?'

'Not necessarily.'

'Oh, good!'

'When Jonathan was killed, I went through everything over and over again. Everything was *if*. If he had left the army, if he hadn't been in that tank… If.. if.. if. And if only…. the list went on and on. I thought it was my fault too, you know. In fact I still do.'

'How could it possibly be your fault?'

'The same reason as why you feel Tamsin's death was your fault.'

'That was different,'

'No it wasn't,' replied Maddy. 'He would have left the army if I had really wanted him to.' Her eyes filled with tears. 'I said it was up to him. If I had insisted he would have left and been alive today. I nearly insisted, but it was his life, he loved it… and it was his death.' She looked down. 'So it was my fault, you see.'

Simon sat quietly looking at the floor. 'That's ridiculous, it wasn't your fault.'

She shrugged her shoulders and replied quietly, 'I think so… sometimes.' He looked at her and she caught her breath when she saw the look of compassion on his face.

'I'm so sorry,' he said. 'When Johnnie died I was no help to you at all. I can see that now. I let him down too, and you.'

'No, I resented the fact that you were alive and he was dead. You did right to stand on your high horse and be detached. Tamsin was brilliant, though.' She smiled. 'Except when she kept sticking up for you and telling me how wonderful you were. It's all water under the bridge now. There is one thing you can do, though.'

'Yes.' He looked a little brighter. 'What's that?'

'Never mention again, or even think, that Tamsin's death was ever your fault.' He smiled and stood up. He held her hands and pulled her on to her feet, and then he put his arms around her and held her close. She felt his muscles through his shirt and smelt his body odour. She relaxed into his arms, remembering the intense pleasure that they had given to each other all those years ago. Her stomach was pressed close to him and she felt his erection. She suddenly jumped away. He released his hold and stood back looking into her eyes.

'I don't deserve this,' he said.

'Deserve what?' asked Maddy, shaken.

'You being so kind and understanding,' he said gently. She looked up at him and the years rolled away again: how easy it would be to reach up and kiss him.

She turned away and said laughingly, 'There is no point in delving into confessions and beating ourselves up over the past. I was horrible to you too remember.'

He laughed. 'Yes, you were.'

'So no more talk about it being our fault then?'

'No,' he answered.

'I must get to bed,' she said hurriedly. 'I expect it'll be another long day tomorrow.'

'Yes, it could be.'

'What are you doing tomorrow?' she asked brightly.

'I'll be off early. Don't worry about me; I can get my own breakfast.' He told her what to do when Colin arrived, and asked if he could come back the next evening.

'Of course you can,' replied Maddy.

'You looked beautiful tonight.'

She felt herself blushing and laughed, saying, 'Looked? You mean I have turned back into a frog?'

'Don't be silly.' He made a move towards her.

'Good night,' she said and fled down the corridor, round the corner and into her room.

CHAPTER NINE

Simon had got up and left long before the others came downstairs. Maddy was talking to Ruth and Judith in the kitchen while she cooked the breakfast when a man suddenly came down the passage from the sitting room.

'What the hell...' exclaimed Maddy.

'So sorry,' he said. 'I'm Colin. I thought you knew I was coming. Can't come in the front door. Mustn't be seen. Smelt bacon cooking and thought...'

Maddy looked at Ruth and Judith and they burst out laughing while Colin stood in the doorway looking a little put out. He was of medium height and in his early thirties with thick fair hair and bright blue eyes. He had the sort of non-descript face that would blend into a crowd, but he had twinkling eyes and an engaging smile.

'I thought the boss told you...' he began.

'Yes, he did,' said Maddy. 'I just thought you would come up the drive and in through the door like a normal person. I don't know what possessed me to think that. How did you get in?'

'The back door was open. I came through the garden. I'm sorry you don't think I'm normal,' he replied with a cheeky grin.

'I'm sure you are very normal,' answered Maddy. 'What were you doing in the sitting room?'

'Setting up my equipment. I hope you don't mind, only the boss said...'

'No, that's absolutely fine,' replied Maddy. 'Sit down... you are allowed to sit down, I suppose? Would you like some breakfast too?'

'Yes please, that would be super.' He grinned. 'Please carry on with your conversation, ignore me.'

They looked at each other and Maddy asked, 'What were we saying?'

'Discussing going for a hack,' replied Ruth.

'Excuse me.' Colin spoke tentatively. 'Does that mean you're leaving the premises?'

'Yes,' said Maddy.

'I think you should stay in the yard. Boss's orders,' he added hastily as everyone looked at him in surprise.

'Well,' said Maddy. 'In that case, training in the sand school it is then.'

***

While Maddy and Ruth were still mucking out, Simon had arrived in the village of Upper Duckworth. He wore slacks, a rugby shirt and trainers. He drove down a lane until he came to an unmade road leading to a farm. He turned into it and slowly drove along until he found somewhere to leave his car.

Then he cut through the wood on foot and headed towards a large brick built manor house. He passed a Nissen hut. He only noticed it because a pheasant flew out of the bushes and made him jump. The hut was surrounded by thick undergrowth and the windows were blacked out. Simon smelt a strange pungent smell that didn't belong to the wood or a farmyard. He frowned; it was almost like strong human body odour. Curious, he tried the door but it was locked. Going round to one of the windows he saw a bright light shining through a crack in the cardboard that had been nailed to the inside. He peered into the hut and saw rows and rows of bushy green plants standing in pots.

He made a mental note of where the little building stood, and shaking his head, he carried on through the wood until he arrived at the back of the imposing manor. He skirted round the extensive gardens and came to the stable yard set in a square around a neatly mown lawn.

Simon walked cautiously through the entrance which lay under an archway. He jumped as the stable clock above him struck the half hour. Flattened against the inner wall and looking out around the large yard, he studied the heads of the horses as they gazed out over their loosebox doors. Not every stable was occupied. He noticed a girl groom mucking out and waited until she had filled her wheelbarrow. He was pleased to hear its wheels needed oiling as the girl pushed it through a door at the back of the yard to the muck heap.

He quietly ran up to a stable containing a big bay horse with a large round white mark on its forehead. The horse jumped back in its stable as Simon opened the door and quietly entered the box. He hastily calmed the startled animal and swiftly undid its rug. His face hardened when he found what he had been looking for.

Simon heard the squeaky barrow coming back, so he stayed in the box waiting for the stable lass to fill up another load. To his dismay he saw a young man arrive. The girl left her mucking out and went to greet him. Simon's heart sank as they walked together towards him.

'Let's do it in here,' said the girl as they reached Simon's door. He flattened himself against the wall and braced himself, but the girl pulled the man into the next door loosebox. Simon let out a sigh of relief.

'Okay, babes,' said the man. 'As long as there's no horse in here; last time it put me off my stroke.'

'I didn't notice.' The girl giggled.

'That's because I'm the best, Susie.'

The walls between the boxes didn't go all the way up to the roof and Simon could hear every word and every movement.

'Yes, you are.' Susie was still giggling. 'I've made up a nice bed in here and look what I've got.'

'I know what you've got sweetheart, and I'll show you what I've got for you.' Simon heard the noise of a fly being unzipped.

Susie said, 'Oh, Jason.' Then they stopped talking and Simon heard straw rustling and the man moaning, then the girl stopped giggling and started moaning too.

He leant against the wall of the stable and raised his eyes to heaven. Eventually both lovers reached a climax and Simon heaved a sigh of relief.

'This is what I've got,' said the girl. 'If you had waited we could have had one before we started, makes it better.'

'That's great, Susie!' exclaimed Jason. 'Why didn't you say so in the first place.'

'I tried to.' Susie laughed. 'But you were too impatient. We'll have to do it again. Have you got a light?'

'Here you are,' he replied. Simon soon smelt the whiff of cigarette smoke mixed with a sweeter herby aroma; it smelt chocolaty with a hint of pine. It was the end product of what he had smelt in the Nissen hut.

He waited patiently while they shared their joint and when they began to make love again he quietly opened the stable door without frightening the big horse and slipped away. The couple were oblivious to everything except what they were doing to each other.

***

Later that day while Maddy was working in her tack room, Simon's lorry, driven by Monica, drove into the yard.

'I've brought you a horse,' announced Monica, smiling as she jumped out of the cab. 'Don't be shocked when I fetch it out. I don't usually deliver horses in this condition.'

Maddy watched in surprise as Monica led a very tall, thin chestnut thoroughbred down the ramp. He wasn't wearing a rug and he was dripping with sweat.

'Good God!' exclaimed Maddy. Did you forget to feed it, or is Simon economising?'

Monica laughed and replied, 'There's a long story attached to him. Simon told me to tell you'.

'Ruth will help you put him away, and then come in for a coffee,' answered Maddy.

Monica and Ruth joined Maddy in the kitchen. Colin stayed out of sight in the sitting room.

'So what happened to the horse?' asked Maddy as they sat down at the table.

'Well,' said Monica. 'It was like this: one of our liveries had seen this horse in Rhona's yard.'

'Rhona Whitehaven?' asked Maddy.

'Yes,' continued Monica. 'You know there's a Veterinary Centre at her place? They rent the premises from her. Anyway, our client had taken his horse in for an operation. They're very good there, you know.'

'Go on,' said Maddy.

'While he was there he saw this chestnut horse in a field. It was during the winter and the horse was only wearing a thin rug. He was standing fetlock deep in mud, there was hardly any grass and he looked dreadful. Alex, our client, complained to the vets about him. They told Alex that they had already spoken to Rhona, and that she had ignored them.'

'I'm not surprised,' interjected Maddy. 'She's like that. Go on.'

'Alex reported the case to the RSPCA.'

'Good for him, so what happened?' asked Maddy.

'Nothing,' replied Monica. 'When Alex went back to collect his own horse he asked the vets what the RSPCA had done about the chestnut horse in the field, and they told him to go and see for himself. So he did. The gelding was still there in the same small paddock, looking worse. The RSPCA had spoken to Rhona, but they weren't going to prosecute because they said the case wasn't bad enough. But Alex managed to get hold of an RSPCA uniform and he went round to see Rhona. He told her that they had reviewed the situation and that if she didn't do something about the horse within the next forty eight hours they would prosecute her.'

'And she believed him?' asked Maddy.

'Oh yes.' Monica laughed. 'Alex said her face was a picture.'

'So what happened next?' asked Ruth.

'Tamsin turned up with her lorry the next day and collected the horse.'

'What, just like that?' Maddy was amazed.

'Well, she said that she had heard that Rhona had a chestnut gelding which she wanted to get rid of, so she had come to pick it up. She gave her a cheque for £500.'

'And Rhona took the money?' asked Maddy.

'Yes. Rhona said she was pleased to see the back of him and that he had been nothing but trouble. Tamsin was welcome to him.'

'When was this?' asked Maddy.

'About eight weeks ago. He's looking a hell of a lot better now. You should have seen him when he first arrived. We had to keep him hidden away in case anyone saw him.'

'What's his name?'

'Rin Tin Tin. We called him Tinny Ribs to start with, but the students said that was an insult, so we changed it to Rin Tin Tin. However, we've since found out that he has a proper name.'

'What is it?' asked Maddy, intrigued.

'Matrix One Over The Top.'

'No!' exclaimed Maddy. '*The* Matrix One Over The Top? The horse that the Australian rider, what's his name… Tom Hargreaves had? It nearly won Badminton. It was one of the up and coming horses, and then it disappeared.'

'That's right. Rhona bought him and couldn't do anything with him,' replied Monica.

'I'm not surprised, she can't ride. How did you find out it was him?' asked Maddy.

'Tom recognised him. He came to our yard the other day.'

Maddy was beginning to see what Simon was up to. She shivered and asked, 'So what's his problem?'

'He's very quirky, and we don't know why. He'll suddenly panic for no reason, it could happen in the stable or when he's being ridden. He wouldn't let two of our students, one boy and the other a girl, near him at all. We also discovered that he wouldn't let Susie, Rhona's girl groom, near him either. That was why he was left in the field.'

'Has he got something wrong with his back, or something else? Is he in pain somewhere?' asked Maddy.

144

'No. We've had everything thoroughly checked and there's nothing physically wrong with him.'

Maddy believed her. Tamsin had top class vets and equine physiotherapists and chiropractors visiting her yard on a regular basis. 'How strange,' she remarked.

'Yes. If he hears chains rattling he goes berserk. Well, I have to get going.' Monica looked at her watch and stood up. 'I've got a long way to go. Good luck with Tinny Ribs.'

'Yes, thanks,' replied Maddy. 'Have a safe journey, and send my love to Emma.' Monica nodded and hurried out to her lorry.

***

That evening Maddy was talking to Colin in the kitchen when he suddenly said, 'We've cracked the horse mutilator's website.'

'I know, Simon told me.'

'Aren't you pleased?' asked Colin.

'Of course I am.' Maddy went cold as she remembered the horrific pictures.

'Horses frighten me,' Colin continued: 'Great big things. Dangerous at both ends and uncomfortable in the middle, as someone once said.'

'Oscar Wilde, wasn't it?' said Maddy.

'I don't think so. Anyway I agree with whoever it was.'

Maddy laughed and said, 'But you're tracking down the people who harm horses.'

'Bullies. I can't stand bullies and cruelty. Sadism and evil. Can't abide it. That's why I do this job. That's why I work for the colonel. He's honest, straight and up front. I respect him. Not many people I do respect, but he's one of them.'

'Oh,' said Maddy and jumped as just then Simon walked into the kitchen.

'Evening boss,' said Colin.

'Good evening Colin,' said Simon. He turned to Maddy and said, 'Hello, have you eaten yet?'

'No.' Maddy was surprised. 'Why?'

'I need to talk to you and I wondered if we could go out to dinner.'

'Yes… yes, I need to talk to you too,' replied Maddy, rather taken aback.

'Good,' he said smiling. 'How about Brinkley Manor? We could finish the meal this time.'

'That would be nice; it was certainly very good.'

'Good,' repeated Simon. 'There are one or two things I need to see Colin about, if you'll excuse us Maddy. You get ready and I'll meet you back down here.'

'Yes sir!' replied Maddy, but Simon was already heading for the sitting room with Colin. She took great care getting ready to go out and it took her longer than usual. Simon was already changed and sitting in the kitchen waiting for her when she came downstairs. He had helped himself to a whisky.

'Hope you don't mind,' he said, holding up his glass.

'Of course not,' replied Maddy, unaware of the effect her entrance had had on Ruth and Colin who were both sitting with Simon. She had put her hair up again and was wearing a turquoise shot silk dress and jacket.

Simon stood up and said, 'You look....'

'Drop dead gorgeous.' Colin finished the sentence.

Maddy smiled and asked Ruth, 'Are you going to be all right?'

'I think we'll manage,' replied Ruth looking at Colin. 'We're going to get a take-away and a bottle of wine.'

***

John watched Ruth drive off to fetch her and Colin's dinner. He was feeling frustrated because he hadn't been able to have another conversation with her and he knew that now Colin was there, and watching the CCTV monitors, it would be virtually impossible. He simmered all through the evening as he thought of Colin alone with her.

Ruth on the other hand became bored with Colin's company. She found him hard going and discovered that they had very little in common. As soon as they had finished eating she went upstairs to her flat, leaving Colin to get on with his work on the computer.

Later she went out into the yard to do the horses' late night feeds at the usual time. She entered a stable and jumped as she saw John crouched on the floor. He had his finger on his lips signalling to her to say nothing. She stared at him, in two minds as to whether to jab him with the stable fork that she had in her hand, or laugh. As if reading her mind he grinned and shook his head.

'What are you doing down there?' she whispered, laughing.

He pointed to the camera on the telegraph pole covering the row of stables and whispered, 'Pretend you're talking to the horse. I want to speak to you.'

Ruth laughed and stroked the horse saying, 'What about?'

'Us.'

'There is no us,' she replied.

'I know, but I would like there to be. I'm sorry I behaved as I did the other day. I want to make amends.'

'How?'

'I don't know, what do you suggest?' he asked.

'I don't know either,' replied Ruth, her heart racing. 'It's a bit difficult talking through a horse to a dwarf on the floor.'

'How was Colin?'

'Boring.'

John's face relaxed a little and he suggested, 'I could come up to your flat and we could talk'.

'All right,' said Ruth slowly, 'When? And how?'

'Leave that to me. I'll come later when Sarah's on duty.'

'Okay, but don't try anything on or I will scream and wake the whole house up.'

'Do you think I'm stupid?' whispered John. Ruth left the loose box smiling.

***

When Maddy and Simon arrived at Brinkley Manor they were ushered, rather like visiting royalty, to a quiet table for two near the window. The head waiter gave no sign of having witnessed the scene the night before.

'Monica told me all about Rin Tin Tin,' said Maddy after they had ordered. 'Apparently he goes berserk sometimes for no reason.'

Simon smiled. 'Yes, I thought a smaller yard would suit him better and maybe you could find out what makes him do it.'

'All right, it'll be a challenge,' replied Maddy. 'I don't know what's happening with Angela. I don't want Jupiter to go to Rhona's yard now, not after seeing Rin Tin Tin.'

'Don't worry about Angela, I'll sort her out. She knows who took the glove but she won't say. I haven't put too much pressure on her yet because I have a good idea who took it anyway. When the time is right she'll do what I tell her to do.'

'You know who did it! Who?'

'Possibly. I went up to the headquarters of British Dressage today and studied their records. I found out another piece of the jigsaw,' said Simon. 'But I don't have enough proof yet. If I had had the glove, maybe with forensic…'

'Thanks for reminding me.' Maddy looked embarrassed.

'No, no,' said Simon, and put his hand on hers across the table. 'I'm so pleased that you took it.' He smiled warmly into her eyes. 'Really I am.' She smiled back and he carried on. 'You know the big bay horse that Rhona is riding at the moment? You said it reminded you of a horse, but you couldn't think which one.'

'Yes I did.'

'I'll give you a clue. Beam me up!'

'What are you talking about?' Maddy laughed.

'Beam me up… Who?' Simon grinned.

'Scotty?' replied Maddy, puzzled. She thought for a moment. 'Scotty! Not Woodleigh's Flying Scotsman? It can't be! He didn't have any white on him, but otherwise… Yes, otherwise it's him.'

'It *is* him,' replied Simon proudly.

'But he went lame and was retired.'

'I know. Tamsin brought him out as a young horse. She sold him to that boy who rode him really well, and then the horse had a fall and hurt his back. He was such a genuine horse,' said Simon.

'I know, I rode him, I loved that horse.'

'So did Tamsin. The owners claimed loss of use from the insurance company and sold it very cheaply to someone just for hacking.'

'What a cow,' said Maddy. 'But what about the white star, and socks on his legs? So how can it be him?'

'Freeze branded.'

'Freeze branded! You mean she freeze branded him on his face and legs? Good God!' exclaimed Maddy.

'Yes, you know when you freeze brand an animal, a horse or a cow, the hair grows back white.'

'Yes, I know that,' said Maddy. 'Some people mark their horses with identification numbers.'

'Well, she made that star on his forehead,' said Simon. 'Didn't you think it looked unnaturally round?'

'Now you mention it, yes. But how can you be sure that he is Scotty?'

'Because he had very unusual whorls behind his elbows on both sides of his body. You know that whorls are where the hair grows into a little circle and finishes in a point.'

'Yes, of course.'

'Well when Tamsin was clipping him behind his elbows, he was always very ticklish just there and when you're clipping a horse you have to use the clippers against the way the hair grows.'

'Yes, Simon, I have clipped out a few horses over the years,' replied Maddy.

'Well, she had to keep changing the angle of the clippers because of the whorls. He used to fidget and kept knocking the clippers out of her hand, so she had to leave it. You know what a perfectionist Tamsin was?'

'Oh yes,' replied Maddy, laughing. 'She would hate leaving that bit unclipped. But no one would notice because the girth virtually covers it.'

'Exactly,' said Simon, 'but Tamsin knew and used to worry about it.'

'She would, bless her,' said Maddy, smiling. 'But how do you know that it is him. Have you examined him?'

'Yes, I went to look at him this morning. Rhona has left that bit unclipped as well.'

'What did Rhona say?'

'Oh, I didn't see Rhona and no one saw me.' Simon grinned.

Maddy laughed and said, putting her hand over his, 'You are clever.' He looked so pleased that she laughed again. 'So how has she managed to keep him sound, and how has she got him a passport with a new name? What does she call him…? Something stupid… Whitehaven Lad, that's it.'

'She forged the passport and registered him with British Eventing quite easily. She keeps him sound in the same way as she did with her dressage horse, Singspiel. She doped him with a really strong pain killer.'

'No! Actually Louise knew about Scotty. She told me that she was going to tackle Rhona about him. Or that she had tackled her about him. I can't remember what she did say now,' said Maddy. 'But I do remember that she told me to ask Rhona about her new horse, but she didn't say why.'

'And did you ask Rhona about him?' asked Simon.

'No, I never did. But I did ring someone to ask how Louise is this morning. They said that she was still in intensive care and her condition was stable, so I suppose that is good news for the moment, although her groom is still in a coma. It makes me so angry I would love to help you nail whoever did it.'

'Yes,' replied Simon. His face darkened and his eyes glinted. 'It'll give me a lot of pleasure too.'

'Judith was right when she said there was no better man to look after me than you,' said Maddy.

'Judith said that?' Simon looked pleased. 'That was a nice thing to say.'

'Yes, I thought she was just being polite or trying to cheer me up at the time. But she's right.'

'Well, thank you.'

'Why do you think so much of her? And why does she say she misses danger in her life?'

Simon's face clouded over and he said, 'Her husband was a Brigadier. I admired him greatly. He was killed by the IRA'.

'Oh, how awful.' Maddy fell silent.

'Yes it was. I went to the funeral. It was a full military service. Judith looked very dignified, and I have admired her ever since.'

'Yes... Yes she would look dignified.' Maddy had tears in her eyes. She stared at her plate, thinking of Jonathan's funeral. Simon had been one of the coffin bearers.

'As did you,' he said quietly, filling up her glass with red wine. She drank some and felt a little better. She wanted to say the same to him about Tamsin's funeral, but she couldn't get the words out.

The main course arrived and lightened the mood. 'There was a time, not so long ago, when wild horses would never have got me to go out to dinner with you,' she said.

'I know,' he smiled ruefully, and then he said out of the blue, 'I'm thinking of selling Moorsend.'

'What!' exclaimed Maddy. 'Why? It's your family home. You can't sell it.'

'It was my parents' home. I was never there very much. I went to boarding school and then into the army. Tamsin liked it more than I did.'

'What about Emma and Richard?'

'Richard is away most of the time and it's a great big house for Emma to be rattling around in. My work is based in London. I travel all over the country, sometimes it's too far to drive home and that's no way to live. I want to find somewhere in the Home Counties, Berkshire, Buckinghamshire, or maybe Surrey.' Maddy suddenly felt pleased.

When they finished their meal Maddy and Simon sat in the lounge having coffee and a liqueur.

'I feel drunk with food,' said Maddy. Simon smiled down at her. They were sitting side by side on a comfortable sofa.

'I know what you mean,' said Simon. 'That's the best dinner I have had for ages.'

'I'm sure it's not. You go to all these highfalutin' places. I'm sure they have better food, not that this wasn't extremely good.'

'I'm talking about the company as well.'

'Oh well, the company was better than last night,' agreed Maddy, who felt very relaxed and completely at ease. 'You know,' she continued, picking up his hand, 'I never thought I would ever like you again. But you are quite nice really. I can see why your staff all respect you. And Emma, she adores you. Never could understand why. She just wants to please you. Colin thinks you're wonderful too... And Judith, there's another one, she thinks the sun shines out of your...'

'Have some more coffee.' Simon quickly poured some coffee into her cup as she nodded.

'Thank you. I was just thinking about Rhona again.'

'Yes?' asked Simon.

'She kept asking me what Louise had said to me. Not just yesterday, but before the funeral. She wanted to go to the funeral with me. I mean, she was very odd. I had to be really rude to get rid of her. Don't you think that's peculiar? We're not friends and I hardly ever see her.'

'Yes, I do.'

'They are a strange couple though. Silly Jilly follows her around like a lap dog. Wherever Rhona is, Jilly is two paces behind her. Everybody thinks that they're a pair of dykes. They could be I suppose. But they don't live together.'

'Don't they?'

'No. Jilly lives in a little semi-detached house, looks a bit like a council house on an estate. She's obviously drawn to Rhona's money.' She picked up Simon's hand again, nearly dropping her coffee cup. 'Ooops,' she said.

Simon gently withdrew his hand, saying, 'My sweet, I think you need both hands to hold your coffee cup: it does seem to be rather lively.'

'Yes,' Maddy laughed. 'I think you're right.' She didn't seem to notice the term of endearment and took a sip of her coffee. 'Actually I think it's quite exciting tracking down this murderer. Colin said he has cracked the website. It can be quite an adrenalin rush, can't it? A bit like riding a horse around a cross country course. I can see why you're addicted to your job.'

'Am I addicted to my job?' asked Simon, looking curiously at her. 'I hadn't thought of it quite like that. I just needed something to take over my whole life as my marriage wasn't very good. Maybe I am addicted to my job now. At the end of the day it's worth it.'

'Pitting your wits against vermin and scumbags and winning. Brilliant,' Maddy enthused.

'We don't always win, unfortunately.'

'Now you tell me!' Maddy laughed.

'Oh we'll win this one, I'm sure of it,' he said seriously. 'We're nearly at the last hurdle.'

They sat side by side in silence for a while, both feeling contented and mellow.

Simon broke the silence by saying, 'I suppose we'd better get home.'

'Yes. I really have enjoyed this evening.' Maddy struggled to get up off the low sofa. Simon gave her his hand and helped her up. 'Thank you.' She fell against him, he put his arm through hers and they walked slowly out to the car.

'Thank you for a lovely evening,' said Maddy, turning in her seat to look at him as he got in beside her.

'It was a pleasure.' Simon looked tenderly down at her. She looked up and he kissed her on her lips. Taken by surprise and throwing caution to the winds, Maddy kissed him back. She gently drew back, smiling at him as he traced his finger round her face.

'You're beautiful,' he said. 'I wanted to say how lovely you looked when you came into the kitchen this evening. You took my breath away.'

'Don't tell me you were speechless.'

'Very nearly.' He bent down to kiss her again. This time she opened her mouth and arched her back pressing her body against his. He tightened his arms around her and she sank back against the door, allowing his tongue to explore her mouth. She felt herself drifting into a sea of desire and her body began to respond to his. He pulled back in order to find more room to manoeuvre when Maddy suddenly thought of Jonathan and Tamsin. She stiffened and sat bolt upright.

'What's the matter,' he asked.

'I don't know... Nothing.'

'There's something wrong. Tell me?'

'No,' she said, her hand on his shoulder. 'I suddenly feel sick, that's all. Too much wine, I think.'

'I'm sorry I have that effect on you,' he replied curtly.

'It's not you,' she said rather lamely. He looked at her but she didn't meet his eyes. He sat up straight and started the car. Unaware of the look on his face, Maddy relaxed again, the images of Jonathan and Tamsin fading. She put her head on Simon's shoulder and before he had driven to the end of the drive, she fell asleep.

Maddy woke up feeling relaxed and comfortable as Simon parked the car in her yard.

'Have I been asleep?' she asked. 'Are we home already?'

'Yes on both counts.'

Maddy turned and looked up at him smiling. 'I had a dream, or did we…?'

'We did.' He grinned down at her, his face soft again lit by the outside light which threw a pale mellow glow through the car windows. He bent down and kissed her; this time she responded again.

***

John watched Simon and Maddy arrive home. Simon came out into the yard to have a word with him and Sarah. After he returned to the house Sarah said, 'That's knocked your midnight tryst on the head.'

'Shut up Sarah.' John scowled.

'Forget her, John. It'll only mean trouble. You can find plenty of other scrubbers.'

'She's not a scrubber. I'll find a way.'

'Not with the Colonel and Colin on the premises, do use your loaf.'

John stared at the house with an inscrutable look on his face.

CHAPTER TEN

When Simon came down for breakfast he found Maddy in a pensive mood. He looked up in surprise as she snapped at Ruth. 'Is Hyps' tack clean?'

Ruth seemed to be pre-occupied and bad-tempered as she replied, 'Yes. I'm sure Gerhardt will be impressed'.

'I'm not bothered if he's impressed or not,' retorted Maddy. 'He's here to give me a lesson, not to inspect the way my horse is turned out. I don't want to have a lesson in dirty tack.'

'It's not dirty.'

'Good.'

'Gerhardt?' Simon questioned.

'My dressage trainer.' Both Ruth and Maddy lapsed into silence. Maddy jumped up from the table, looking at her watch. 'I'll go and warm up, he'll be here soon.' Ruth left the table, too, without a word.

Simon spoke to Colin and then went outside. He stood and watched Maddy riding in the school. She didn't seem to notice him and continued warming up her horse. He got into his car and drove slowly down the drive, wondering what was so special about this Gerhardt. He saw another car coming towards him so he pulled over in order to let it pass. As the driver of the other car lowered his window to say thank you, Simon froze. At the wheel sat a blond, blue eyed man with white flashing teeth. He was the spitting image of Jonathan as a younger man.

'Sank you,' said Gerhard. Simon managed some sort of gesture of acknowledgment and sat stunned. *So that's it,* he thought. He felt a surge of anger and wanted to go back to the yard but he realized that that would look a bit strange, and anyway he had to drive to Hampshire. He put his car into gear and accelerated away, throwing up a shower of gravel. He turned into the lane screeching his tyres, narrowly missing a car coming the other way. He was too angry to see who it was.

Simon sped down the main road fuming. 'All that looking at her watch. She couldn't wait, could she?' he said to himself, his mouth set in a thin grim line. He was becoming more and more angry, but luckily the traffic was building up and he was forced to slow down

He knew his wife had never been interested in other men, and he had never cared enough about another woman to bother what she was up to when she wasn't with him. In fact he had been pleased to use the hint of another man in order to get rid of one or two of them. This burning feeling was new to him and he didn't like it.

He made record time to the Hampshire hospital where Louise had been admitted, and found his way up to her ward. What he saw when he got there took his mind off his own problems. Louise looked terrible; she had one leg and an arm in plaster. The parts of her face that weren't black and blue looked like stretched white parchment. 'Hello,' he said gently. 'I'm Simon Coulson.' Louise stared at him. 'You knew my wife Tamsin,' he continued, patronizingly, thinking that she wasn't *compos mentis.*

'I know who you are,' replied Louise. 'What are you doing here?'

'Are you up to answering a few questions about your accident?'

'Yes,' she replied. 'Why?'

'Can you remember what happened?'

'I was driving along. I asked Vicky, my groom, something. She didn't answer and then I woke up in hospital. That's it, I'm afraid.' She tried to smile but grimaced instead. 'The police have already asked me what happened. Why do you want to know too?'

'Where was Vicky sitting?'

'She was lying down in the living compartment, asleep I think.'

'Was the door open between the cab and the living compartment?'

'Yes,' replied Louise.

'How do the police think it happened?'

'They don't know. Why are you asking me these questions?'

'I'm trying to piece something together. I think your accident could be connected with another.'

'What accident? You mean Tamsin, don't you?' she exclaimed.

Simon smiled kindly at her. 'Yes,' he answered gravely.

'Who would want to do something like this? I don't know anyone who would want to... kill me.' She spoke quietly.

'What did you say to Rhona Whitehaven about her horse?'

'Rhona? This has nothing to do with her!'

'Why do you say that?'

'Because she's just a pompous rich fool.'

'I agree with you, but what did you say to her?'

'Only that it was obvious that that bay horse she's riding isn't what she says it is. It looks exactly like Woodleigh's Flying Scotsman; I used to train the boy who rode him. I told Rhona to stop riding him or I would go to British Eventing and tell them. I also said that Maddy would recognize the horse because I remember Tamsin rode him when she stayed with Maddy once. When you watch a horse a lot you remember how it goes, and that horse is Woodleigh's Flying Scotsman…'

'Or you're a Dutchman.' Simon finished the sentence for her.

'Don't make me laugh,' replied Louise, smiling. 'But you're quite wrong if you think my accident is anything to do with Rhona. I've known her for years. Something happened and I ran off the road. I killed two horses and Vicky is seriously ill.' Her face looked tragic.

'Believe me, it really wasn't your fault,' said Simon firmly.

'I don't know, but it was nothing to do with Rhona. She sent me a card, look.'

'Oh yes, so she has.' Simon stood up and studied the card on Louise's bedside table. 'I have to go now. Please don't blame yourself for this and thank you, you've been very helpful.'

'I can't think why.' Louise tried to smile. Simon left the ward feeling very uneasy. He found a senior member of staff, flashed his card at them and asked questions about Vicky the groom. He was not happy with what he found out.

***

Maddy was standing in the yard talking to Judith when her phone rang.

'How did your lesson go?' asked Simon.

'It was great, thank you. Hyps went really well.'

Simon could hear the smile in her voice and felt himself becoming annoyed again. 'Has Gerhardt gone?' he asked, in spite of himself.

'Yes,' said Maddy. She turned to Judith, who was on the point of leaving, and mouthed. 'It's Simon, wait a moment.'

Simon could tell there was someone there. 'Are you sure?' he snapped.

Maddy retorted, 'What's it to you if he's still here? Why would I say he isn't if he was?'

'Maddy, we're supposed to be looking after you and I need to know who's there.' Simon pulled himself together.

'Ask Colin then, or your men.'

'Kindly don't take that attitude. I'll speak to you later,' he said through gritted teeth.

'There's no need to get on your high horse,' replied Maddy, but he had rung off. She turned to Judith and said, 'Honestly, whatever's the matter with him?'

'He doesn't seem to be in a very good mood today,' replied Judith. 'He drove out of your drive like a maniac. He nearly hit my car.'

'I don't know what his problem is. He obviously hasn't got his own way over something. Let's hope he calms down before he gets back.'

'Well, come to dinner tonight, both of you together, or on your own if he's still in a bad mood. Maybe you need a break.'

'Thank you Judith, that would be lovely. Ruth seems to be in a bad mood today as well. I don't know what's got into everyone. But I'll see how the land lies.'

***

That afternoon a young man was riding around on his trail bike looking for easy access to paddocks and stables with no living accommodation close by. He sped through a wood until he came out along a path opposite the drive to October Farm. Seeing the sign *CCTV CAMERAS IN OPERATION HERE*, he halted and turned left up the lane. He rode along slowly until very shortly he came to a gap in the hedge. Something caught his eye. A tall chestnut horse was being exercised in circles on a lunge line in a sand school. He stopped to watch, while the thought of the CCTV gave him an extra frisson.

When the big horse heard the motor bike engine he reared up, twisted round and pulled back. The pretty dark-haired woman who was holding him had a job to keep him under control. The boy sat mesmerised, with a smile on his face. He revved up his bike and each time the motor roared the horse reared up on to his hind legs. He twisted and turned and threw himself about until he set off in a straight line towards the rails enclosing the school. The woman had no chance of holding him and had to let go of the lunge line. The horse sailed over the rails and careered off across the field.

The boy looked round and saw an angry girl running towards him. He put his bike into gear and roared away.

Maddy and Ruth had managed to corner Rin Tin Tin in the field when another trail bike sped up the road after the first. The horse, dripping with sweat and shaking in fear, charged past the two women and set off at a gallop around the field again.

'Bloody motorbikes!' yelled Maddy. 'Did you see his face?' she asked Ruth.

'No, he was wearing a helmet and he drove away. I didn't get to speak to him.'

'A pity. I wish we could follow him.' She turned her attention back to the horse that had stopped galloping and stood trembling. His sweat was now transformed into the white foam of stress and fear. This time he allowed them to approach him and to catch him.

'Well,' said Maddy. 'We now know he doesn't like motor bikes. And look at this!' She pointed to the curious scar on his chest. It looked as if something had gone right through the soft tissue at the base of his neck. Maddy touched the scar and the horse reared up again, almost knocking her over with his front legs.

'Something very odd has happened to this horse,' exclaimed Ruth. 'Whatever does Rhona do to them?'

By the time they had cooled him down and dried him off, Maddy heard Simon arriving back. She put the horse away and, forgetting about her earlier conversation with him on the phone, went indoors, eager to tell him what had happened. Simon met her with an unsmiling face. 'Hello,' she said cheerfully.

'Well, you look happier,' he snapped.

'Yes, I am.' She had still not read Simon's dark mood. 'I had a good lesson and I've just had your rescue horse out on the lunge and do you know what...'

'I bet you did,' Simon butted in.

'What are you talking about?'

'I'm talking about your boyfriend.'

'What?'

'Don't look so naïve Maddy,' Simon sneered.

'How dare you,' retorted Maddy, her hackles rising.

'Don't deny it. It's as obvious as the nose on your face.'

'He's married!' gasped Maddy, almost lost for words.

'When has that ever stopped anyone?' said Simon, now in full flow. 'You've been in a funny mood all morning. Your good looking "*trainer*" appears, and you're suddenly in a good mood. What do you take me for?'

'I'll tell you exactly what I take you for,' replied Maddy, icily calm and speaking very slowly and very clearly. 'I'll explain in extremely simple language. I take you for someone who has the morals of a tom cat. I take you for someone who screws anything in a skirt, and who collects notches on their bedpost.' Simon stood staring at her. 'Please stop me if there is a word you don't understand,' she continued, 'I have *not* and *never will* sleep with a married man. But I don't expect you to understand the moral implications of such a statement, because it's clearly far and away beyond your field of imagination or comprehension. There is, of course, one exception to my rule, and that is if I happen to be married to the man in question.' She paused. He still said nothing, so she continued, 'I am now going upstairs to get ready to go out'.

'Huh!' said Simon, seething, 'What did I say? You're going out on a date.'

'Yes, I am actually, and it's none of your business with whom,' Maddy answered, as she marched out of the kitchen and upstairs to change.

She took great care as she got ready to go round for supper with Judith. When she came downstairs again Simon came out of the sitting room. He stood and stared. Maddy looked amazing: she was wearing a tight fitting dress, her hair was up and she wore her very high heels again. She walked past Simon as if he didn't exist and straight out to her car. She drove down the drive spraying gravel in all directions.

Simon stood in the kitchen doorway and watched her speed away. He picked up his phone and called Sarah. 'Follow her and don't let her see you,' he barked down the phone. Then he stalked back to the sitting room and sat down at the TV monitors connected to the CCTV cameras. He fiddled around with them until he found that morning's tape of Maddy in the school with Gerhardt. He watched her lesson. He studied the body language between her and her trainer. He kicked himself. It was quite obvious that it was a lesson, exactly as she had said. The more he watched, the more he realised what a good rider she was. *This German bloke certainly knows how to get the best out of her and her horse,* he thought.

He suddenly relaxed and smiled as Sarah reported in to say that Maddy had arrived at Judith's house and that she was eating there.

***

'That man,' stormed Maddy to Judith as she marched into the house. 'How dare he!' She paced up and down Judith's beautiful sitting room. 'I've never been so insulted. And to think last night...' she recoiled. 'It doesn't bear thinking about.'

'Maddy dear, whatever has happened?' asked Judith.

'You may well ask,' replied Maddy. 'Of all the nerve! Judging me by his own standards. Just because he screws everything in a skirt, how dare he!'

'Calm down. Sit down and have a drink.' Judith hastily poured a whisky.

'How could I have even considered...? '

'Considered what?' asked Judith. 'You look lovely tonight. Please sit down.'

Maddy sank into a comfortable old fashioned arm chair and took a gulp of her drink. 'Thank you Judith.'

'I take it Simon isn't coming?'

'Certainly not. I didn't ask him to come out with me... The thought of it... Well!'

'Oh dear. What's he done?' repeated Judith, laughing.

'It's not funny.'

'No, no I'm sure it's not,' Judith replied calmly. 'Please tell me what's happened?'

'He only accused me of having an affair with Gerhardt. I mean, how dare he?'

'Oh I see.' Judith sounded relieved. 'What did you say to him?'

Maddy told her. 'Well that should certainly have left him in no doubt.' Judith smiled.

'Yes, so I should think.' Maddy began to calm down.

'How did his trip to see Louise go?'

'I don't know. I'm not interested,' replied Maddy. 'I'm fed up with the whole thing. I don't believe a word he says and the sooner he clears off the better as far as I am concerned. Another notch on his bedpost, that's what he's after.'

'Maddy, don't you think that all this would be rather an elaborate plan for him just to get another notch. I'm sure there would be easier ways,' said Judith.

'He likes a challenge,' retorted Maddy. Judith couldn't help laughing. Maddy suddenly saw the funny side and laughed too, then added ruefully, 'I wish I had asked how Louise is, but I didn't think.'

'I'm sure he would have said if there had been any developments.'

'Well at least he thinks I am out with some man tonight.' Maddy laughed. Judith nodded. She didn't mention that she was sure that Simon would have had her followed.

They passed a pleasant evening and when Maddy left to go she felt much calmer. She drove home slowly, unaware of the car following her.

Suddenly a trail bike appeared from nowhere and shot past her. The tone of the engine and the rattle of the machine when the rider changed down a gear sounded like the bike she had heard earlier that day. She put her foot down and followed it along a lane leading away from October Farm. The rider kept up a steady fast pace then suddenly slowed down. Maddy jammed on her brakes and switched off her lights as she saw the bike stop beside a gate to a field.

She parked quietly by the side of the road, still unaware of the car behind her. She watched a beaten up old Ford Escort pull up beside the trail bike rider. The two young men left their vehicles and went on foot into the field. One was carrying a bucket and a tripod, the other was carrying a variety of other things, but Maddy couldn't make out what they were.

She quickly took off her high heels and put on a pair of old boots which were lying in the back of her car. She slid out of the 4 x 4. The boots were a loose fit over her stockings and clomped as she walked. She pulled her tight dress up above her knees and hurried to the gate.

She peered into the meadow, and as her eyes grew used to the darkness she saw the two young men catch a horse and take it into a field shelter. They had a powerful light with them and she could clearly see them tie it up and, while it ate the food in the bucket, they sorted out their equipment. Maddy went through the gate and crept nearer to the shed, keeping close to the hedge. She saw that they had a crossbow, a sword and a length of rope. One of them was putting a video camera on to the tripod.

Maddy stepped forward and opened her mouth to demand what they were doing when someone suddenly grabbed her from behind, clamping their hand over her mouth.

She started to struggle violently until a voice hissed in her ear, 'It's me, Sarah, keep very quiet.' Maddy nodded and Sarah let her go.

'We have to stop them,' whispered Maddy, 'You know what they are going to do?'

'Yes, just wait,' hissed Sarah. 'I've called the boss, I'm waiting for orders.' Maddy stared at her in amazement, realising that Simon must have sent Sarah to follow her. She was now seething again, but she kept quiet. She jumped as she heard the sound of a phone ringing.

'We've got to get out of here, Danny,' yelled one of the men. They grabbed their equipment and untied the horse.

'What is it?' gasped Danny as they hurried past Sarah and Maddy who were crouching in the hedge.

'Jason's coming down the lane and he says there are two cars parked on the road outside,' replied the other in a hoarse voice.

'Fucking hell,' yelled Danny. 'Leg it!' They fled out of the field to their vehicles, threw their equipment into the Ford Escort and drove away at speed.

Maddy ran, as best she could in her tight skirt and ill-fitting boots, to the field shelter to look at the horse. Sarah followed her. They found the horse unharmed but very drowsy.

'You followed me to Judith's house.' Maddy confronted Sarah furiously.

'Yes, boss's orders, sorry.'

Maddy drove home in a temper and stalked into her house.

'Hello.' Simon smiled at her as she entered the kitchen. She glared at him and went to walk past but he stood in her way and said, 'You were lucky Sarah was with you tonight, you could have been seriously hurt.'

'Really,' she snapped back at him. 'What are you going to do about those two thugs? I suppose you're going to ignore the fact that they were about to attack the horse. Have you found out who they are and have you contacted the owner?'

'Yes, I have.'

'Well, are you going to arrest them? One of them is called Danny, by the way, he was on the bike. And they have a friend called Jason.'

'All in good time.' Simon smiled.

'I'm glad you think it's all so funny,' retorted Maddy.

'I don't find it in the least amusing.'

Maddy scowled at him and saying, 'Excuse me,' she walked straight past him and up the stairs.

***

The next morning Maddy woke early; she couldn't get back to sleep so she got up, tacked up her dressage stallion, Hyperion, and went out for a hack. She followed a bridle path through the fields. The grass was wet with heavy dew, the sun was coming up and the air smelt fresh.

She cantered along the side of a field, enjoying the powerful horse beneath her. He suddenly shied at a trail bike leaning on the fence. Maddy pulled up and looked around. She saw a young man coming towards her across the field. As he came closer she was astounded to see that it was Danny, the same man whom she had seen the night before. Maddy felt the anger flood through her body and a red mist came down in front of her eyes. She gathered up her reins and kicked her horse forwards. He responded and gathered momentum as she rode straight at the young man standing on the ground. He stared at her, mesmerised like a rabbit in the headlights of a car. Just as she was about to cannon into him he turned and ran.

Maddy galloped after him. He dodged from side to side trying to avoid her. She checked her horse, and cantered just behind the running figure. As he ran first left then right she asked her horse to move sideways, still following him and gaining on him until he could feel her horse's breath on his back. He waited for the pain of the thundering hooves but instead he felt Maddy's long dressage whip cut into his cheek. He stopped dead in his tracks and spun round. Maddy, taken by surprise, overtook him, but turned her horse sharply on his haunches and faced the enraged boy. He briefly reminded her of someone she knew, but she was far too angry to even think or remember who.

Danny stood facing the incensed woman and her steaming black mount. He wanted to pull her off the horse, but he saw the wild look in the eye of the stallion. His great neck arched and his nostrils flaring red, he reminded Danny of the Angel of Death and he faltered.

Maddy, surprised to see him turn and face her, saw the look of fear in his eyes and her anger briefly left her.

He stepped back, turned and ran for his life, back to his bike. He started it up and roared across the field. Maddy, her fury returning, urged her horse into a gallop and followed him.

Once mounted, confident now that he had his wheels beneath him, he rode his trail bike straight at her. Maddy held her nerve and waited until the bike was nearly on her and then swung her horse sideways away from the path of the machine. He shot past, turned and came at her again; she cantered directly at him. They rode towards each other as in a game of chicken. The horse snorting, his hooves thundering on the turf and his eyes locked on to the motor bike as if he knew it was his prey. The bike roared and bounced over the rough surface, the back wheel throwing up a mixture of earth and grass.

Maddy had her back to the road and the field gate. She was unaware that that was where the biker was heading. She waited until he was nearly on her and then ducked to one side and circled to come at him broadside on. As she caught up with him she lunged at his wheels with her long dressage whip. It caught in the back wheel of the bike. The bike skidded and veered to one side, nearly throwing its rider, but he stayed in the saddle and skidded through the gateway and on to the road. The whip, broken in two, lay on the ground. Maddy stared after the retreating figure and listened to the roar of the bike as it became fainter and fainter.

Hyperion suddenly neighed and swung round. Maddy jumped as another horse answered his call and she saw Simon riding towards her on Highwayman.

'What the hell are you playing at?' he bellowed.

'Catching your criminal,' she yelled back. 'I nearly did too.'

'You nearly got yourself killed and your horse damaged.'

'What are you doing on my horse? You look ridiculous in your suit trousers, I hope you've ruined them,' retorted Maddy.

'You bloody little fool,' shouted Simon, as he rode up to her. He had been more shaken by her encounter with the biker than he liked to admit.

'Don't you call me a bloody fool,' replied Maddy angrily. 'He's got away again. I've come to the conclusion that you and your men are bloody useless. I'm going back home. And be careful with my horse, he's worth a lot of money.' She turned Hyperion towards home and walked across the field. Simon joined her.

'Don't you realise the danger you're putting yourself in?' asked Simon.

'We'll walk quietly home.' Maddy ignored his question. 'I'm not going to argue. I don't want to upset the horses. I want to cool them off.' She patted Hyperion. 'You were so good and so responsive.'

'I watched your lesson with Gerhardt on the video from the CCTV cameras,' said Simon walking along beside her.

'Huh!' said Maddy. 'So you saw us having it off on the floor of the school then?'

'I'm sorry,' replied Simon contritely. 'I had no right to say what I did. I thought you rode beautifully and I don't think Emma is far wrong when she says you should make the British team.' Maddy looked up and stared at him. 'That's if you don't injure your horse first by making him play silly games,' Simon added.

Maddy smiled in spite of herself but said nothing. Simon, seeing the smile, continued, 'You looked lovely last night and I'm sorry that I missed out on a good evening'.

***

164

When Judith arrived to ride her horse later that morning, she was relieved to see that Maddy and Simon seemed to be on good terms again.

As Maddy's two horses had already been out, Maddy gave Judith a lesson in the school.

They were just finishing when Maddy's mobile rang. She looked at the display and exclaimed, 'Oh bugger, it's Rhona!'

'Answer it,' said Judith.

Rhona said abruptly, 'Someone told me you have a horse that belonged to me. I want to come and check if it is true. Jilly and I are over your way this morning. I'll call in... Say in about an hour?'

'Really,' said Maddy. 'I... I didn't know. Hold on.' She put her hand over the phone and said to Judith 'What shall I do? She's found out about Rin Tin Tin. She wants to come and look'.

'Stall her and tell Simon.'

Maddy spoke into her phone. 'Let me go into the house and I'll check my diary. I'll ring you straight back.' She sprinted into the house and breathlessly gasped to Simon, 'Rhona... wants to come here in an hour... to look at Rin Tin Tin.'

'Good,' replied Simon cheerfully. 'I made sure she would find out about the horse. We're all ready for them, aren't we Colin?' Colin nodded.

'You mean you set her up?' Maddy was astonished.

'Yes. Ring her back and tell her to come. But make out you don't know anything about the horse.' After Maddy had done that, Simon said, 'Now calm down and let me explain'. As Judith arrived in the sitting room he asked her, 'Do you want to stay and join in as well?'

'I certainly do.'

'Right, this is what I want you to do.' He sat them down and talked them through his plan of action.

'That seems to be quite simple,' replied Judith. 'I think we can do that, don't you Maddy?'

'Yes I suppose so,' answered Maddy.

'Oh come on. It'll be a piece of cake.'

'Yes,' replied Maddy hesitantly, as Colin fitted her with a microphone and an ear piece.

'They'll be here before long,' said Simon. 'Go and wait in the kitchen.'

Maddy and Judith sat nervously watching the time. Maddy wanted to tell Judith about her escapade that morning, but her microphone was switched on so she didn't say very much at all.

Eventually Simon's voice came into Maddy's ear. 'They're here, go out and greet them.'

'Here we go.' Maddy took a deep breath.

'Smile,' said Simon's voice in her ear.

Maddy put a smile on her face and went outside to meet their visitors. She introduced Judith to Rhona and Jilly, and then said, 'I'm delighted to see you both, but why...?'

'Someone told me you had a horse that belonged to me. I wondered if it was true.'

'Well, I'll show you our horses. I can't think which one.' Maddy hoped she sounded genuine.

As they walked past Hyperion's bull pen Rhona stopped and asked, 'Isn't this your stallion?' Maddy nodded. Rhona walked towards the box, but Judith put herself between the horse and the large lady.

'Isn't he gorgeous,' tittered Jilly. 'He's got a lovely head. Isn't he beautiful, Rhona?'

'Yes.' Rhona nodded condescendingly. 'What a good idea, putting him in a loose box like this. Do you shut this outer door as well?' she asked, looking at the old outside pen.

'Oh yes, always at night. Not always in the day time though.'

'I see by the sign at the end of your drive that you have CCTV here?' said Rhona. 'Very sensible. I do in my yard.'

'Yes, but I usually forget to turn it on, don't I Judith?'

'Yes,' agreed Judith. 'Quite often I have to remind her. Dear Maddy is so forgetful sometimes.' Maddy gave Judith a look but managed to keep a straight face. They walked on.

'What have you got in here?' asked Rhona, as they went into the barn.

'That's a livery,' replied Maddy pointing at the different stables, 'and this is Judith's horse...'

'What, this coloured thing?' Rhona rudely butted in.

'He's worth his weight in gold,' retorted Maddy a little heatedly.

'Keep your cool,' came Simon's voice in her ear.

Maddy smiled. 'Of course he suits Judith very well.'

'Oh yes,' said Judith. 'I'm such an amateur you know. I can hardly tell which end the ears are on.' She gave a silly tinkling laugh. 'Isn't that right Maddy?'

'Yes, I'm afraid so.' Maddy looked at Rhona and tried not to laugh.

'Well done,' said Simon, in her ear. Rhona was too busy having a good look round the barn to be aware of anything odd in Maddy's behaviour. No one took any notice of Jilly.

'What lives in these empty stables?' demanded Rhona.

'The horses are out in the field,' replied Maddy.

'What horses?'

'My youngsters, and Sally's horse. The old warm blood…'

'What old warm blood?' Rhona butted in again.

'The one belonging to Serena Poulston-Hayes. The Grand Prix horse.'

'Oh, that old thing. I'm surprised she hasn't had it shot by now. It must be thirty if it's a day.'

Maddy bristled. 'Keep smiling,' said the voice in her ear. 'He's twenty eight and a star,' retorted Maddy, remembering how he and his rider had beaten Rhona on her dressage horse several times in the past.

'I wouldn't keep a horse for ever,' blustered Rhona. 'Put it down, I say. I had my old Singspiel shot.'

'Yes, you did,' said Jilly, everyone turned in surprise to look at her. 'You were so brave about it too, weren't you Rhona?'

Rhona ignored her and said, 'Are these the only horses you have?'

'No, no.' Maddy took them round the back to Rin Tin Tin's stable. Rhona stared at him, horrified. It was obvious that she recognised him. He put his head over the door. Jilly went up to him and touched his nose. He shot to the back of his stable.

'Very odd behaviour. He doesn't like you Jilly,' remarked Rhona. 'Well, I can't see any horse here that I've had. We've had a wasted journey.' She glanced at Jupiter who was in the next stable and demanded, 'What's this?'

'This is Jupiter. He belongs to Angela Tidebrook. I spoke to you about him,' replied Maddy.

'Oh yes, he's coming to my yard,' replied Rhona. Maddy stiffened.

'Stay calm,' said Simon in her ear. 'You're doing very well.'

'Why are you holding your ear?' asked Rhona.

Maddy jumped and replied, 'I've got a bit of an earache. I think I've got a foreign body in it.' She heard a chuckle.

'Oh.' Rhona turned away disinterestedly.

'Let's go in for a coffee,' suggested Maddy. They walked slowly back to the house. Rhona's eyes were everywhere.

'I heard you might become a Director of British Dressage, or was it British Eventing?' Maddy asked as they drank their coffee.

'British Dressage have already approached me.'

'Really. Things seem to be going well for you.'

'Oh yes, it's not a question of good luck, it's a question of one's ability and one's standing in life. I'm a born leader, always have been. Things always go my way. I make sure they do.'

Maddy gasped. 'Keep going,' said Simon.

'What happens if someone comes up against you and opposes you?' asked Maddy.

'They don't.'

'It must happen sometimes.'

'Well if it does, I deal with it,' replied Rhona.

There was a silence.

'Ask about Scotty,' said the voice in Maddy's ear.

She took a deep breath. 'That horse you were riding the other day, Whitehaven Lad. Louise Parkway told me it looked very like a horse Tamsin Coulson had called Flying Scotsman.' Rhona's face clouded over. Jilly looked nervous and started fidgeting.

'Really?' Rhona's voice hardened. 'How extraordinary.'

'Yes,' Maddy carried on, 'I remember Scotty. Tamsin brought him here once. I rode him. He was a lovely horse. I would know him anywhere and your horse is exactly like him except for the white bits. But I remember he had very unusual whorls by his elbow.' Jilly gasped, and this time Rhona glared at her.

'They're probably by the same horse,' said Rhona. 'That's why they look alike. How was it bred?'

'I think he was by a horse called Highland Fling.' Maddy made up the name on the spur of the moment.

'Well, there you are then, so was my horse. Problem solved.'

'Go on,' said Simon.

'But,' Maddy continued while the large woman looked daggers at her, 'I would know Scotty anywhere, and your horse looks exactly like him.'

'I just told you it's obviously in the breeding,' snapped Rhona.

'How's he going?' asked Maddy.

'Very well.'

'Where are you going with him next?'

'Up country somewhere. I've forgotten the name of the place.'

'I thought you said…' started Jilly.

'You think too much,' barked Rhona. 'Hurry up and finish your coffee. We've got to get back. Can't sit here talking all day.'

'Yes Rhona,' said Jilly, getting up to go. Her friend was already on her feet and walking through the kitchen door.

'We'll find our own way to the car,' said Rhona. 'Don't bother to get up. Thank you for the coffee.' Maddy and Judith rushed out after them. The large lady turned to take another look at Hyperion's loose box, then got in her car and drove away.

Maddy and Judith stared after her. 'What a nasty piece of work,' said Judith, 'and so blatantly aggressive.'

'I know; she gives me the creeps. Thank goodness we have Simon and his team here.' said Maddy, forgetting she was still wearing the microphone. 'Don't you think so, Judith? But don't tell him I said that, it'll go to his head and he'll become impossible.'

'I agree with you,' replied Judith, laughing. 'But you've already told him yourself.'

'What do you mean?' asked Maddy.

'Thank you for the compliment, Maddy. I'll try and live with it,' said Simon's voice in her ear.

When they returned to the house he said, 'You did brilliantly, both of you'.

Maddy gave Simon back her ear piece and microphone, and he gave her a hug.

'You did superbly, Maddy. And you, Judith, were splendid too. Now, the horse harming people are going to meet tonight.'

'Where?' asked Maddy.

'Not very far away, do you want to come with us?' he asked.

'Yes, I do,' she said.

'It might get violent.'

'Good. I hope it does.'

'I don't think you should come Judith…' Simon started to say.

'No, nor do I,' she added quickly. 'But what about Maddy's yard?'

'Don't worry, I'm leaving Sarah here. Anyway, as luck would have it our chief protagonists are busy tonight.'

'How do you know?' asked Maddy.

'Never mind. I'm calling in some extra personnel for the raid tonight. I'm taking John and two other men who'll meet us at the venue. You can bring Ruth for company if you like.'

'Okay,' said Maddy.

'I would like to use your 4 x 4 if that's possible?' asked Simon, his tone becoming distant as if he were talking to a subordinate. Maddy nodded. 'Thank you,' he carried on. 'Please make sure it's full of diesel. We'll leave here at 20.00 hours; I want you all assembled here in the kitchen at 19.45 wearing dark warm clothes.'

Maddy looked at him and replied, 'We're supposed to say "*yes sir!*" are we?' Simon smiled briefly at her and walked out of the kitchen. Maddy stared after him. She wasn't quite sure what to think because as soon as he had mentioned the raid his attitude had changed. He now seemed to be very remote.

CHAPTER ELEVEN

Maddy was still wondering why Simon had become so remote and withdrawn. He had been ensconced with Colin in the sitting room for most of the day, and she hadn't seen him since Rhona's visit. She couldn't understand why he had been so full of praise one minute and so cold the next. Determined to have it out with him, she marched up to the sitting room door, knocked and walked in.

Simon looked up, annoyance showing on his face. 'Yes,' he said curtly.

Maddy looked around the room; it was full of wires and electronic equipment. Television monitors from the CCTV cameras stood on a table and Colin sat surrounded with laptops and computers. 'And you called my room untidy before Colin arrived,' she said.

Simon gave her a brief smile. 'We're very busy, what do you want?'

'I just wondered if I could talk to you, but I see that it is an inappropriate moment, so I'll leave you in peace.' She swung round to go, when Colin said, 'Perhaps I could have a cup of coffee?'

'Of course.' Maddy marched back to the kitchen. She turned round in surprise to see that Colin was following her.

'Don't worry about the colonel,' he said.

'I'm not.'

'He's always like this before an operation.'

'Like what?'

'Snappy and uptight.'

'I hadn't noticed,' Maddy lied.

'All right, pretend I said nothing.'

Maddy had to smile in spite of herself. 'You're not as silly as you look.'

'Thank you and may I say that you're not just a pretty face.'

Maddy relaxed. 'Is it going to be dangerous tonight?'

'It could be these men are extremely vicious, with what they do to horses, that is. I don't know what they would do to humans. Maybe they're cowards, most bullies are.'

'They look so young.'

'Yes, they are. No more than boys.'

'It's quite exciting. I'll be pleased to see them caught.'

'So will I.' Colin paused while he watched Maddy put the kettle on and get out the mugs. 'I think I ought to tell you something.'

Maddy's heart sank. 'What?' she asked.

'Your girl Ruth.'

Maddy felt relieved. 'What about her? Do you fancy her?'

Colin blushed and looked away.

'You do!' Maddy laughed.

'No… of course she's a very pretty girl. No, it's not that. Anyway I wouldn't stand a chance with her; I'm not her cup of tea at all.'

'What is it then?'

'John.'

'John. The security guard, our minder?'

'Yes. He's been talking to her and I believe she takes him food. The colonel would sack him on the spot if he knew.'

'Well… I thought she might be doing that. Does it matter?'

'Yes, it does. He's a good operative and I would hate to see him dismissed, but unfortunately he's taken a liking to Ruth. He is a womanizer you know; I wouldn't like to see her hurt.'

'Like employer, like employee,' said Maddy under her breath.

'What did you say?'

'I'll tell her. How far has it gone?'

'They only have chats in the yard and, as I said, she takes him food.' Colin paused. 'I believe he was going to go up to her room one night but I think he thought better of it. He didn't go.'

'Well, thank goodness for that. I'll have a word with her.'

'Thank you.'

'How do you know all this?' Maddy asked.

Colin touched his nose. 'My job.'

'Yes, I suppose it is.' Maddy smiled.

'Colin,' Simon called irately from the sitting room. 'Are you going to be all day? What the hell are you doing?'

'I'd better go,' said Colin.

'Yes you had.'

'Don't worry about the boss, this is normal before a raid.'

Later Maddy and Ruth, dressed in black as instructed, sat waiting for Simon well before 7.45 p.m. Maddy felt the tension in the air; nevertheless, she said to Ruth, 'I've heard you're seeing John'.

'What do you mean? He's supposed to be invisible.' Ruth laughed.

'It's not funny Ruth. He'll get the sack if he's caught.'

'Who told you?'

'So you are seeing him.'

'I don't know what you're talking about.' Ruth looked away.

'Ruth, he's a notorious womanizer. He's probably filling in time between girlfriends. Do be careful.'

'Has Sarah been talking to you?'

'No! Does she know about this as well?'

'What do you mean, as well? Who told you?' Ruth raised her voice.

'It doesn't matter.'

'It does.'

Just then Simon strode into the kitchen. 'What doesn't matter?' he asked.

'Nothing,' said Ruth, quickly.

'We were talking about… a horse,' said Maddy, taking care not to meet his eye.

He gave the two women a long look, and said curtly, 'Come on then'.

Ruth glared at Maddy as they followed him out to the 4 x 4.

The tension built up as Simon drove; nobody spoke until he broke the silence. 'I'm glad to see you both followed my instructions and dressed correctly for the occasion.' Neither of his passengers answered. 'Cat got your tongues?' he added. 'If you're frightened and don't want to come I'll take you home again, but tell me now before it's too late.'

'No,' they both replied in unison. 'I wouldn't miss it for the world,' said Maddy.

'Neither would I,' added Ruth.

That's because you want to see John, thought Maddy. 'How far is it?' she asked Simon.

'Not far.' They all lapsed into silence again.

Simon suddenly turned off the road. 'This is Watersleigh Park, isn't it?' asked Maddy.

'Yes,' replied Simon.

'It's a horse sanctuary.' Ruth was horrified. 'The park is full of old retired horses.'

'Yes it is. They make good targets, decrepit horses.'

'That's horrible,' said Ruth.

'Despicable,' exclaimed Maddy.

Simon drove down a track running alongside the parkland. He reversed the 4 x 4 into the undergrowth facing the way they had come. Then he got out his mobile and made a call.

'Right, everyone is present and correct. Now make sure you wait here. You can come to the edge of these trees, but don't make a sound, don't show any lights and keep well hidden. And on no account go into the field. Is that clear?'

Ruth nodded and quietly said, 'Yes.'

'Maddy!' Simon snapped. 'Have I got your assurance on that? I brought you here against my better judgement. Don't let me down.'

Maddy was furious. 'You didn't have to bring me if you felt like that.'

'Don't be childish,' he retorted. 'Ruth, make sure she behaves herself.' He left the car and walked into the park without another word.

'Well!' said Maddy, 'of all the overbearing, arrogant prigs. If only he knew what you've been up to, he wouldn't think you're so wonderful.'

'I suppose you're going to tell him, seeing as how you're probably jealous, because my friendship with John is going better than yours.'

Maddy knew she was being unreasonable and nasty but she couldn't stop herself from saying, 'Going better than yours? That's a laugh. I hear John was supposed to go to your bedroom, but he didn't quite make it, did he?' Ruth said nothing. 'I'm right. I said you should take care. But then once he's shagged you he'll lose interest.'

'How dare you! What's got into you Maddy? You're being a right bitch. Anyway, the same goes for Simon; once he's had you, you'll see the back of him.' Ruth was close to tears. 'I'm getting out of here. I'm not sitting with you any longer. The horse mutilators will be better company.' Ruth got out of the car and stalked off into the park.

'Ruth, come back,' called Maddy.

'Piss off.' Ruth kept walking towards the outline of a building at the end of the field.

'For goodness sake,' Maddy ran up behind her.

'Leave me alone.'

Maddy saw her tears. 'I'm sorry. I didn't mean what I said.' Ruth kept walking. 'Take cover.' Maddy grabbed her arm. 'I can see some people in the field.' Ruth allowed herself to be dragged behind a tree.

They stood peering into the darkness until their eyes became used to the dim light. They could just make out a group of three men, one of them leading a horse back towards an old barn in the far corner of the pasture.

'Let's follow them,' said Maddy. 'I'm not going back to the car. Simon can get stuffed. How dare he speak to me like that?'

174

'Yes, it'll be all right if we stay hidden,' agreed Ruth. Maddy looked at her and gave her a hug. Ruth smiled back.

They started to walk across the meadow towards the building. The men, following the same procedure as they had before, took the horse into the barn and gave it some food from a bucket that they had brought with them.

'That's drugged,' whispered Maddy.

'What are they going to do?' hissed Ruth, looking with horror at their equipment. It was the same as the previous night, a crossbow, a sword and a video camera. She was shocked at how young they were, not much more than teenagers.

'Hobble him, Jason,' said the youth with the crossbow.

'Okay, Danny,' replied Jason, producing some rope hobbles from a rucksack and fixing them around the horse's front legs. Danny lit a gas camping lamp and placed it on a box so that the light fell on to the horse. He then set up the video camera on a tripod.

Maddy and Ruth crept nearer to the barn. A ladder led up to a hay loft constructed of precarious planks resting on thick oak beams. A tractor was parked in one corner of the building, while at the other end stood an old mower, a set of harrows and a large roller. The barn smelt of hay mixed with engine oil.

'What shall I do?' asked the third young man, who stood watching them with his hands in his pockets.

'You keep watch, Mark,' replied Danny.

As Mark ambled towards the entrance, Ruth and Maddy hastily flattened themselves against the wall of the barn. But the lad only gave a cursory look outside and mooched back saying, 'Nothin' there. I'm going to miss the action.'

'Where's Simon?' mouthed Ruth. Maddy shrugged her shoulders.

'What are you going to do, Dan?' asked Mark.

'I wish you would stop asking questions,' snapped Danny. 'Jason's going to cut his ears off. Then he wants to push his sword in one eye and see if it comes out the other eye. I told him that wouldn't work 'cos it would have to go through his brain and that would kill him. So I'm going to bolt him to the floor first, like the pony, you remember?'

'Oh yeah,' replied Mark, his eyes lighting up. 'That was good.'

'Okay, Jase, you can start now,' said Danny.

'Why don't you mark him with a Z, like Zorro?'

'Why don't you shut up,' snapped Jason. 'I'm not Zorro.'

'Well a J then, for Jason, or a D for Danny.'

Jason picked up the sword. 'I'll mark you if you don't keep quiet.'

'Yeah, mark him Jason.' Danny laughed.

Jason waved the sword in the air. 'Where shall I start?' It's a bit difficult to cut his ears with this; perhaps I should use my knife.' He began swinging the sword in circles above his head. 'But if I do it like this…' He swung the sword lower and lower until it almost touched the horse's ears. The horse heaved a sigh, lowered his head, and his eyes glazed over.

Maddy saw red. 'If Simon isn't going to do anything, I will.'

She made a move towards them. Ruth made a feeble attempt to stop her by pulling on the sleeve of her coat, but Maddy brushed her aside and marched up to the doorway of the barn.

Simon, who was crouched behind the tractor, watched her in fury. John was in the hay loft and the other man, called Steve, was hiding behind the roller. Simon had no way of stopping her. He kicked himself for bringing her along.

Maddy stepped inside the barn and yelled, 'What the hell do you think you're doing, you fucking bastards?'

Pandemonium broke loose as the three men spun round. Danny recognised her and shouted, 'She's mine. I know that bitch.' He ran at her, picking up a sledge hammer that was propped up against the tractor wheel; he passed within a whisker of Simon, who sprang after him. Simon rugby tackled him to the ground, but not before Danny had swung at Maddy with the hammer and caught her with a heavy blow on her arm. She fell to the ground and hit her head on the concrete floor. She passed out.

John dived at Jason, who was running away with his sword still in his hand. Ruth was now standing in the doorway of the barn rooted to the spot. As Jason ran past her he lunged at her with his sword and caught her upper arm. John, spurred on with anger, took a flying leap and landed on top of Jason, throwing him face down on to the ground. He tied his hands behind his back.

John glanced at Ruth and saw that blood was running down her arm over her hand and dripping on to the floor. He turned Jason over and shouting, 'You fucking bastard,' sat astride him and punched his face. 'You're lucky I don't have more time,' he snarled. Then he secured the boy's feet with parcel tape and ran to help Ruth.

Steve had easily overpowered Mark who had been standing rooted to the ground with fear. Simon dealt with Danny and tied him up too. Nobody seemed to notice Maddy lying on the floor.

Ruth had also sunk to the floor. John picked her up, carried her to some hay bales and gently set her down. The sword had hit an artery and blood was pumping furiously out of her arm.

'Hold her,' ordered Simon. He carefully removed her coat and wrapped it around her shoulders. 'That bloody fool, Maddy. Look what she's done. I told her not to leave the wood.'

Ruth looked up at Simon as she leant weakly against John. 'Not Maddy, I…'

'Don't speak,' said Simon gently. 'We'll soon have you patched up.'

John cradled her in his arms and held her blood soaked arm above her head while Simon pressed a pad to the wound, staunching the blood. 'Don't worry,' he said quietly, 'the ambulance is on its way, you're going to be fine.'

He turned and yelled, 'Maddy!' By now she had come to and stood leaning against the wall of the barn, holding her arm and watching him attending to Ruth. 'You nearly lost us the whole operation. You've got Ruth injured. Just go back to the car. I don't want to see your face in this barn any more. I'll talk to you later.'

She felt dazed and was in agony, but Simon's words had so incensed her that in spite of her pain she walked all the way back across the field to her car. She opened the back door and collapsed on to the back seat, cradling her injured arm. She felt something hard sticking out through her jumper but she was in too much pain to know or care what it was. She started shaking with cold and passed out. She came to briefly, hearing sirens, and then she passed out once more.

Eventually Simon strode up to the car and flung open the back door. 'That's right; you sleep in the back while we clear up the mess.' The car rocked as he opened the door and Maddy let out a cry of pain. Simon saw a trickle of dried blood on her ashen face. She was shaking with cold and her eyelids flickered over her half-shut eyes. He noticed with horror that her left arm was soaked in blood. He tried to roll back the sleeve of her coat but something hard was protruding out of her forearm. Maddy screamed with pain as he tried to remove the object.

'Oh my God!' he exclaimed as he realised that the object was a piece of bone. He hastily rang to recall the ambulance that had taken Ruth, but it was well on its way to the hospital and refused to turn back.

'I'll bring her in,' he snapped.

'We'll meet you halfway, if her condition is as bad as you say.'

'It is.'

'Then I can't understand why you didn't tell us earlier.' Simon had no answer to that. He took off his coat and threw it over Maddy, and then he drove very slowly and carefully out of the wood and up the road. 'I'm so sorry,' he kept repeating.

As soon as he heard the sirens coming towards him he frantically flashed his lights and the ambulance stopped. He stood and watched as the paramedics transferred Maddy with great care to their vehicle. They soon had her comfortably installed with an injection of morphine and saline drip into her vein. She opened her eyes, looked unsteadily at him and said, 'Go away, you murderer'.

'What does she mean?' asked one of the paramedics.

Simon shrugged his shoulders, feeling foolish. 'I don't know.'

Both men gave him a strange look and drove away with their lights flashing. Simon got in the 4 x 4 and drove swiftly after them.

***

Time passed slowly as Simon waited while they attended to Maddy. Eventually a doctor came out to the waiting room.

'Well,' he said, 'Mrs Richards has a compound fracture to her left ulna and concussion from a very nasty cut on her forehead, presumably caused by a fall on to a concrete floor. She was suffering the first throes of hypothermia and was in deep shock when she arrived. She's lucky to be alive. We've stabilised her, set and pinned the bone in her arm. She's now on the ward.'

'Good,' said Simon, 'may I go and see her?'

'No, I'm afraid not .She's sedated and asleep just now, but in one of her more lucid moments she gave us instructions that on no account were we to allow you to visit her. You are Colonel Coulson, are you not?' Simon nodded bleakly. 'The police are waiting to see you,' continued the doctor. 'I believe they want an explanation as to this lady's condition and injuries.' The doctor turned and left. Simon looked up and saw two uniformed officers advancing towards him. He suddenly felt very tired.

***

Maddy woke to find Ruth and Judith by her bedside. She smiled and tried to sit up but winced in pain.

178

'Don't move,' said Judith, thinking how awful Maddy looked. A nurse arrived and propped her up on her pillows. Ruth sat on a chair, her arm in a sling.

'Why are you both staring at me as if I'm a ghost?' demanded Maddy. 'Do I look that bad?'

'No, no, of course not,' Judith quickly answered. 'We're just not used to seeing you in bed and doing nothing.'

'I'm not doing nothing. I've worked out who killed Tamsin.'

'Who?' exclaimed Judith and Ruth in unison.

'Well, Simon, of course.'

'I… Do you think… I'm sure…' said Judith.

'Of course it was him, everything points to him. He's free of her now, he can do what he wants, screw as many women as he wants, not that being married ever stopped him before. I think he hoped the horse mutilators would kill me. That's why he took us along. He was quick to save Ruth, but he left me to die.' The tears started to run down Maddy's face.

'No, no, Maddy,' said Judith. 'Of course he didn't and why would he anyway?'

'I've thought of that,' replied Maddy tearfully, 'because he knows that I know he did it, that's why.' She paused and added, 'And he hates me, he always has.' She began to sob.

'Maddy, he doesn't hate you; quite the opposite I would say.'

Maddy wasn't listening. She sat trying not to cry but the tears were coursing down her cheeks. 'I want that bastard out of my house. Where is he?'

'I'm not sure,' replied Judith.

Turning to Ruth, Maddy ordered, 'Go back home and keep an eye on the place.' Then she added, 'Are you all right?'

'Yes, yes I'm fine. I've had a couple of stitches and I'm fine.' Ruth didn't say that she had had over twenty stitches in her arm. Jason had caught her with the sharp edge of his sword and it had made a long deep cut through her coat and thick jumper.

'Good. Well go back home and get rid of Simon. I want him and his minions out.'

'Maddy, is that wise?' Judith asked.

'Of course it is,' snapped Maddy. 'I don't want him in my house or in my yard. He's too full of his own importance. He's had too much authority over people who can't or daren't answer him back, obviously with good reason if they value their lives. Now please go and get rid of him.' Ruth and Judith sat and stared at her in surprise. 'If you don't, I'll call in the police to do it.' Maddy became more and more worked up. 'Go, go!' she shouted.

A nurse came hurrying into the ward saying, 'What's going on?'

'Nothing,' answered Maddy. 'These two ladies are just leaving.' Turning to Ruth and Judith she said more calmly, 'You know what to do?'

They nodded and left the ward.

***

Judith told Simon about their visit to Maddy as soon as they arrived back at October Farm. She told him that Maddy was furious and wanted him to leave her house. She didn't tell him that Maddy thought he had killed Tamsin, or that she thought he had tried to kill her.

Simon put his head in his hands and said, 'I'm so sorry. I didn't realise she was injured. I was so angry with her because I feared for her safety. I thought she would get seriously hurt. I didn't realise that she actually had. She nearly jeopardized the whole operation. I should never have taken her along in the first place. I don't know why I ever thought she would do as she was told. It was a serious error of judgement on my part.'

'Well, I'm sure she'll calm down in time,' said Judith. 'Why don't you and Colin move into my house for now? Leave John and Sarah here. They can help Ruth as well.'

'I've sent for one of my girl grooms from Moorsend. She'll be arriving soon. I don't want Ruth to do any work at all, but she could oversee things. I'll go along and see Maddy this afternoon.'

'No!' replied Judith. 'That would not be a good idea.'

'Well I think I should make my peace with her as soon as possible.'

'No,' repeated Judith. 'She has already mentioned the police in connection with you.'

'Yes, I know.' Simon smiled wryly. 'She sent them to see me in the hospital last night. It took all my influence to stop them arresting me.'

'Oh dear,' said Judith quietly.

***

That afternoon, true to his word and ignoring Judith's tactful remarks, Simon walked into the ward. Maddy opened her eyes and on seeing him at her bedside started in fright and pressed her red alarm button.

'Get him out of here,' she yelled as a nurse came flying in. 'He wants to kill me. Call the police.' Simon fled out of the ward and down the corridor. The nurses and patients stared after him.

He returned to Judith's house and told her what had happened.

'I've never been so embarrassed in all my life,' he said, with an ironic smile. 'Whatever's the matter with her? You'll have to go in and persuade her that I'm not out to kill her.'

Judith looked at him and said, 'It's not funny Simon, she thinks you killed Tamsin'.

He stared back in horror. 'How can she? Of course I didn't. She seems to have gone mad... paranoid at the very best.'

'It could be the shock and the drugs,' said Judith. 'She's been through an ordeal you know.'

'I do know that, and I caused it. In fact she blames me, doesn't she?'

Judith put her hand on his arm and said gently, 'Yes she does, but I'm sure she'll come round, because actually I think she's very fond of you, fonder than you know and fonder than she realises'. Simon grunted. Judith continued, 'I think she feels that you let her down just when she needed your help. It's made her very angry and she can't forgive you at the moment.'

'I can understand that.' Simon sighed. 'I'm close to finding Tamsin's killer. When I'm sure and get the person arrested, then perhaps she'll change her attitude.'

'Yes, I think you're right. Who is her killer? Could it be this Danny person they have in custody?'

Simon answered kindly, 'You know better than to ask that question'. .Judith smiled, and he added, 'I have reason to believe that they'll attack Maddy's yard, but not until she's there to witness what they have planned. For some reason they blame her for a lot of things.'

'But Danny's in prison.'

'They don't need Danny. He has a lot of friends. I'm not saying any more. When is Maddy due out of hospital?'

'I don't know; I'll go in tomorrow and find out.'

***

When Judith went to see Maddy the next day she was in a buoyant mood, sitting up in bed and looking much brighter.

'Hello.' She smiled at Judith. 'Have you got rid of Simon? The bastard came to see me. I mean, what a nerve.'

'Yes,' Judith replied truthfully, 'he's gone.'

'How's Ruth?'

'She's fine. Someone has come in to help her, as well as Sally.'

'Yes, Sally came to see me. She's forgiven us for the Nigel incident.' Judith didn't mention that the help had come from Simon's yard. 'I'm coming out tomorrow,' Maddy announced.

'That's marvellous news.'

'Yes. So I'll be able to continue my investigation; isn't that good?'

'Y…Yes.'

'You know that boy Danny, the one who's now in custody?' Judith nodded. 'He reminds me of someone, but I can't think who.'

'I expect it'll come back to you.'

'Yes, I intend to find out who he is as soon as I'm home. And don't think I'll leave any stone unturned,' replied Maddy. Judith's heart sank.

***

As soon as Maddy arrived back home she went to look at her horses. She found Ruth talking to Pat, the girl groom who Simon had sent from Moorsend.

Maddy drew Ruth to one side and demanded, 'Who the hell is she?'

'Oh, a friend I knew years ago. She was free and came to help.' Maddy gave her a searching look but accepted her answer.

'Are Simon's people still here?' asked Maddy.

Ruth looked at the ground. 'I don't know.'

'Yes you do. They are, aren't they? I told you to get rid of them.' She turned angrily to Judith and said, 'Come on,' and marched into the kitchen. The dogs ran around her in frantic circles.

Maddy sat at the table and dialled Simon's number while Judith made some coffee. 'Hello,' she snapped when he answered. 'I want your men out of here and that girl Pat, as well, if she has anything to do with you.' She paused. 'No I won't listen, I don't want you here or anyone else connected with you. You're a bully, a liar and a murderer.' She slammed the phone down.

Judith looked up and said, 'He is helping you, you know.'

'I don't want a two timing womanising bastard helping me, thank you,' retorted Maddy. 'To think I was beginning to like him again. I mean I... Well it doesn't bear thinking about.' She shuddered exaggeratedly. 'I can't stand him and I'm well rid of him. Look at the life he led poor Tamsin. He tried to make excuses for his behaviour but I don't believe him. He just had to have anything he fancied in a skirt.'

'I'm going to put you straight about Simon's women.'

'I don't want to hear, thank you,' snapped Maddy.

'Well I'm going to tell you anyway, whether you like it or not.' The firmness in Judith's voice made Maddy sit up. 'I think you're a lot fonder of Simon than you like to admit.'

'I hate...' started Maddy.

'Don't say it,' interrupted Judith, holding up her hand. 'I can see what you feel about him. Please don't insult my intelligence.' Maddy subsided and looked away. 'Simon is devastated by what has happened.'

'Huh,' grunted Maddy.

'I'm not going to argue about it, he is and that's that. He did not kill his wife, and he's very close to finding out who did. He needs your co-operation.'

'So that's it.' Maddy smiled. 'He needs my co-operation. Now we're getting to the point. I can believe that; he wants my help for his own ends.'

Judith sighed. 'You cannot continually throw his past women in his face. That is his past. You can't change it, and neither can he. If you can't accept it then you must walk away, which would be a shame because I know that he's very fond of you.'

Maddy looked up. 'How do you know? Have you discussed my prowess in bed?'

'Don't be so stupid, of course not. I know by the way he looks at you and the way he talks about you.'

'So you have discussed me.'

'Not in the way you are talking about. I know how he was with the women he had affairs with.'

'What do you mean?'

'I knew someone whom he had an affair with very well,' Judith continued. Maddy stared at her but said nothing. 'She was married to an officer, rather a dull man actually. She said that she had had a good time with Simon. He took her to expensive restaurants in London, and to the theatre. He was good company and he had beautiful manners. She enjoyed going out with him, but he had told her right from the start that that is all it would be; a good time. He also told her that if she wanted anything else then she must look elsewhere because he would never leave his wife, and that she must not expect him to. He didn't use terms of endearment, nor did he buy her presents. Not once did he send her cards or flowers. When he was with her he was always charming, but there was a coldness to him. He put up a barrier and it never came down. At the end of an evening he would switch off. She always knew when he was about to go home, because half an hour before he left his mind was already on something else. He always dictated everything within the relationship, when they met and where, etc. She enjoyed the physical relationship.' Maddy blushed and looked at the floor. She knew only too well what he was like in bed. 'But he was never affectionate;' Judith went on, 'sometimes this lady said that she would have liked a hug or a cuddle instead of sex. But that never happened.'

Maddy breathed again and remembered how affectionate he was with her, which was another of the reasons why she had found him so hard to give up, until she found Jonathan. 'It all sounds very clinical,' she commented.

'That's exactly what this woman thought,' replied Judith. 'When he left her bed he would give her a polite peck on the cheek and she would almost expect to find money on the bedside table in payment for services rendered.'

'That's awful.' Maddy shuddered.

'He stuck by his word and never became emotionally involved,' continued Judith. 'Although she did try hard to make him fall for her, but she had no success and she decided that he was totally devoid of any emotion. He never got angry with her and he was never radiantly happy. He was always pleasant and charming. .She ended up calling him the ice man. She also thought he was a very unhappy man.'

'He sounds like a nightmare.'

'He said he had fallen in love once when he was young and had blown it, and that he was never going to fall in love again. This woman stopped seeing him in the end because she said it was like going out with a robot and it was wearing her down. A friend of hers took over from her because she fancied him too. She told the same story.'

'It all sounds rather boring.' Maddy sighed.

'Yes, even Simon became bored with it all in the end.'

'I feel sorry for the women. Well, no I don't actually, more fool them for putting up with it. They must have been leading very boring lives.'

'They were, and they had boring husbands who were often away from home. That's why he chose them.'

'He sounds like a predator, preying on bored housewives.'

'He was in a way, but, to be fair to him, they actually preyed on him. I mean, you must admit, he is good looking,'

'Oh yes.' Maddy smiled for the first time.

'So now you've had an insight into his affairs. Can you live with them?'

'I don't know what you mean.'

Judith smiled, shook her head and said, 'Can you let him back in your house to finish his enquiries?'

'No,' replied Maddy.

***

Maddy was awoken by a noise in the yard. She scrambled out of bed and looked out of the window but the security lights hadn't come on. She pushed her feet into her slippers, wrestled with her dressing gown, drawing it on with one hand as best she could, and went downstairs. She picked up a torch, opened the back door and hurried down the garden path.

She could hear Hyperion snorting and swung her torch at the bullpen. She thought she saw a figure and opened her mouth to cry out. Someone grabbed her from behind and pinned her arms painfully behind her back while another person tied a handkerchief tightly over her mouth. One of them then shone the torch at Hyperion. Maddy felt faint as she saw a boy in his loose box with a knife and a bucket of feed.

'We're going to blind him,' said a voice behind her. 'Then castrate him. He won't be any good to you then.' Although the person had disguised her voice, Maddy knew who it was and she tried to speak, but she couldn't. She was pushed to the bullpen and tied to the railings. The woman stood behind her taunting her while the young man in the loosebox offered the food to Hyperion. Maddy silently willed the horse not to eat it. As if he understood, he reared up and knocked his attacker over.

The lights in the yard sprang to life. The woman behind her gasped and then began to shout and swear. Someone untied Maddy and released her hands from behind her back. She saw a figure running away, and as she pulled off her gag she saw Simon holding Jilly Rich. She stared at Maddy, her eyes wild and her mouth set in an ugly line. She snarled and spat like a wild cat as she wrenched her body to and fro trying to get loose.

'Enough of that.' Simon yanked her hands and tied them together behind her back with parcel tape.

Jilly cried out in pain and tried to kick him. 'You're breaking my arms, you bastard,' she screamed. 'Fuck off. Let me go.'

Simon shook her. 'Shut up. Maddy, tie the handkerchief she used on you around her mouth.' Maddy did so, pulling it tight, knowing how much it hurt. Jilly kicked out at her but missed and caught Simon again.

'You're beginning to annoy me,' he snarled and slammed her into the bullpen. She knocked her head against the railings and her body went limp.

'For Christ's sake Simon, you've killed her,' gasped Maddy.

'No, I don't think so,' replied Simon. Jilly's shouts were muffled by the handkerchief. 'No, she appears to be alive,' continued Simon grinning at Maddy.

Maddy looked at Hyperion. John had overpowered the young man in the inside railed area. The bucket of feed rolled around on the concrete.

'Handcuff him to the railings,' yelled Simon, 'and then go round the back to the young horses.'

'Sir!' barked John. He manhandled the struggling youth to the side of the pen. Maddy could see that he was no more than a teenager but he shouted and cursed like an old lag. He jerked his hands and the handcuffs dug into his wrist. He screamed in pain.

'Hang in there,' shouted Simon. 'I've brought you some company.' He then handcuffed Jilly to the outside of the railings on the opposite side of the pen.

'Check that the horse doesn't eat anything, and take the bucket away,' Simon threw at Maddy. 'Stay there and listen to what they say to each other. It's important. Don't go within reach of either of them. Will you do that for me, please?'

'Yes.' Maddy smiled in spite of the situation.

The black stallion snorted, his eyes flashed and his ears flicked back and forth. Maddy gathered up the contents of the bucket that were strewn harmlessly over the floor. Then she stroked his neck and stayed by the stable door, well away from the two prisoners.

'Ere, you said there would be no police,' shouted the boy. 'But they're everywhere. We walked right into a trap and it's your fault.'

Jilly made frantic muffled noises and shook her head. Maddy watched her and realised why the boy Danny had looked so familiar. She was staring at his mother.

***

While Simon was dealing with the two intruders at the bullpen, Ruth had come downstairs and walked nervously towards the barn. She heard a scuffle and the sound of a bucket flying into a wall. She started to run and entered the barn in time to see Sarah leap into the air and land a kick in the face of a teenager.

The horses were nervously stamping and snorting in their looseboxes. The boy fell sideways into a stable door, and as he turned to face Sarah she saw that he was holding a knife. He lunged forwards. She ducked out of the way and the boy, carried forward by his own momentum, fell against Panda's door. The knife embedded itself into the neck of the horse. Sarah grabbed a shovel and hit the lad on the side of his head. He fell to the floor like a ton of bricks and she quickly secured his hands behind his back before he had time to come to.

Ruth ran to the black and white horse who was shaking his head and neck, desperately trying to rid himself of the knife. 'Should I pull this out,' she shouted agitatedly to Sarah. Panda shook his head violently one more time and the knife fell on to the stable floor. Sarah gingerly picked it up and put it on a ledge. Blood was oozing out of the wound, running down his neck and staining his white patches red. As Ruth frantically searched for the first aid box, Simon came bursting into the barn with Pat close on his heels.

Simon glanced at Panda and turning to Pat ordered, 'Go and get some towels from the house. Tell Maddy to call her vet. Come back here and press the pads on to the wound.' He grabbed some rolled up white exercise bandages and handed them to Ruth. 'Hold these over the cut until Pat comes back and then come inside.' Ruth pressed the bandages one by one to the horse's neck. They changed from white to crimson as they soaked up the blood.

CHAPTER TWELVE

Sarah and John brought in the two intruders and Simon sat the captives down at the kitchen table. 'Right, let's have your names.' No one answered. Simon moved round the table to the youth who had been handcuffed to the railings. 'Let's start with you, shall we.'

'Say nothing,' shouted Jilly.

'Not a good idea,' said Simon. 'John, come here.'

'Sir!' John marched up to the boy. He grabbed hold of his hair and roughly yanked his head back.

The boy croaked at Jilly, 'You fucking stupid woman, you didn't tell us the filth was going to be here'.

'Keep your mouth shut, and say nothing. They're not the police,' she snarled back at him.

'Who are you?' he asked Simon. John slightly released his head as Simon showed him his card; he also showed it to the other boy and to Jilly.

'My name's Sean,' John's captive said very quickly. 'You can let me go.' John released his hair and the boy turned towards Jilly and shouted, 'You fucking bitch, what do you want to mess with these people for? I ain't keeping my mouth shut. It's your fault. I done this for Danny, not you'.

'I said shut up,' yelled the woman. Maddy stared at her. She couldn't believe the transformation of the down trodden, subservient Jilly into a spitting, snarling wild cat. Jilly glared at her. 'What's your problem, you stuck up tart?'

'Enough of that, Mrs. Rich,' barked Simon. 'We've found drugs, knives, a sword and a crossbow in your car. What have you got to say about that?' Jilly said nothing.

Simon moved on to the next boy, who sat looking pale and frightened. 'What's your name?' he barked.

'Ashley. I ain't done nothin' neither. It was her.' The boy pointed at Jilly.

'They seem to agree that this was your idea,' Simon sneered at Jilly. She still kept silent. 'John.' Simon indicated with his head. John went over to Jilly and pulled her head back by her hair as he had done with Sean. She cried out in pain, and Maddy winced.

'Fuck off, you bully,' Jilly yelled. 'You can't intimidate me.'

'Can't we?' said Simon. 'You come here to torture and maim

Maddy's horses, trying to cover up for the work of your warped little son. All you've done is to incriminate his clients.' He turned to the two boys. 'You do buy drugs from Danny, I take it?' He paused. 'Well, you'll have to deal with your addictions when you're in custody.' He looked at Jilly, who was beginning to show signs of weakening. 'I don't think Danny or his mates are going to be best pleased with you, do you?' Jilly stared at the floor. 'What were you going to do to the horses?' Simon snarled. 'Especially Maddy's stallion, what had you in mind for him?' He walked to the kitchen drawer and pulled out a knife. Everyone's eyes followed him. He took a plum from the fruit bowl on the kitchen table, sliced it round the edge and gouged out the stone. 'Castration was it?' Everyone watched the plum stone roll out on to the table.

Maddy jumped up in horror. Simon quietly and gently pushed her back into her seat where she sat glowering at Jilly.

Feeling everyone's animosity, Jilly suddenly began to whine. 'It wasn't me, it was Rhona Whitehaven. She gave me the orders.'

'You can discuss it with her in a minute,' replied Simon. 'She'll be joining us shortly.' Jilly looked at him in astonishment, fear showing on her face for the first time.

'Rhona?' gasped Maddy. 'Was it her…?' Simon looked at her with an inscrutable look on his face. Silence fell.

They all heard the scrunching of the gravel as a car drew up. Jilly tried to get up out of her seat. John roughly pushed her back down. Maddy and Ruth got up and went to the back door as Rhona came striding up the path followed by a tall, plain-clothes policeman. Angela Tidebrook came reluctantly after them, escorted by a uniformed police officer.

'What…?' Maddy looked at Simon.

'Patience,' he said, smiling at her. 'Not something you're blessed with.'

'What on earth's going on?' demanded Rhona as she marched into the kitchen. 'I've been woken up in the middle of the night by this person.' She turned and glared at the tall plain-clothes detective who stood behind her. 'I was brought here in some sort of cloak and dagger manner, against my will I hasten to add. I have had to put up with this snivelling woman,' she glanced at Angela, 'and what are you doing here?' she asked Simon. Then, catching sight of Jilly, she exclaimed, 'Good God. Jilly's handcuffed! Let her go at once. Have you all gone mad?'

'I don't think so.' Simon coolly ignored her outburst.

'Who are these boys?' blustered Rhona.

'Friends of yours, apparently,' replied Simon.

'They're nothing to do with me. Just who do you think you are, and what do you think you are doing? You can't treat people like this. Let them go at once.'

Simon showed her his card and said abruptly, 'Sit down'. The wind left Rhona's sails as she read his card. She sat heavily on a chair at the table. 'What's Jilly doing here?'

'She was caught acting on your orders,' sneered Simon.

'My orders? What orders?'

'To dope and harm Maddy's horses and ultimately, I believe, to kill Maddy.'

'Are you insane?' exclaimed Rhona. 'I'm a magistrate. I don't go around issuing orders like that.'

'No, but you do dope horses. You've changed the identity of at least one if not two horses, so why should I believe you?'

'I would not and have never killed anyone, nor indeed have I given orders to do so.'

'Mrs. Rich says you have,' responded Simon.

'What the hell are you talking about?' Rhona looked daggers at Jilly. Jilly scowled back at her.

'These people were caught red-handed trying to dope the horses here.' Simon turned to Angela and added, 'But nobody seems to have gone near your horse Mrs. Tidebrook. Why would that be?' Angela stood near the back door beside the uniformed officer. She looked terrified and her eyes darted from face to face as everybody turned to stare at her.

'Well?' barked Simon.

'I... I don't know,' Angela stuttered.

'Oh, I think you know very well, Mrs. Tidebrook. It would be something to do with a certain glove that went missing from the fridge in this very room, wouldn't it?' Angela went pale. She rocked backwards and forwards. The policeman held her arm to steady her.

'You knew who came in here, drugged the dogs and took the glove,' continued Simon. Angela shook her head.

'What glove?' protested Rhona. 'Drugging dogs? What are you talking about?' Simon ignored her.

He walked towards Angela. 'I suggest you answer unless you want to be implicated in murder.'

'Murder? I... I don't know anything about any murder.' Angela blanched and stared at Jilly. 'She...she said that Maddy had been saying horrible things about me, and wanted to get me out of her yard because I didn't fit in any more with her new found friends like Judith. She said Rhona had left something in her kitchen and she was going in to fetch it. She told me she was going to play a trick on Maddy, and that I was to say nothing. I was angry and upset. I didn't know what it was she did in here or what she took.'

'You silly bitch,' snarled Jilly. 'No wonder they don't want you here with that useless horse which you can't even ride.' Angela started crying.

'What trick?' Simon asked, more kindly this time.

'I don't know. She didn't say.' Angela sobbed. She turned to Maddy. 'I'm sorry Maddy; I didn't know she was going to drug your dogs.' Maddy smiled at her.

'I never left anything in Maddy's house!' exclaimed Rhona. 'I haven't been here for ages until the other day. What do you think you're playing at Jilly?' Turning to Simon, Rhona demanded, 'I need to speak with Jilly in private'.

'In order to match your stories? I hardly think so,' replied Simon.

'My dear good man, as I've been trying to point out to you, these boys and whatever it is that they are doing here are nothing to do with me.'

'Jilly tells me that they're acting on your orders.'

'Then Jilly is lying. I have never seen them before in my life.' Rhona turned to Jilly. 'What's going on? Don't just sit there looking dumb. I know you're an idiot but you're going too far this time.' Jilly ignored her and stared down at the table.

Simon turned to Sean, the boy who had been handcuffed to the railings, and asked kindly, 'You mentioned earlier that you did this for Danny. What did you mean?'

'Oh, well,' snorted Rhona. 'I might have guessed it would be something to do with that layabout.'

'Why do you say that and what do you know of Danny?' Simon asked her.

'Shut up Rhona, you bitch,' yelled Jilly.

'He's her good-for-nothing son.'

'Yes, I know,' replied Simon. 'We have him in custody.'

'Best place for him.'

'He's your nephew, remember,' snarled Jilly.

'Unfortunately my silly brother made the ultimate mistake of fornicating with you and produced that wastrel. At least he had the good sense to die after he had discovered his mistake.' Everybody stared aghast at Rhona and then at Jilly. Maddy didn't know whether to be horrified or to laugh.

Simon looked a little taken aback. 'Go on,' he said, unsteadily.

'Well, Jilly lived in the village,' continued Rhona as if Jilly wasn't there. 'She was quite pretty when she was young; although it's hard to believe now.' Everybody looked at Jilly. 'My unfortunate brother fell for her. We managed to put a stop to the relationship, but not before it was too late. The wretched girl got herself pregnant. My brother was sent abroad, South America, I believe. He caught some disease and promptly died. My father died soon after. The foolish man thought he was responsible for his son's death. I was left as head of the family because my mother, who was as weak as my brother, wasn't capable of being head of anything. I felt that I owed some sort of responsibility to the sprog, so I have helped Jilly financially over the years. Recently I understand he's developed a liking for drugs. I've told Jilly that I will not finance his habit.' She turned to the two boys. 'I suppose you're his junkie friends. If you come up in front of me you can expect harsh sentences.'

'No one will be coming up in front of you again, Miss Whitehaven,' declared Simon. 'There are too many other issues at stake. In fact you might be coming up in front of someone yourself.'

'Rubbish.'

'I think not. Are you aware that there's a cannabis factory on your property?'

Rhona stared at Simon. 'What are you talking about? I want a lawyer before I say anything else. I want to go home. I've told you all that you're going to get out of me tonight. I categorically repeat that I've had nothing at all to do with this charade. Come along Angela, we're going home.' She stood up. Simon nodded at the man plain-clothes policeman.

Rhona turned to Jilly. 'You can consider that our association is now finished. Good night to you all.'

'One moment please,' interjected Simon.

'What?'

'Who will inherit your money, should you die?'

'That's none of your business.'

'Sit her down again,' Simon addressed the detective.

'Well really,' said Rhona as the man moved closer to her. 'If you must know it would have been the sprog, because there is no one left in the family. But after this latest performance I'll certainly be leaving it all to someone else.'

Jilly let out a scream. 'You bitch. You can't break the Trust Fund.' She tried to jump up but John roughly pushed her back down again.

'No? You've just invalidated it,' replied Rhona. 'I'll see to that.'

'You can't! You can't, I know you can't,' screamed Jilly.

'Oh yes I can, but I'm not staying here to argue with you.' Rhona moved towards the door.

'Thank you for your help, ladies. You can go now but the police will be speaking to you again,' said Simon. Rhona strode out of the kitchen like a tall ship in full sail. Angela scuttled after her.

A tense silence fell in the kitchen after Rhona and Angela left. The two boys were getting edgy and started fidgeting. Simon looked taut and grim, his mouth tight and his eyes like steel. He stared over the heads of the people sitting at the table. Maddy had never seen such a look on his face and she felt frightened.

She turned to watch Jilly, who glared back and said belligerently, 'What are you looking at, you silly stuck up tart with your flash horses. You think you're better than everyone else. Well you're not. You know nothing'. Turning to Simon she added, 'and neither do you. I want to go home. You can't keep me here'.

'You'll sit here as long as I say.' Simon stared at her. Maddy thought he resembled a coiled snake ready to strike. She shivered.

'So,' he growled. 'It was your son who killed my wife.' Everybody in the room froze.

'You're talking bollocks,' Jilly sneered. 'Why would he do that?'

'You wanted to implicate Rhona, so you attacked and killed my wife.'

'You're mad!' Jilly glared at him. He walked up to her, stood in front of her and grabbed her by the shoulders. She cowered away from him.

'I don't think so. You made your son go down to Devon and kill my wife. Why?' Jilly said nothing. 'Why?' he yelled; his face was inches away from hers. Jilly continued looking at the floor.

'So which one of you helped him?' Simon left Jilly and walked slowly up the other side of the table past the two boys like a lion selecting its prey, looking for the weakest person. The two teenagers shuffled in their seats. Simon stopped opposite Sean, who was on the verge of tears. He leant across the table, saying menacingly, 'It was you, wasn't it?'

Sean shrank back. 'No, not me mate. I don't know nothin' about that.'

'So what do you know about?' snarled Simon.

'Nothin', I know nothin''.

'You're here aren't you? You brought drugs here to sedate the horses. Were you going to torture them?'

'No, no. I ain't into that.'

'So what are you into?' snapped Simon. 'Drugs... you have an addiction and you need the money to fund it. You buy your gear from Danny, right,' he shouted. The boy jumped and so did Maddy.

'Ye... I dunno,' he answered.

'You know why Danny's mother brought you here. So tell me.' The boy said nothing.

Simon turned to John. 'I'm losing my patience. Take him into the other room, soften him up. You know what to do.'

'Yes sir. I can't stand junkies. It'll be a pleasure.' John advanced towards the boy.

'No, no.' Sean cringed. 'I'll tell yer.'

'All right Sean,' Simon continued pleasantly. 'Why did you come here tonight?'

'Don't say a word, or it'll be the worse for you,' snarled Jilly.

'Shut up,' said Sarah suddenly. She had moved beside Jilly's chair.

'You don't frighten me,' said Jilly. Then she screamed as Sarah jabbed her in the face with her elbow.

'Want another one?' hissed Sarah. Jilly kept quiet.

'Sorry about that interruption.' Simon smiled at Sean. 'Please carry on.'

'She told us,' he said, looking at Jilly.

'Mrs. Rich told you what?' asked Simon.

'That it was her,' Sean nodded towards Maddy, 'who got Danny banged up.'

'Why was that lady responsible for Danny getting locked up, Sean?'

'Because she grassed everyone up.'

'What do you mean?'

'She told the filth about Danny and she grassed up her posh friend Rhona about 'er ringin' 'er 'orses. You know, changin' 'em, makin' 'em look different. Well Auntie Rhona has all the money see...' Jilly made a move but Sarah pushed her back threateningly into her chair.

'Auntie Rhona has all the money?' repeated Simon interestedly. He walked round, picked up a chair and sat next to Sean. Turning to face him, and giving him the impression that he was now his best friend, he leant towards him as if sharing a secret. 'So did Danny benefit from her money then?'

'What?'

'Did she give money to Danny?'

'No, but 'is Mum used to get some out of the old trout every now and then, and she give it to Danny.' He looked at Jilly, who was seething. Sarah's elbow was hovering dangerously near her face.

'Really,' exclaimed Simon. 'And that helped you then, did it?'

'Yeah, then 'e would give us some gear, see. He was good like that, Danny was. He'd share his money wiv us.' Seeming to fall for Simon's disarming manner, he continued, 'She's Danny's auntie. Danny was going to inher...in.....'

'Inherit,' prompted Simon.

'Yeah, inherit, that's right. He was going to get all the money and the big 'ouse. We was goin' to be alright, 'cos 'e's my mate, see. We was goin' to get a car and all sorts.'

'What sort of car were you going to buy, Sean?'

'We was going to 'ave a Ferrari. You can pull a lot of skirt in a Ferrari.'

'Yes, good choice.' Simon smiled. 'But how was Danny going to get the money?'

'They said,' Sean looked at Jilly, 'that his Auntie Rhona was going to go to prison for a long time and that we would move in.'

'How could Danny move into the big house and have the money if Auntie Rhona was still alive?'

''Cos she said,' Sean looked at Jilly again, 'that it would be alright, if she was in prison. 'Cos of the trust thing.'

'The Trust Fund?'

'Yeah, somethin' to do with that. It says in that.' Jilly sagged like a rag doll and looked at the floor.

'Thank you, Sean.' Simon smiled. 'You've been really helpful.' He gave him a pat on the back and the teenager looked pleased.

Simon walked towards Jilly. He stopped in front of her and looked down. 'So that's why you wanted to implicate Rhona. There's a clause in this trust fund that would allow Danny to inherit if Rhona was in prison. But things didn't quite work out as planned, did they?' Jilly said nothing. 'You thought you would incriminate Rhona, but it didn't work. Now you've lost everything, your son, the money and your freedom. Was it worth it?' Jilly continued staring at the ground.

Simon gazed mockingly down at her. 'You were waiting for an announcement after my wife's accident saying that there had been foul play. But I put a stop to that.' Jilly moved in her seat. 'You thought that the inquest would bring a verdict of unlawful death. But it didn't, did it?' Again Jilly shuffled and avoided Simon's eyes. 'Then you were going to tell everyone how Rhona had been down in Devon that day, because you were down in Devon that day with her, weren't you? You managed to get away from her to put Danny in place on the top of the Ridge. Your car was seen by a member of my staff.' Simon resorted to a shot in the dark, hoping that it would have an effect, and it did. 'You have quite a distinctive car, don't you? It's yellow. Not a good colour for a car if you want to be discreet, is it?' Jilly began to look frightened. 'You were waiting for the story of the accident to hit the newspapers. When they mentioned foul play, you were then going to tell everyone the story of how Rhona had seriously fallen out with Tamsin. There was indeed a very strong case. The fact that Rhona had changed the identity of a four star horse that she was now riding as a novice. The cruelty charges that could be brought over the big chestnut horse, Rin Tin Tin, and doping charges over her dressage horse Singspiel. All this would be disastrous for a magistrate, and it would put paid to any prestigious position in British Dressage.'

Simon paused for breath. Jilly tried to make a lunge at him, but Sarah rammed her back down in the chair.

'You were going to say how Tamsin knew all about it, and had challenged Rhona concerning it,' Simon continued. 'You would tell the police that Tamsin was going to grass her up, as our friend Sean would say. You would have then gone on to say that Rhona slipped out that day when you were in Devon, but you didn't know where she went. You would also tell them that Rhona has access to any medication she wants through the veterinary centre on her property and that she uses these drugs on her own horses whenever she feels like it.' The silence in the kitchen was almost tangible. Everybody watched Jilly. She sat very still, staring at Simon. All the colour had drained out of her face.

'But you never got the chance, did you?' continued Simon in his cultured voice, 'because I put a stop to all that. It must have been very frustrating. You tried to get Maddy to go to the funeral with you, God knows why. Then you found out by accident that Maddy had the glove in her kitchen. How did you manage that?' Jilly said nothing.

'Oh yes, when you were in the pub, the evening before the funeral,' continued Simon. 'You listened to a conversation that Maddy had with her friend Sally. Also, to your horror, you heard them talking about the website. That immediately put Maddy in danger. You made a mental note to fix her as soon as you could.' Simon paused. He opened a cupboard, picked up a glass then went to the sink and filled the glass from the tap. Nobody spoke but everyone's eyes were on him as he drank the water.

When he was ready he carried on, 'But your plans all went awry'.

'Went to Rye?' asked Sean curiously, breaking the tension. 'Why did she go to Rye?'

'Went pear shaped.' Simon smiled.

'Oh,' said Sean.

'With your plans going pear shaped, you had to do some quick thinking. The Eastleigh Horse Trials would provide a good opportunity to get rid of Maddy. So you got Danny to fix her lorry and while you were there you had a stroke of good luck. You found out that Louise Parkway had challenged Rhona as well. Not only that, but she also knew about the horse harming society. That made it necessary for you to kill her too. Things very nearly worked out for you, but thankfully Maddy saw the footprint.' He paused again; everyone watched Jilly as she slumped in her chair.

'You're a ruthless and cold blooded murderer,' continued Simon. 'You've killed one person and seriously injured two more. You cleverly managed to send a "Get Well" card to Louise in hospital, forging Rhona's signature. You must have delivered it by hand. It was too quick, it made Rhona look suspicious. Why would she do that to herself? No one would, it had to be someone framing her. Louise Parkway is on the mend now, thank goodness, but her poor groom will be a vegetable if she ever comes round. Does that make you feel good?' Jilly said nothing and sat with her head bowed.

The two captive youngsters were looking from Simon to Jilly and from Jilly back to Simon with incredulous expressions on their faces.

'To return to the matter of the drugs again,' continued Simon, 'Danny, like you, steals them from the veterinary centre. But of course he's been doing that for a long time now, hasn't he? He uses them in his vile and depraved horse mutilating operations, doesn't he? You stole strong pain killers and tranquillizers for Rhona; whatever she wanted. It was easy, you worked there for a while as a veterinary nurse and you did their book keeping. The books are going to look very interesting, especially the drugs ordered against the ones used legitimately. But you would have sworn blind that Rhona bullied you into it. You might have been believed: your act of the downtrodden little skivvy was a good front and fooled a lot of people.' Jilly looked broken.

Simon paused, picked up his phone and dialled a number, saying, 'Coulson here. You can come and fetch them now'.

There was a long silence in the kitchen. Nobody moved. Simon stood looking down at Jilly, an unfathomable look on his face; then he moved to the Aga and leant back against it, holding on to the rail and staring straight ahead. His eyes glazed over and he had the hint of a smile on his face. Maddy suddenly thought of Tamsin. She shivered; it was almost as if she was in the room.

The wailing of police sirens as two cars sped up the drive broke the silence in the kitchen. A commotion followed as several police officers burst into the room. They read the prisoners their rights and whisked them away.

Simon left the room with Sarah and John. Ruth and Maddy stayed in the kitchen.

'I don't know what to say,' said Maddy,

'Neither do I,' replied Ruth.

They both jumped as the vet walked into the room, saying, 'I see you've had some chaos here tonight'.

Maddy smiled weakly; she had forgotten all about calling him out to Judith's horse. 'How's Panda?' she asked.

'He's fine, just a few stitches. I don't need to tell you to keep him off work until the wound has healed: you'll know when. I'll leave you to remove the stitches.' Maddy nodded and he continued, 'I have the results of the drugs test on your dogs. I've told Colonel Coulson and I thought you might like to know too'. Maddy nodded. 'They used Phenobarbitone, it's a drug for epilepsy in dogs. We found it in the blood samples of both dogs.'

Simon walked in at that moment and said, 'Yes, it probably came from the veterinary centre on Rhona's property'. Addressing the vet he continued, 'They used Ketamine on my wife's horse, and we have reason to believe that Danny gave it to him on a piece of bread, then stabbed him as he stood by the thicket. Judging by past horse mutilations we think that Danny used ketamine at least twice to drug horses. When they suffered pain they went berserk. So that is why he used it on Troubadour, and it certainly worked'. His face became hard and he turned away.

'Can you prove the mutilations were all Danny's work?' asked the vet.

'Hopefully, because the police have DNA samples.'

'Really?' questioned Mike. 'How come?'

'They smoked cannabis and left their cigarette ends lying around at the scene of the horse mutilation sites.'

'That's excellent. Congratulations, Colonel Coulson, a good result,' replied Mike briskly. 'I have to get back, now. Good night to you all.'

'The police have taken the buckets of feed that they brought with them here tonight. They'll get them analysed,' said Simon as he left with the vet.

Ruth went off to bed and was soon followed by Pat, who came in looking tired. Maddy sat in the kitchen, mulling things over in her mind as she waited for Simon to come back in.

When at last he appeared she said nervously, 'I want to say sorry'.

'No,' replied Simon sitting down beside her and taking her free hand in his. 'It's me who has to apologise. I can't believe how crass and stupid I was. I cringe and kick myself whenever I think of you lying in the back seat of your car. You could have… It doesn't bear thinking about.'

'You have Tamsin's murderer now,' said Maddy gently.

'Yes.' He looked away. 'I do and it has brought everything home to me. The reality of it all and the finality. Now it's all come to a head I need to put things back into perspective. I want to spend time with my children and talk to them about selling Moorsend.'

'Yes, I understand.' Maddy paused and then added nervously, 'Will I see you again?'

'Yes, of course, why ever not?'

'I….Us… that night in the car. Was it just a crazy moment? A lot has happened since then.'

Simon turned and touched her face, smiling tenderly at her. 'No it wasn't a crazy moment.' He leant over and kissed her tentatively on her lips. She moved, trying to stand up.

'What's the matter?' he asked, standing up too.

'Nothing,' she said smiling. She stood in front of him and put her good arm around his neck. 'I was just uncomfortable sitting there.' He bent down and kissed her again. She moved her body against his and felt his breath coming quick and fast. He pressed his hips hard against hers and she felt her legs beginning to tremble.

'Let's go upstairs,' he whispered, but Maddy sat down again.

'When will you be back?' she asked.

'I don't know.' He sat down beside her and looked her straight in the eye. 'I'll definitely be back. I want to do things properly this time. Leave a decent gap. I don't want to be seen out in public with you...'

'Why, am I that ugly? Do you want me to put a bag over my head?'

'Don't be so ridiculous! I mean that I don't want people gossiping about us, or the tabloids writing about us. I want a reasonable time to pass. I owe that to Tamsin and I owe it to you. I hope you understand.' Maddy nodded. 'I won't ask you to have a hole-in-the-corner affair. I don't want that and neither would you.' She shook her head. 'So I'm asking you to wait. Will you wait for me please?'

Maddy nodded. 'How long?'

'I can't answer that,' he said smiling. 'But I give you my word that I'll be back. I love you. I have always loved you since we first met. I found it very hard watching you with Jonathan, knowing that he ...' He turned away. 'We were always good together...'

'Yes,' Maddy smiled, 'we were. But you loved Tamsin.'

'That was a different sort of love, almost brotherly. With you it is an all-consuming passion. We're two of a kind, you and me. You have a temper, you say what you think, and you're not frightened of me. If I ask you a question, I know that I'll get a truthful answer, however difficult that might be to swallow. I hope that you can find a place in your heart for me because I know what you felt for Jonathan.'

'I loved Jonathan. But...' She paused and looked away. He touched her hand. She smiled and turned back. 'You were my first love, and you know what they say about that.'

Simon sighed. 'I hope, my darling, I'll also be your last love.'

Maddy stood up; she suddenly felt very tired. He put his arms around her and held her tight. 'Let's go upstairs,' he whispered again.

She hung on to him and then she broke away, saying, 'I thought you didn't want a hole-in-the-corner affair?'

'I don't.'

'Well how "hole-in-the-corner" is this then? Ruth and Pat are upstairs, it's nearly morning. I've got to tell Judith about her horse very soon, and I need some sleep first. I'm all in.'

Simon laughed briefly and said, 'All right, always the truthful answer; point taken. I'd better go. Actually I have a confession to make,

I'm staying with Judith, and Colin is there too, so I expect she already knows.'

'Oh.' Maddy suddenly laughed. 'I've been a bitch, haven't I?'

'Yes, my darling, just a little, but I deserved it and I wouldn't have wanted it any other way.'

'Will I see you tomorrow morning?'

'No, I'll leave early.'

'So this is goodbye then?'

'Au revoir, not adieu!' Maddy stood with tears in her eyes. He tenderly put his arms around her and held her close. 'I'll be back as soon as I can.'

'Yes,' she whispered. He gently let her go, kissed her on her cheek, and turned and walked out of the room without looking back.

***

It was eight weeks since Simon had left, and Maddy's arm was now out of plaster. She was sitting at her kitchen table with Judith one morning having their usual coffee.

'You seem so much better now that you're riding again,' said Judith.

'Yes,' replied Maddy. 'There's nothing like horses for helping you recover from things.'

'No, I agree. Have you heard from Simon?'

Maddy sighed. 'Only a brief text about ten days ago saying he was coming back soon. Nothing since then. I don't believe what he said about coming back anymore, and I don't believe what he said about loving me. It's all talk.'

'He gave you his word, didn't he?'

'Yes, but what does that mean?'

'Everything where Simon is concerned,' replied Judith brightly.

Maddy laughed wryly and said, 'I used to think so once'. She paused and then continued, 'I know it's silly and a bit unfair…'

'Yes?'

'It doesn't really help with Ruth becoming so close to John. I found out that she was seeing him on the quiet, making him sandwiches and things like that, but I thought it would a nine day wonder, given his job and everything. In fact I told her to ditch him, but they seem to be making a go of things. I mean, who would have thought it? However, I don't want

201

to sound ungenerous, I'll be really pleased for her if it works out.'

'I know,' replied Judith. 'I think Simon was a bit surprised. John's a changed man, now, where women are concerned.'

'Let's hope it lasts,' said Maddy. 'They're going sailing next week, down to the South of France on a yacht.'

'That might be a make or break situation.' Judith laughed. 'The yacht's very small.'

Maddy smiled and then sat in silence munching a biscuit and tracing patterns in the crumbs on the table.

'Angela's being very friendly.' Judith broke the silence.

'I know. She follows me about like a kicked spaniel. I almost wish she was grumpy again.'

'I know what you mean, but at least her horse didn't go to Rhona's yard.'

'No, thank goodness. Anyway, Rhona is selling up and moving away now that she can't be a magistrate anymore.'

'Is she? I hadn't heard, but I understood that she took the disgrace of everything very hard.'

'Yes. She's going to live in Scotland. She has distant relatives up there apparently, going to make a new life for herself. She's lucky she's not in prison, but at least she won't be allowed to keep any animals for a very long time.'

'I feel a bit sorry for her concerning Jilly, because she knew nothing about her activities, or Danny's cannabis factory on her land or indeed the horse mutilating.' Judith shuddered.

'I know,' agreed Maddy. 'You know we discovered why Rin Tin Tin went berserk sometimes?'

'Yes, it was when he smelt cannabis on someone, because Danny had tortured him once and made that awful scar. Although why did he take a dislike to the grooms at Moorsend?'

'They smoked cannabis!' replied Maddy laughing.

'Good Lord! The police could use him as a sniffer horse.'

'I offered him to them, but they didn't want him.'

'Thank goodness Danny and his mother are behind bars now. Did Jilly know about his mutilating gang?' asked Judith.

'I think she pretended it wasn't Danny, but I guess she knew in her heart that it was.'

'That's appalling. How could she be a horsewoman and put up with it?'

'Because she knew it was her fault.'

'How could it be her fault?'

'She was horrid to Danny when he was little: she used to ignore him and spend all her time with the horses. He had to fend for himself at a very early age, you know, get his own meals, let himself in when he came home from school. She was a dreadful mother. She knew that he resented it and she knew he blamed the horses. It would be sad if they weren't so vile.' Maddy sighed, stood up wearily and continued, 'Well, this won't get the horses exercised, we'd better get on. Now who's this?' she added as she heard a car pull up. 'I hope it isn't Angela come to ride. I don't feel like her today, or Sally for that matter.'

'Talking of Sally,' asked Judith, 'has she got a man?'

'Several, I think. I know she's met at least eight through the internet.'

'Eight?'

'Yes, one a week since my accident.'

'What does she do with them all?'

'Goes out to dinner with them, I think. She doesn't like all of them, she just likes going out. I don't know what else she does with them.'

'Heaven forbid.' Judith looked out of the back door and added, 'Well your visitor is neither Sally nor Angela. I'll leave you to it'. She smiled and promptly disappeared.

'What?' asked Maddy wondering what she meant. She heaved another sigh, walked disinterestedly to the sink and rinsed out the coffee mugs.

'Don't I get a "hello"?' asked a familiar voice. Maddy spun round.

'Simon!' she exclaimed, suddenly feeling shaky. 'I didn't expect to see you again.'

'Why ever not? I gave you my word, didn't I?'

'I know but…'

'Aren't you pleased to see me?'

Maddy sensed the tension and worry of the last eight weeks leave her body and felt a smile break out. 'Of course I am.' He took her face in his hands and gently kissed her. Tears welled up into her eyes as she threw her arms around his neck. 'Of course I'm pleased to see you,' she repeated quietly.

'I'm glad to see you've lost your plaster.' He drew back, holding her at arm's length. 'You looked a little peaky as you stood at the sink, although you look happier now.' He smiled. 'I think a nice holiday in the sun would do you the world of good.'

'Fat chance of that.'

'Well, I had hoped that you would accompany me to Italy next week.'

Maddy stared at him. 'But I can't leave the horses, and Ruth is going away.'

'All taken care of, I've got a groom coming. Pat enjoyed her stay here so much she wants to come back and John has agreed to spend his leave here as well. They're going to postpone their sailing trip until we get back; that's if you want to come with me of course.'

Maddy beamed and flung her arms around his neck. 'Just try stopping me.'

'So, you've forgiven me.'

'I exonerated you on the night that you caught Jilly. Have you forgiven me for being such a bitch?'

He bent and kissed her. 'I deserved it, as I said before. But enough of the past, we need to plan the future.'

'What future?'

'Ours. Emma hopes that you'll become her step mother, as do I.' Maddy stared at him. 'Well, my darling, may I have an answer?'

'I thought you had forgotten me. It's been eight weeks. I'll have to think about it.'

'I know, I'm sorry. I needed that time. So now you're making me wait.'

'Are you sure that it's what you want? We'll argue all the time.'

He smiled. 'Not all the time. We can make up in between times.'

'I'm very untidy in the house, it'll drive you mad.'

'I forgot to say Anna is hoping for a new mistress too. She'll look after the house.'

'I have a temper.'

'I'm sure I'll cope.'

'What can I say then, if you're ready for all eventualities?'

'Yes. I know that you'll drive me mad, but I don't want to live without you.'

Maddy relaxed and smiled. 'I agree. I don't want to live without you either.' She fell into his arms.

He whispered, 'Can we go upstairs now?'

'Yes, I don't see why not.'

THE END

Printed in Great Britain
by Amazon

78042800R00120